Hindsight Bravo

Hindsight Bravo

Book 1 in the Dreams of Victory Series

J.R. Mosby

Rand-Smith Books

CONTENTS

CONTENTS

CONTENTS

Rand-Smith Publishing
www.Rand-Smith.com
USA

First Printing, 2023

One

Waiting for the green light to snap on was always stressful for Mike. That's the signal that the plane is over the drop zone, and it's time to exit the aircraft. Paradropping always filled him with anticipation just moments before the door swung open. He especially enjoyed the first few seconds when his body was solely supported by the air beneath him. The sense of stability never failed to surprise him. The cushion of air never failed to give him a sense of empowerment as he hit terminal velocity.

Since this was a night mission, the jumpmaster didn't have any visual recognition points to cue Mike in on the track of the aircraft. In such instances they used a CARP (Computed Air Release Point), putting the team at the mercy of the aircrew and the instruments, as well as a healthy dose of luck.

By the time the team jumped, the first plane had already launched its payload of heavy drops, including most of the equipment they would use for the mission. He hoped that had gone without a hitch—there was really no telling what they would find waiting for them on the ground. As he steadied himself, he went through his mental routine: relax, make sure the equipment is ready, and prepare for all possible outcomes. No matter how many times he performed a drop, he never failed to follow that mental checklist, and it kept him safe throughout his military career.

Master Sergeant Mike Mann was a perfectionist, and he always told his guys that he would have been a textbook case of ADHD if it had been a viable diagnosis when he was a kid. His mind ran double the

|1|

speed of most people's, making him an excellent team leader, but a difficult person to befriend.

He anxiously trained his attention on that light as if he were a racer waiting to launch his dragster down the strip, albeit without the cheering crowds or adoring fans. And although it was expected, the bright green light always sent a jolt of adrenaline through his body as the loadmaster pushed out the pallets, signaling to the team that it was go time. Mike felt the familiar rush, and then he was out the door in a flash. His thoughts were immediately on getting a visual of the rest of the guys and zeroing in on the drop zone.

From his vantage point, he could see all nine members of his team, so it appeared that everyone had made it out successfully, and they were all tracking him. So far so good, but it was still early, so he remained cautiously optimistic. He hoped that the equipment wouldn't burn in and that it would hit the mark or at least come relatively close. He saw the big cargo chutes billowing below him and quickly verified that all of them had deployed. *Going smoothly*. Mike knew that it never went exactly as planned, but he was still proud of his team for its effort thus far.

Not one to dwell on the present, his mental channel flicked to the next phase of the operation as he neared the ground. His descent was flawless, and he flared at the last moment, making a perfect landing. With the crew of ten men planted on terra firma, Mike secured his weapon and set about organizing the drop zone security. His men knew the drill, and he had complete confidence in their execution.

However, as the team sergeant, he still had to reign over the entire operation. He remembered a quote he'd learned as a young sergeant: "You can delegate authority; you can't delegate responsibility." Fortunately, he had a strong group of self-starters who understood the concept of responsibility. They knew he wasn't there to hold their hands or wipe their asses, and for that, Mike was grateful. He checked with everyone via radio, and no one reported seeing any activity. Next on the agenda was securing a manageable, defensible site where they could collect and consolidate the equipment.

Cpt. Kevin McKenzie walked over and heaved a sigh of relief as he patted Mike on the shoulder. "How you doing, buddy?" he asked rhetorically.

The two men couldn't have been more different, but their working relationship was rock solid. As team sergeant, Mike was usually all business. He had to be, although occasionally, he'd let down his guard and show the guys his sense of humor, complete with goofy dad jokes.

At 6 feet tall and 30 years old, Kevin was two inches shorter and eight years younger than his sergeant. While he could be as serious and focused as Mike, he had no problem sharing facts about US history, his major at American University in Washington, DC. He also had a deep love of jazz and took every opportunity to hang out in local dive bars and smoky clubs that he encountered on his deployments. Allowing the rhythmic patterns of swing, cool jazz, and world fusion to wash over him in a strange land gave him the comfortable feeling of home.

His father had been an accomplished horn player before putting his dream career on the back burner to earn a living as an accountant to support his wife and two boys. Kevin knew it had been a huge sacrifice, but he loved when the family got together every Sunday after dinner and listened as his father played living room DJ, spinning records by greats like Miles Davis and Louis Armstrong. He would typically finish up with one of the jam sessions he'd played on in his prime. Kevin, especially, was transfixed. He loved everything about the genre, especially the improvisation and how the music veered off in one direction for what seemed like an eternity before abruptly righting itself and finding the groove once again. Unfortunately, Kevin might not get a chance to hear his favorite tunes for a while because his focus was on this mission for the next few months. He had to keep his head in the game.

He knew Mike wasn't usually one for small talk, but he felt they could afford to take a brief moment to relax before digging in for the night and waiting for daylight, at which point dawn would bring the ultimate test. Before it got too busy, he knew it was important to touch base with Mike, for his own well-being. Neither expecting an answer nor waiting for one, he asked what he could do to assist. Mike had already located an area to set up camp and pointed it out to Kevin. Mike also asked the young captain to grab Tom Kay, the senior communication (commo) sergeant, so he could position the gear in the center of camp for maximum reach.

The others rounding out the team were Joseph Strong, junior commo sergeant; Senior Engineer Sergeant Jack Morrison; Staff Sergeant Frank Holland; Senior Weapons Sergeant Dave Woods; Staff Sergeant Dennis Ayala; Senior Medic Jan Stanton; and finally, Staff Sergeant Jon Silverheels.

With the area properly secured, Tom wrote up the preparatory report to advise HQ of the team's progress. In turn, HQ would notify Naval and Air Force elements to cease overhead flights, and everyone could rest easy, at least for now.

The update would be a huge relief to the commander in the rear, so Mike and Kevin were eager to send it out. However, it was important that they take their time to make sure they felt secure enough in their surroundings to release the undetectable aircraft flying high above them.

Mike and Kevin conferred, decided that they were happy with their position, and advised Tom to proceed with the report.

Once he received the nod, Tom powered up the radio and went to work. "I'm not detecting any enemy chatter," he declared into the handheld transmitter. "No sign that we've been detected. Continue ground operations."

Tom had an affinity for single-channel radio because it was flexible, securable, mobile, and reliable. As senior commo sergeant, it was one of his tools of the trade, and he took pride in sharing his knowledge with Joseph, the cocky millennial still honing his craft. Tom was careful to instruct Joseph that while radio was their primary communication, there were limitations.

Radio is the most detectable means of electronic communications and is notoriously subject to interference, both intentional and unintentional. When surprise is of utmost importance, radio communication should be used sparingly and only with established contacts. Once an attack is launched, restrictions can be removed since radio communications play an important role in relaying information to all parties. Joseph absorbed the information and looked forward to taking over Tom's position one day.

Now that HQ had been contacted, Mike tracked down Sergeant First Class Jack Morrison, a tall, dark-haired man of few words, which he articulated in a deep Alabama accent. When he spoke, everyone listened intently, and he took full ownership of the team's engineering operations.

"I want you to set up the tactical operations center (TOC)," Mike told him. "We need to keep track of all remotely controlled equipment. Thanks, Jack."

Next, Mike and Kevin began hammering out plans for the next day while the rest of the team established a security perimeter and consolidated the remaining equipment. Both men knew that it was critical to get a feel for the lay of the land and set up a defense plan in order to protect it. The intel briefings during isolation and planning had indicated that the area was extremely remote and thus sparsely populated. Problem was, Mike's experience had taught him not to rely on the intel, at least not fully.

During wartime, it's natural for people to flee the area and repopulate elsewhere. Since no infrastructure existed, it was difficult to track those areas. Besides that, Mike had always harbored a well-earned mistrust for the intelligence community. After all, it was easy to sit back and issue predictions from the safety and security of a faded leather swivel chair. Mike's experience had taught him to never take anything for granted, especially when assessing a new location. This team knew he lived by his commonly shared refrain: "We get paid to be pessimistic."

Mike was perhaps the ultimate pessimist. Jack sometimes joked with him about this in the way that buddies do, hinting that it was contributing to Mike's premature graying. However, his ability to foresee complications that might arise, stemming from his inability to stay focused on one thing for too long, had helped his team avoid many a pitfall in the past. If one thing was certain, it was that he was always wary of a sure thing.

That being said, it was time to get a visual of the progress his team had made in securing their new environment. He walked around until he found Dave, his senior weapons sergeant. He asked for an update, more for his own information than to check on the SSG's progress. Although Dave was young by Special Forces standards, in his three years with Mike, he had distinguished himself as a competent weapons man and had learned a lot from his more-experienced team members, who now held him in high regard.

In fact, he and Jack, the senior engineer sergeant, became fast friends who parlayed their areas of expertise into a solid working relationship. Mike knew that Jack had taken Dave under his wing and helped guide him as their bond grew stronger. As a result of their teamwork, Mike trusted that the layout and defense plan would be a well-coordinated effort.

After talking to Dave, Mike walked around and checked in with each team member just to satisfy himself that all was well. He hated to go to sleep while the men were still busy, but he knew the morning would bring fresh demands. He rounded up Cpt. Mackenzie and convinced him that there was nothing else the two of them could do, suggesting they get some sleep. Mike tried to bring the day's events into focus and convince himself that things were on track. Surely, they could afford a couple hours of shuteye. The early April air was colder than they had expected, so Mike and Kevin pulled out their sleeping bags, hunkered down, and drifted off to sleep.

Jack continued on where Mike had left off. As the next senior man, he stepped in and took charge when he felt it was necessary. He and

Mike had occasional disagreements that sometimes resulted in surprisingly intense arguments, but Mike knew that Jack's heart and head were always in the right place. He also knew that the rest of the team looked up to Jack and trusted him as much as Mike did. Even with night vision capabilities and the briefing the team had received about the terrain, Jack knew that he would not truly be able to survey their surroundings until he had done so with his own eyeballs in the light of day.

In contrast to Mike, Jack referred to himself as a realist. Rather than getting paid to be a pessimist, he elected to "trust but verify." How else could he expect his teammates to do their jobs if he were micro-managing the shit out of them all the time? The answer was he couldn't, and for that reason, the other members of the team held Jack in high esteem.

He continued to survey as he and Dave walked the perimeter again to decide on the final emplacement of the crew-served weapons and the claymore mines. The hill they were on was solid, defensible ground, even though it wasn't on the highest elevation. The mountains to the east were too far off for the enemy to use them to initiate fire, but still close enough for the team to use their enhanced optics to observe them. They could also, if necessary, employ the X-ray Laser IMage TRansporter (XLIMTR), the experimental invention that purportedly scanned the area, detected the molecular composition of objects, and then deconstructed and reconstructed those objects (or beings) to a designated location. It was explained as operating like the transporter teleportation machine from the *Star Trek* series.

The approaches were made up of open, rolling terrain so this would be relatively easy ground to observe and defend. The vegetation was mixed with trees and underbrush and had a nice carpet of grass. With the perimeter roughly encompassing 75 square meters, it was tight getting all of the equipment and supplies situated, yet still segregated enough to ensure that if the ammo and mortar rounds cooked off, the rest of the perimeter would survive.

On each corner of the base, they placed one M-2,.50 caliber machine gun, effective out to 1800 meters at a rate of 600 rounds a minute. In addition, they mounted four Mk 19 grenade launchers capable of propelling a 40mm grenade out to 1500 meters at a rate of 60 rounds per minute, and four M-134 mini guns, each with the ability to fire 6,000 rounds per minute, to the corners of the small base. Each position was reinforced by an M-240 machine gun and an M-249 automatic weapon.

The staggering amount of ammo that these weapons could consume was stored next to each machine. The sum effect of this arsenal was the ability to stop an attack by a small army. Pretty impressive firepower for a small but mighty 10-man team.

All of these weapons could be fired manually, as well as automatically by a remote weapons system. The 120mm mortars were set in a pit in the center of the perimeter to allow them a 360-degree field of fire. The mortars required a loader but could be aimed remotely to fire up to four rounds per minute at a range of five miles. The XLIMTR was in the center of the mortar pit, collocated with the Forward-Looking Infrared Radar (FLIR) and the infrared camera. They were all elevated to allow them to swivel in any direction without interfering with any of the other weapon systems. The combination of systems gave the team the ability to see the entire perimeter and zoom in on targets and areas of interest at unbelievable distances. Later, when the sensors were emplaced, they would remotely slew the cameras to any sensor that indicated a disturbance, thus giving the team forewarning of any approaching enemy.

The M-18 claymore mines were set one hundred meters out from the perimeter. These were directional mines containing seven hundred steel ball bearings that, when detonated, were projected in a sixty-degree arc out to one hundred meters. They were well within visibility but far enough out to stop an assault dead in its tracks while still allowing the team to react, should enemy forces encroach beyond that point. The ground sensors were embedded even farther out, depending on the terrain. In the event of vehicles approaching during an attack, the hand-held AT-4 anti-tank missiles were placed around the perimeter.

These were key because the enemy was known to employ vehicles laden with explosives to attack bases. The procedure had become so common that it had its own special acronym, VBIED (Vehicle Borne Improvised Explosive Device). The men felt they had minimized their exposure to this type of attack by bringing in all the supplies necessary for the duration of the mission, thus eliminating the need for any incoming traffic, and hence, any roads to service the base. Overall, the team felt good about its chances of defending the remote little piece of the planet.

Jack and Dave knew that there would be no sleep for either of them for quite a while. They would be busy modifying and reinforcing the perimeter as soon as they got a good look at the ground. Getting all the equipment set up was coming along well, and all of the critical equipment would be operational by daylight. The four-wheelers they had dropped in would be busy all night ferrying boxes of ammo and supplies recovered from where they had landed in the soft dirt. None of the team members had ever deployed with, and certainly not jumped with, this much gear, but their initial concerns about bringing the four-wheelers were a thing of the past, as they were making the work much quicker and easier. The team was on autopilot recovering the gear and supplies and not overly concerned about a possible attack. The fuel was moved to the western edge of camp near the ammo areas. Food and water were stored, and extra ammo was distributed to all of the weapon systems. Dave and Dennis went about inspecting, lubricating, and performing function checks on all the weapons to make sure they were ready for use.

Meanwhile, Joseph and Tom set about checking the XLIMTR. They were not quite sure if it would be needed, and if so, whether it would even work. It was experimental, but it was worth a shot. Even without it, they were now confident they could not only hold off a rather large enemy force but even prevail if given the chance. They were in as good a position as they could be and eagerly anticipated the first tentative rays of sunlight creeping over the mountains far to the east.

With an hour or so left before sunrise, Mike and Kevin arose and shook off the night with a cup of coffee that Joseph had already brewed. Then they walked around the base perimeter and inspected all the fortifications and gun emplacements. They saw that the gun positions were stocked with ammo and supplies, and after satisfying themselves that the team could sustain a fight and survive, they told everyone to catch some shuteye. They would stand watch while staying in contact by using the team radio that everyone was expected to monitor until further notice. The team's designated positions were assigned and henceforth would become their permanent places of residence for the duration of the mission. With sleeping mats unrolled, the rest of the team settled in for some well-deserved rest.

Kevin and Mike decided to take turns patrolling the area and manning the array of cameras and sensors. Mike took the first shift, and Kevin settled in to take stock of all the equipment he had at his disposal. It was amazing how much he could observe and control from one chair. Old-school guys like Mike still didn't feel comfortable relying on this technology, but Kevin was duly impressed as he scanned the area from near to far.

The system was flawless as it panned from close up to miles away, automatically achieving focus so there was no delay in the picture. The only thing that could defeat this setup was a power outage, but that, of course, had been taken into consideration. The triple redundant generators, as well as the battery backup, should keep it up and running. Every detail was covered, every contingency considered. The generators were spread out, and the batteries would be buried to prevent an incoming round of fire from destroying all of them.

The team would be roughing it without many luxuries in order to conserve electricity for the surveillance and weapons systems. It had become routine for the army to provide air conditioning, gyms, internet cafes, TV rooms, and even coffee shops for soldiers serving in combat zones, but none of that was provided here. These men were SF, and that meant they were used to sleeping on the ground without electricity or any other amenities.

An important mission like this was all business. Kevin considered how this assignment would affect his career, and he wanted no mistakes or missteps. He was just beginning his career in Special Forces, also referred to as Green Berets, and he was honored that his team had been selected to conduct this critical and highly classified mission in the arid terrain of Afghanistan.

Their operation was to be dropped in a remote area near the Pakistani border to afford them a view of a suspected missile site being constructed by Al-Qaeda. Intelligence sources indicated that, unbeknownst to the Pakistani government in Islamabad, radical elements of the Inter-Services Intelligence (ISI) and the Pakistani army were currently and covertly supplying long-range missiles with undetermined warheads to the secret base. It was a sensitive assignment since the outright destruction of the site would be an international incident. The ISI is the Pakistani intelligence agency that was reinforced during the 1980s with American money in an attempt to aid Afghanistan during the Russian occupation. Kevin remembered how that war of attrition lasted from 1979 until the US pulled out 10 years later, in no small part because of the US weapons that were funneled through Pakistan via the ISI. All manner and means were employed to deny US involvement, and as such, the ISI was given the task of delivering the weapons and materials across the border into Afghanistan. The ISI was hesitant to relinquish its newfound position of power and influence, inherited on the world stage from its surrogates, the CIA.

Kevin understood that this mission was to observe that base and determine what stage the construction was at, and if it was deemed possible, to employ the XLIMTR and render the missiles non-operational while maintaining plausible deniability for the US. That is the reason why this elite team was selected to carry out the mission, to keep it low-key and above suspicion. They were simply an Operational Detachment Alpha (ODA) team on the edge of Afghanistan, no different from the many others that dotted the length of the Af-Pak border and roamed the country. They were under relaxed grooming standards to keep them in sync with their fellow operators. They would stop shaving and let their hair grow out. Even though they wouldn't be interacting with the locals, anyone who happened to spot them would just assume they were doing the same thing as their counterparts and would avoid the area.

If the XLIMTR did what it was created to do, there would be no evidence left, and the ringleaders responsible for delivering the missiles certainly couldn't report them as destroyed. Captain Kevin McKenzie had his doubts about the XLIMTR, but who was he to say? The science was way over his head, but he thought it sounded plausible. Besides that, an order was an order.

Two

The first crashing boom startled Master Sergeant Mike Mann. He was angry with himself—had he fallen asleep? He asked himself how he was caught so off-guard. A veteran of several tours with Special Forces in Afghanistan and Iraq, Mike was accustomed to war, but this was an unfamiliar sound, something altogether different. The crescendo of explosions, the overwhelming noise, and the acrid smell of gunpowder assaulted his senses. *What the hell was going on?*

As the fog cleared from his head, the noise grew more intense. Mike struggled to sort out the situation. Then he thought he heard the sound of men stampeding toward him, a rousing chorus of screams, cries, and feet pounding the earth. He couldn't imagine what massive force of humanity was creating such a maelstrom. He stood up to get a better look and was amazed to witness thousands of men in blue uniforms armed with bayonets and charging straight at him and his men. A group of men clad in ragged gray uniforms was running in the other direction, many of them bloody and bandaged. Their haunting screams and cries competed with the nonstop gunfire. Mike couldn't make sense of the situation as clouds of dust and gun smoke billowed in every direction. Hell had arrived at his sacred half-acre, and Mike was instinctively analyzing the situation.

How were we surprised, and why aren't we returning fire? he wondered. Without any answers, he still needed to come up with a plan and take charge of the battle that raged in front of him. Just as he put out a call on the radio, he was rocked by an explosion that knocked his feet from under him.

"Status," he barked, and each member of the team methodically called in and gave his call sign and condition, just as Mike had taught them. The radio rattled off the call signs in order until the last man was due.

The radio crackled back to life when Staff Sergeant Dave Woods called in with a calm but rapid transmission, announcing, "Advancing troops, Dennis is hit, situation critical, need a medic, requesting permission to open fire."

Although Dave was young, he was far from green, and a deadly shot to boot. He decided not to wait for the reply that he knew was coming. He opened up with everything he had, and what he had was a devastating array of modern weaponry and an arsenal to feed it. There was a tremendous blast as he cracked off the dozen claymore mines that were emplaced a hundred yards in front of their position. Each mine unleashed its 700 steel balls, and they shredded the secondary wave of the advancing force. Then he cranked up his mini guns and they belted out their deadly tune of 6,000 rounds a minute, dropping the fast-approaching enemy at a staggering rate. The noise was deafening, the effect immediate. The men were stopped in their tracks, and the few survivors were trying to retreat as they stumbled over their fallen comrades.

There was a momentary lull in the shooting as the approaching troops searched for their next target. Mike was able to hear the distant sound of a bugle as incoming artillery commenced. Before the first rounds made impact, he launched his own mortars to deal a massive dose of death to everyone who had made the mistake of opening fire on his men.

Meanwhile, the ballistic computer made adjustments to dial into the acoustics and heat signatures of the incoming rounds and return fire to the source. The .50 caliber machine guns established their own rhythm of long-range fire, causing horse-mounted soldiers to drop like flies on the distant hill over a mile away. That onslaught was followed up with the Mk 19 grenade launchers that were capable of sending an explosive to an equal distance at the rate of 40 per minute. Snipers picked off the remaining soldiers who hadn't taken cover. The effect was dramatic and decisive. The incoming fire stopped abruptly, and the remaining soldiers were in full retreat. In their wake was a bloody battlefield littered with the dead and dying, as primal screams and moans filled the air.

Next, the ground started shaking and a low rumble built behind the stunned team of soldiers. Out of nowhere, a cavalry on horseback was charging toward them from the tree line almost five hundred yards away, the opposite direction of the previous attack. Their numbers were too many to estimate, but there was no denying the thunderous hooves of the massive steads that were fast approaching the bewildered men. They charged headlong and even plowed down several of their own men who made their way on foot. Following the urgent commands of their riders, the horses lurched forward and picked up speed, clearly intent on charging the team's position.

Mike wasn't going to risk having another teammate wounded as he grabbed the radio transmitter and bellowed: "Reverse position and fire!"

With enviable precision, the SF Team swiveled 180 degrees and took its spot on the opposite side of the perimeter, strategically placed artillery still within reach. In seconds, they were delivering another deadly dose of firepower at the aggressors. It was over in seconds. The soldiers on horseback were no match for the ten-man Special Forces A-Team; nevertheless, the effects were equally devastating. A nightmare of screams from the injured horses and wounded men filled the air.

What the hell just happened? Mike wondered. *Why were they armed with sabers and revolvers?* "I'll sort this out later," Mike said to himself before barking, "How's Dennis?" over the radio.

"Serious" was the immediate reply.

Mike was the senior enlisted member of the team, second in the chain of command to Kevin McKenzie, who was an eager but inexperienced captain. In the SF world, officers like Kevin came and went while the team's core remained together for years, usually the span of their military careers. The team sergeant—in this case, Mike—was in charge of the day-to-day operations, whereas Kevin oversaw the operation's big picture. Mike had spent years in the bush with most of these guys, and they respected his experience, often deferring to him, rather than Captain McKenzie, when the chips were down. A good captain recognized this delicate dynamic and prized the respect and buy-in of his team sergeant above all others.

As this was Captain McKenzie's first mission in charge, only time would tell whether he was the type to get in where he fit in and gain his men's respect, or storm the castle, wielding his rank with the subtlety of a battering ram. Coordinating the medevac pickup would be a joint effort between them, and they both knew that hierarchy was irrelevant at a time like this. Mike knew his men needed his composure and guidance now, and Kevin was grateful that Mike had those things nailed down at present.

Mike turned to Sergeant First Class Tom Kay. "Dial in the frequency to get a medevac bird spinning up and headed this way." Tom was as competent a communications sergeant as you could ask for, and Mike and Kevin had complete confidence in his abilities.

Meanwhile, Sergeant First Class Jan Stanton was tending to Dennis' wounds. He was Tom's medical counterpart and equally respected and trusted as the senior medic. The wound was serious: a large caliber bullet had lodged in his chest, and Dennis needed surgery immediately. While the three remained focused on stabilizing the soldier and getting him choppered out, the rest of the team pulled security to guard against further attacks. Judging by the carnage spread around them, the odds of that happening seemed remote, and the men were finally able to take stock of the massive devastation that they had wreaked.

The puzzling thing was, who had attacked them? The last thing any of them remembered was their Special Forces team had parachuted in and established a firebase hard along the Afghanistan border in preparation for the mission to monitor a missile site in neighboring Pakistan, but the men who littered the ground did not look like Pakistanis.

Mike was operating on instinct and adrenaline, but he forced himself to reflect back on the chain of events that had led up to the battle. *What the actual hell had happened? Where did these guys come from and what did they want with a fledgling crew like us?* There were a lot of unknowns, but Mike was certain of one thing: he had to devise a plan to secure the trust and confidence of his men and quickly assess the level of danger that remained.

Three

Mike couldn't reflect too long, for they still had a serious casualty to manage and a fierce, albeit temporarily halted, enemy probably aching for revenge. While the team's thoughts may have been scattered, their actions were deliberate as they set about securing a landing zone for the medevac helicopter. While Jan tended to Staff Sergeant Dennis Ayala's gaping wound, Tom was trying to raise someone—anyone—on the radio to secure a helo with little success. Meanwhile, Joseph was having similar difficulty with his equipment.

"Permission to borrow your GPS?" he asked Tom.

"Granted with reservations," Tom barked.

Joseph was momentarily worried that he had overstepped, but his superior was likely frustrated, and with good reason. Making contact with the outside world was paramount, especially for Dennis. His survival likely depended on it.

Joseph had a tendency to internalize such interactions. After all, he was still learning not only his job, but how to navigate his relationship with Tom, a mathematics major who could seem standoffish due to his analytical nature. It was a relationship that Mike kept an eye on as he watched the two men develop a productive working relationship. He would step in, if necessary, but for now, Mike was content to supervise from a distance.

Joseph quickly snapped on the device and waited for it to acquire enough satellite links to give him an accurate grid coordinate for their location. He had always been fascinated by the military's Global Navigation Satellite System (GNSS) and its benefits when used to track convoy movement, search for injured soldiers, and accurately pinpoint enemy locations.

Joseph knew the GPS would allow him to determine their three-dimensional position, speed, and time anywhere in the world no matter what the weather, but this time, something was different.

"What you got?" Tom barked, already impatient for an update.

"Neither GPS is working, but here's the grid," Joseph informed him.

"What?" Tom shouted in exasperation. "First the radio and then the GPS...what's going on?"

Without any answers, Joseph simply replied, "I can't raise anybody on the radio. I know we're transmitting, though. Mike is monitoring his radio and he copies us."

Tom then ordered his junior sergeant, "See how Jan is doing with Dennis while I brief the others."

Tom walked over to where Mike and Kevin were talking with Jack. All three of the seasoned veterans wore a worried look that Tom had not seen before.

"I have bad news to report," Tom said. "Neither the radio nor the GPS units are working. How should we proceed?"

Mike said, "I know you and Jan were busy with Dennis and haven't looked around but take a moment to do so now. Something's up."

Tom took a few moments to survey his surroundings and was alarmed by what he saw. "What the hell is going on? And what the hell just happened? I know we just unloaded a shit ton of ammo, and there are enough dead out there to prove it. But something doesn't look right."

"Exactly," Mike said. "The question is, who were we fighting? They are not like any soldiers we've ever encountered. And another thing, you see the terrain? It's different. The mountains of sand have been replaced by leafy green trees that are certainly not indigenous to the area."

"I guess I was distracted by the GPS malfunction," Tom said. "My question is not only who did we battle, but where the hell are we?"

By now everybody was wondering the same thing.

Jack, a Civil War buff, broke the brief silence. "Guys, I didn't want to say anything because it doesn't make any sense, but I thought those uniforms looked familiar when we were in the heat of battle. Upon closer inspection, I'm confident in saying that they are reminiscent of those worn in the War Between the States."

"The Civil War?" Kevin asked. "How is that possible? Is this some kind of joke?"

"I don't have those answers," Jack responded. "I just know the blue and gray when I see it. Did you get a good look at those men? That was an infantry armed with muskets and bayonets. I can't explain it, but we have to understand what we are dealing with."

After a brief silence, Kevin broke in. "Seriously, we've got to get Dennis out of here."

"Out of where and to where?" Mike wondered. "Let's assess our situation. We fought an unidentified enemy, our surroundings have somehow been altered, and despite our state-of-the-art communication equipment, we can't get a signal, much less contact headquarters. In fact, we don't know if there's anybody out there *to* contact."

As the words sunk in, they were jolted back to the more imminent situation at hand: they still had a man down. When the team approached Jan for an assessment, the look on his face was nothing short of alarming.

"Any improvement?" Mike asked hopefully.

"Negative," Jan replied. "We are trained in trauma care, but unfortunately, that's just not enough. Dennis has sustained at least two puncture wounds as far as I can tell without a full assessment. One entered his chest, but there's no way to tell if it punctured a vital organ. There's another in his leg which I fear may have severed his femoral artery. Again, there's no way to verify this information without the use of a properly stocked trauma unit."

"As you all know, blood loss is the number one preventable cause of death on the battlefield, but that's only if the proper tools are available to treat the injury. So, the first priority was to manage the bleeding, which I believe we have done for now. Yet, without knowing the extent of his injuries, all we can rely on is a little luck and a lot of prayer."

Jan had been so wrapped up in treating Dennis that he had missed out on the team's recent revelations.

"Jan, I have some news for you as well," Mike said.

"Yes?"

"Despite several attempts, we have exhausted all communications options and were unsuccessful in making any contact whatsoever."

"Are you saying there is no helicopter on the way? No medical help for Dennis?"

"Affirmative. In fact, it's time to pull the team together," Mike said as he put his hands to either side of his mouth to amplify his voice. "Guys, fall in over here! Let's regroup!" Mike watched as all eight of his men gathered around while Dennis continued to rest under the makeshift medic tent.

"OK, team, it's time to assess our situation and update everyone on the information we have thus far. Tom and Joseph have made every attempt to establish contact with no success. Of course, they will keep trying, but the fact is, the longer we go without reaching anyone, the less likely we are to do so."

"Fortunately, we are able to use the remote monitoring equipment to keep an eye on the battlefield so at least our perimeter is secured for now. As for the rest of the news, I'm just going to be as direct as usual. The fact is, we're not exactly sure what happened over the last 24 hours, but here's what we do know. We were forced to battle an aggressive, unidentified enemy that is alarmingly reminiscent of those who fought in the US Civil War. In addition, we have confirmed that our surroundings have somehow been altered, the foreboding mountains and arid desert being replaced by lush foliage not found in Central Asia."

Mike's announcement was met with complete silence. "Men, I don't pretend to have the answers. To be clear, I don't know what happened, who we fought, or where we are. The only thing I do know is that our two main priorities are to keep our perimeter secure and do everything we can to obtain help for Dennis."

Mike also knew that the dead bodies strewn outside of camp would soon start to decay, flies would then command this killing field and disease and vermin would rapidly follow, creating a hazardous situation for his team. Then there was still the possibility of enemy reinforcements. Not surprisingly, that was the least of his worries. They had plenty of ammo and adrenaline to deal with any future show of aggression.

Mike and Kevin paired up and stepped to the side for a quick huddle. "I'm proposing we establish a recon party to scour the vicinity for a suitable site to relocate the team," Mike proposed. "What are your thoughts?"

Kevin nodded. "I concur. We need to secure a defensible position that the entire team and all of our equipment can occupy for a stay of undetermined duration."

With that, Mike turned to his left and shouted, "Dave! Jack! Bring it in!"

The two men jogged over for a quick briefing. Kevin updated them on their plans and advised them to loop in anyone they need to assist with the mission.

Dave and Jack spent some time strategizing, discussing the requirements, and assessing urgency before deciding to take Joseph to assist with communication and Frank for an extra set of hands. As they geared up, the two men briefed Mike and Kevin on their plan. The four would strike out to the north since that seemed to be the shortest distance through the gruesome morgue stretched out in every direction. They would check in with the team via radio every hour on the hour as they searched for a suitable site, and of course in the event of an emergency, such as making enemy contact.

When it was time, they struck out on their mission with guns at the ready but no idea where they were headed or what might lie ahead. They moved in single file with Dave up front, followed by Jack and then Joseph, with Frank bringing up the rear. The normal SOP was for the first man to walk point, meaning he would keep an eye out for any sign of danger, and the last man to "watch their six," which refers to the 6:00 position on a clock being at your back if you're facing the twelve. The front and back are crucial positions to make sure the team is properly protected throughout the mission.

The foursome swiftly navigated the grotesque human landmines that littered the first leg of their route. The team maintained their focus on the mission but couldn't help examining the carnage and wondering who had attacked them. As Jack had pointed out, the dead were indeed wearing what appeared to be Union Civil War-era uniforms. All the weapons and paraphernalia also seemed consistent with that time period. They exchanged puzzled glances but continued to move in silence. Moving at a good clip, they covered six miles in less than two hours, only stopping to call in their progress as instructed.

Dave was the first to spot a structure up ahead, which the men promptly decided to recon as a possible base camp. They moved swiftly but remained vigilant. As they got within a quarter of a mile, they could see that the structure was what appeared to be a two-story clapboard house complete with a white picket fence, painted shutters, and potted plants on either side of the door. There was also a small band of people walking slowly along a primitive dirt road toward the house.

Dave held up his right fist to signal the men to stop and stay quiet as he pulled out his binoculars and observed the subjects. Then he motioned to the men to move in closer as he whispered, "Guys, we've made soft contact. There appear to be six unarmed civilians approaching the white structure which is clearly a residential home. The people are moving slowly and do not appear to be talking to each other. They are in a single-file line, led by two African American males, then two Caucasian females in dresses that fit snugly at the top and billow out as they reach the ground, and two African American females bringing up the rear."

The team remained out of sight, observing as the small band of travelers proceeded up the road, entered the gate, and ascended the porch steps. Dave signaled the team to keep alert as they moved slowly toward the house. When they were within 200 yards, they stopped in their tracks. One of the Caucasian females standing on the porch was pointing in their direction.

The team stopped once again as Dave spoke in a hushed tone. "They've got a visual on us, but they don't appear to be aggressive. However, we must approach with caution and establish contact. Jack, as the history expert, it's probably best if you make the first move."

Once the team reached the fence, Jack approached. "Hello," he said in a non-threatening tone. "We would like to speak with you, with your permission of course."

The woman who appeared to be in charge seemed surprised at his request but acquiesced, nonetheless.

"You may approach, sir," the woman said with a strong southern accent. "However, I do request that you leave your weapons by the fence as a gesture of goodwill."

"We can't do that, ma'am, but you have my word that we will remain at ease," Jack responded with a nod.

The men strode up to the porch with deliberate caution so as not to startle the group. It was hard to tell who was more confused, the four soldiers or the six people on the veranda.

"I am unfamiliar with your uniforms," the woman said as she wiped dust from her ruffled gown in an attempt to make herself more presentable. "Might I trouble you to identify yourselves?"

The small band of soldiers stood silently until Frank whispered to Joseph, "What in the *Gone with the Wind* is happening?"

Jack was used to Frank's wisecracks and ignored the comment as he stepped forward but remained at the bottom step as a sign that he was not the aggressor. "It's our pleasure to meet all of you," he said. "We are soldiers in the United States Army. We are on a peaceful mission to find medical assistance for one of our men who is wounded."

This time, the younger of the white women spoke. "It's a pleasure to meet you. I'm Mrs. Elisabeth Drummond, this is my mother," she said with a sweeping motion. "And these men are our servants."

Jack bowed in reverence and asked, "If I may ask, where is your husband?"

Her face momentarily sunk as she hesitated, then said in a faltering voice, "I'm afraid I'm not used to such direct questions from a stranger. However, the Union Army killed my beloved husband not more than a week ago." The team exchanged glances at the mention of a "Union Army."

Jack pressed her, "When was that specifically, ma'am?"

"Sir, I don't believe you've introduced yourself. May I suggest that be the first order of business?"

"You are so right," Jack said. "My apologies. My name is Jack Morrison, this is Dave Woods, Frank Holland, and Joseph Strong."

"Wonderful to meet you lovely folks," Frank said in his strong Alabama accent.

"Mr. Holland, the lilt in your voice echoes that of a true southern gentleman. And is Mr. Strong truly a soldier, an equal?"

Jack had anticipated this question with Joseph the only African American in their group. "Yes, ma'am," Jack responded. "Where we come from, everyone is equal, based on their military rank, of course."

"I do understand, Mr. Morrison. A pleasure to meet you, Mr. Strong, and the rest of you. As for your question, my husband was killed eight days ago," she replied, "on March 30."

Jack paused to consider how to phrase his next question without directly asking the obvious. He finally settled on a simple, "When did you marry him, Mrs. Drummond?"

She reflected briefly and then quietly replied, "September 15, 1852."

Now it was the team's turn to look dumbstruck. Their faces collectively turned ashen, and no one could utter a reply. Judging by their reactions, the woman assumed the four men were expressing their sorrow or regret.

She quickly said, "I know you had nothing to do with his passing. He was shot by Union soldiers on horseback when he went out to see what the commotion was outside. We fled out the back door into the woods, and the Union soldiers stayed in the house until only a few hours ago. Since all is quiet, we decided to come back. We're tired, thirsty, and hungry." As they listened to the woman speak, it was clear to all that this was a strong, confident woman who, even under such awful conditions, maintained her poise and dignity.

"How can we assist you?" Jack blurted out without even realizing it.

"I'm not sure you can," she answered. "But first I have a question for you. Since you aren't with the North, are we to conclude that you are Confederates?"

Jack was taken aback and not sure how to answer. He finally replied. "It may be difficult to understand, but we are on neither side. We are bystanders. What I can tell you is that we have food and water, and we can guarantee that nobody else will cause you further harm," Jack offered. "That is, if you will allow us to set up camp in your barn temporarily," Jack said with a grin.

She returned the smile and nodded. "You are welcome to stay as long as you like. Now, if you'll excuse us, we need to assess the condition of our house and get to work putting things in order."

With that, Jack and the other three walked out to the barn to check on its condition. To their surprise, they found it to be in excellent shape. Despite whatever else they had done, apparently, the Union soldiers had chosen not to ransack the barn. The men discussed using it as a base camp, but all quickly realized that their priority was to stay and render assistance to the six civilians. Jack decided that he and Dave would return to home base, leaving Frank and Joseph behind to secure the site. He briefed them and then radioed back to camp with his decision and course of action. Jack and Dave would leave immediately with an expected arrival of two hours, tops. The men would remain in radio contact with both sites and notify Mike before approaching his position. Despite their utter confusion about the events that had just transpired, they made their way swiftly back without incident. Their next task was to inform the others of what they had seen.

Although Frank and Joseph were not worried, they were unsure of their next move. They could easily defend the homesite if it were attacked. That wasn't an issue. Hell, they carried more firepower in their hands than a couple hundred of the fallen soldiers they had seen on the way there. What really had them scratching their heads was the awkward situation they'd found themselves in.

Frank was in his late 20s and had grown up in Alabama. Joseph was 28 but had grown up in Ohio. As the only African American in their troop, he was starting to grasp the totality of their situation. If he could believe his eyes and ears, they were standing outside a barn in Confederate territory in the middle of the Civil War. The woman they had just spoken with must have been the owner of the two Black men and two Black women. They were slaves. He couldn't believe that he was witnessing such horrors in person. It was the stuff of history books, not to mention the talk of family reunions. He had relatives who'd been slaves before making their way to the freedom of Ohio. How could he stand by and let those Black folks remain in servitude?

"I could singlehandedly free all four of them," he thought to himself. However, his deference to his team leadership is what kept him focused on just protecting the place until the others returned. They would sort it all out then. He was sure of it.

Frank interrupted his thoughts when he said, "Let's go up to the house and check things out."

"Do you think it's OK?" Joseph replied.

"Why not? Looks like we're bunking here for a while, might as well get to know our neighbors," Frank offered.

As they strode up the dirt road, Joseph was apprehensive. How would he deal with his first encounter with slaves? What could he do? What would *they* think about him?

In just under two hours, Jack and Dave approached the firebase cautiously and radioed in that they were preparing to enter friendly lines.

They met with Mike and Kevin and each duo filled in the other on the latest information they had obtained.

Mike called everyone together, and all seven men circled around the fire for some coffee as Dennis remained motionless.

Kevin couldn't resist asking, "Do you guys know where the hell we are?"

"I have no idea," Jan said. "To be honest, I've been so focused on Dennis."

Kevin continued, "Based on the intel Dave and Jack collected along with our investigation of the troops we defeated, we've come to a conclusion. However, before we get to that, everyone needs to keep an open mind and stay focused."

The men remained silent as Kevin continued, "I think we are in the middle of the US Civil War. In fact, the year is 1865. April, as a matter of fact." The men shared stolen glances as they pondered what it all meant.

"How is that possible?" Jan piped up. He knew that no one had an answer, but he felt it had to be addressed.

Kevin continued, "There's not much we can do about where we are. The most important thing is figuring out what we are going to do about it."

Mike quickly cut in to make sure the men were not alarmed, "The most important issue is getting the hell out of here before we're carried off by buzzards. Anyway, we can sit around and discuss all this later. It's getting late." Turning to Jack he asked, "Jack, can you fill in the others about what you encountered?"

"Small farm with six non-threatening residents, water and shelter available. Frank and Joseph stayed behind to establish camp in the barn with permission from the homeowner."

"Alright," Mike responded, "we're burning daylight, so let's get this show on the road."

"Oh yeah," Kevin said, "we've got some guests to transport with us." Jan and Jon Silverheels had been busy rendering medical treatment to some of the surviving soldiers they had discovered. It would be necessary to move them due to the risk of disease.

"How many are alive?" Dave asked.

"Twenty-six," Jan replied, "18 Union and eight Confederate. We'll treat them all the same, of course."

Jan and Jon had come to realize that, if they were indeed in the 1860s, the two of them likely possessed more medical training than any other people on the planet. They had medical supplies and equipment that were nonexistent for that period. The gravity of the situation and the impact of what they had done so far, coupled with what they were capable of doing, was starting to sink into their collective minds.

Everyone was eager to move, but they were just as keen to discuss everything that had happened. As they started working in teams of two to unload and break down the weapons systems, it became apparent that they could not move everything before nightfall set in.

"I hate to split us up with all the turmoil and uncertainty, but I see no way to avoid it. I'm not worried about our physical security. It's everyone's mental state that concerns me," Mike announced. "Dave and I will remain here until all the gear are moved. Let's work until darkness shuts us down. He and I will sleep here, and we'll resume in the morning."

With that said, the team set about loading and bundling the gear to be hauled on the four-wheelers to the other site. Jack and Tom took the first loads to the farmhouse and dropped off the equipment before setting off for another load, leaving Joseph to start setting up the commo gear. They repeated this drill again and again. They wore a path between the two sites that a blind man could follow. They kept this up until well after dark. At first, the four-wheelers frightened the folks at the farmhouse, along with the soldiers they were treating and transporting. They were in total disbelief at the beams of light emanating from the front of the vehicles.

Those reactions further reinforced to the team the impact they were having on these people, these times, and this moment in history. They all fell asleep that night with their imaginations soaring, each with his own dreams and visions of what lay ahead. They left two men awake at the farm while Dave and Mike took turns sleeping back at the battle-field. Jan and Jon steadfastly alternated tending to Dennis while the others stopped by to check on him as they rotated shifts.

Morning broke for the team. The men awoke slightly disoriented, wondering momentarily if it had all been a horrible dream. All they had was the comfort of one another and the familiarity of their weapons and gear. The only choice they had was to keep going with their routine. Get up, check their weapons and gear, then fuel their bodies with food and water. They took turns doing this so that someone was always alert with hands on a weapon. Kevin checked on Dennis and then rallied the men, attempting to keep everyone focused on moving the rest of the equipment. He had to tell himself just to keep putting one foot in front of the other. Once they got everything moved, they would figure out the rest.

The men methodically went about their tasks and had everything moved by early afternoon. While the rest of the team continued orga-nizing and setting up the gear and equipment, Kevin and Mike huddled up for a discussion. Dennis was not doing well and would likely not survive without surgery. Kevin's primary concern was treading lightly over history, whereas Mike's focus was on the fundamentals of staying alive and healthy. Unable to reconcile their differing opinions at the moment, they agreed to have a sit-down with the rest of the team later that night.

Meanwhile, everyone had gotten at least some exposure to their hosts at the farm. While there was no outright distrust by either party, it was still as if two alien life forms were coexisting. They observed each other warily, not sure where each other stood. Joseph and Frank had helped with a few chores and cleaned up while they waited for the rest of the team's arrival, and thus, had gathered a bit of information about the kind folks who had agreed to house them. Joseph had learned that the elderly Black man and woman were Edwin and Mattie, husband and wife. The younger two were their children, Silas and Annie. They were slaves that had belonged to Elisabeth's husband and had worked on his family farm for years. Silas and Annie were born in Virginia, where they had been taught to read and write. Joseph felt uncomfortable knowing that they were slaves and figured they were not yet ready to ask him about his status as a free Black man. Neither was he prepared to deal with the topic, and Joseph wasn't sure how or even if he could help them. He decided to bide his time.

That night, lots of questions and very few answers hung in the air as the meeting kicked off. Captain McKenzie started, "Men we're not sure what happened or how we arrived here. However, it appears as though we are in Virginia in April 1865. In our estimation, we landed in the middle of the Battle of Sayler's Creek. I did my master's thesis on this period of the Civil War, and this battle was instrumental in Lee's surrender at Appomattox a few days later. Grant had chased Lee's army as he tried to move south to recover and refit after being driven from Richmond. This was the final battle of the Civil War. What this means, of course, is that we may have seriously altered the course of United States history."

He continued solemnly, "On another note, Dennis is not doing well. We need to lay low here until we figure out how to travel back to our own time and get him the help he needs." Glances flew around the barn as questions simmered in everyone's minds.

"What do you mean 'lay low'?" asked Jack.

"We need to refrain from disturbing history as much as possible," replied Kevin.

"Ha!" Jack scoffed. "You just said we were in the middle of a decisive battle, and as I walked here and back from the battlefield, I saw thousands of Union soldiers dead and dying. I think we have already disturbed history. Lee is not going to surrender now, and Grant's army is devastated."

"I know," Kevin replied, "but I think we need to do our best to avoid any further interference. Our actions could alter history!"

"Think about what you're saying," said Frank. "The history of the United States just underwent a huge revision, and you want to stop now to minimize the impact." That prompted several nods of agreement from the team.

"Think of it this way," Jack said. "We just changed the course of the Civil War. The South won't surrender. Lincoln probably won't be assassinated. Neither side knows why or what happened, so the war may continue."

"We can't stop now," Jon added. "We have a moral obligation. Besides, who's to say we'll figure out how to get back to our time?"

It was Dave's turn to interject. "We may be stuck here for the rest of our lives. What do we do, twiddle our thumbs, hoping the switch is thrown to get us back so we can start all over? Are we really going to right the wrongs of history? Save a president from assassination?"

Tom brought up the point that because they had already changed history, even if they did make it back by some miracle, they may have killed some of their relatives and might not even exist in the altered future. Then he explained that all of their electronic gear was somehow still functioning.

"Radios are fine and continue to work even though we're the only ones with them. Computers, as well, but there's no internet or connectivity obviously. Range finders and sensors still work."

"Great, we have some commo equipment that is marginally useful," Mike said. "In the meantime, we stand out like aliens from outer space. We have no money or clothes, other than what we brought. How are we going to go about assimilating with these people?"

Jon, a Native member of the Mohawk nation, spoke up. "Hey, Captain McKenzie, remember back at the battlefield you mentioned that while we were walking around you saw that Cavalry officer? And that when you examined his uniform you said that it was General Custer and that he had been present at that particular battle?"

Kevin responded, "Yeah, I did say that. In fact, I looked in his saddle bags to confirm his identity."

Jon went on, "Well, I'm no history major, but while I was at Sturgis one year, I went down to Deadwood, and I read something that said Custer discovered gold at French Creek around 1874. That ended up being the Homestake mine. Turned out it was the largest in the US."

Now Jon was getting visibly excited. "Custer is no longer with us, and that gold is just sitting there. That would give us a pretty good stake to survive on until we can get everything sorted out."

"Great idea," said Frank. "Somebody's gonna discover it someday. Might as well be us." This wasn't what Mike had in mind, but the more he thought about it, the more it made sense.

Captain McKenzie was resistant to the idea, reiterating, "I said we need to refrain from upsetting history any more than we already have. We need to stay here until we figure out how to return to our time."

When Jack spoke next, he brought up something that no one had considered. "Captain McKenzie, when were you commissioned?"

"2006," Kevin answered.

"So," Jack continued, "you have another 150 years or so by my reckoning before you become an officer. I mean no disrespect, but none of us is even *in* the army now." That sent everyone reeling, and a telling silence fell over them.

When it came Mike's turn to speak, everyone listened closely. "Men, we possess the ability to significantly alter history for better or worse with our knowledge, technology, and weapons. Let's all take some time to consider what we intend to do with this power. As Jack said, we're not really in the army anymore. The army we joined does not exist. There is no means to discipline, promote, demote, discharge, or pay anyone. I hope that doesn't mean we're not still a team though."

Elisabeth, who had been nursing Dennis while the team conducted its meeting, hesitantly approached the men. Her face was drawn, and she seemed despondent. She looked at the team in sorrow and quietly announced that Dennis had died. It was not unexpected as the news brought with it a moment of reflective silence. Elisabeth left the men to process their loss. Death was an inescapable part of this line of work.

Every soldier knew that, and Mike had coached them to visualize these events in their minds so that when injury or death invariably occurred, it would not be such a shock. Perhaps more critically, this exercise prepared them to drive ahead with the mission at hand. What they were not prepared for were the finality and isolation. There was no one to call and inform; no body bag to be recovered by a helicopter; there was just the team, their memories, and the task of conducting a burial and ceremony for Dennis.

The guys walked up to the farmhouse and asked if there was a graveyard nearby. Elisabeth informed them there was a family plot a little piece up the road, with the freshly dug grave of her husband. She also told them that she would be proud to have Dennis buried there. Silas and Edwin went out to the barn, retrieved two shovels, and accompanied the team as they carried Dennis' remains to the burial plot. They took turns digging in the dry soil in silence. They gently placed the body in the grave, and Jan gave a brief eulogy before closing with a prayer. Edwin and Silas were touched by the kind words that Jan had spoken, especially the prayer.

On the walk back, Silas struck up a conversation to break the tension. He asked where the nine men were from. Glances immediately darted among the team. Kevin, first to speak, told him they hailed from North Carolina since that was where they had been stationed. It would be easier than trying to explain they were from places that may not even exist yet. Naturally, Silas was particularly curious about Joseph.

"Are you a freed negro?" he asked.

All Joseph could think to reply was "yes."

He couldn't or wouldn't offer any further explanation. It would be too confusing, at least for now. Silas asked how he might go about becoming free. He would volunteer to help the team, doing anything that needed to be done if they would help him and his family gain their freedom. Joseph searched for an answer as he looked at Mike.

"Done," said Kevin, "You, your parents, and your sister are now officially and irrevocably free."

An earthshaking revelation, yet so simple and straightforward for these strangers from North Carolina. Silas and Edwin smiled from ear to ear and kicked up their heels as they hurried back to the house to share the news.

Mike was first to break the silence. "I thought we were going to be careful how we use our position of power. I understand and agree with your sentiment, but how are you or any of us going to enforce this decree you just put in place? And what about Elisabeth and her mother? Shouldn't we have warned them? They've been incredibly gracious to us."

Kevin's answer was matter of fact: they would simply have to keep them all on board with the team to ensure that they would remain free.

"And how the hell are we going to do that when we don't even know how long we'll be here?" Mike asked. "This just reinforces the problems we will incur if we are not careful with our decisions and our power. We can either accomplish great achievements or conversely, we can create stunning failures."

As one of the oldest members of the team, Jack was seen as the resident voice of reason, albeit with a strong southern drawl. "Guys, I'm not sure we all share the same expectations of what our goals should be at this point. As y'all know, we have tilted the Civil War in favor of the South. Do you understand what that means? Our responsibility now is to focus on what is in front of us. I think we can use this opportunity to practice some statesmanship, eliminate slavery, and influence both sides to reach a peaceful resolution to the war. We can even ensure that President Lincoln will not be assassinated, and the South will not suffer through the oppressive measures it endured during reconstruction."

The others looked on as he continued. "Neither side will have to harbor the ill will that still existed when we left our own time. We can—quite frankly, we must—take this opportunity to revise history in a positive manner to the best of our ability. We're all human and have our own wants, needs, and desires distinctly separate from our wishes to return to our own time. While we're here, and God only knows how long that will be, whether it is five more minutes or the rest of our lives, let us behave in a manner that puts history on the path to right all the wrongs that we have studied all our lives. Let us make a path to correct all of the injustices we have witnessed ourselves."

The men were silent as they considered the gravity of Jack's words. He had a way of seeing the bigger picture when others were mired in the minutiae of the present.

Finally, Jan responded with a hearty, "Amen."

Tom was next to take the torch and speak his thoughts. "That is a much more complex goal than we know," he allowed. "There are second- and third-order effects to every decision we make."

Mike summed it up with a question he put to every man. "Let me put it this way: who thinks we should live as if we will find a way back to our former time, and who believes we should focus on the here and now? The former will involve leaving history undisturbed, whereas the latter will necessitate that we take matters of the world into our own hands. Let's all think about it. Let's have a barbeque tonight, at which point we'll reconvene and discuss the next steps."

They decided to have a big celebration. For their part, Joseph and Frank were tasked with finding something to cook. They walked up to the house and asked if there were any chickens, pigs, or cows to be bought anywhere. Elisabeth replied that the Union soldiers who had been there had stolen them all.

"What they didn't kill to eat, they took with them," she lamented. "We had twenty head of cattle, a couple of dozen pigs, and about 30 chickens. They took the guns we had and left us nothing. We've been scrounging around while Edwin has been trapping rabbits."

Moved just as much to help their hosts as he was to have some fresh barbequed brisket and pork, Joseph asked, "Do you know where they took the livestock?"

Elisabeth answered, "We heard they were camped over the other side of Amelia."

"How far is that from here?" Joseph asked.

"Edwin said it was 10 or 12 miles east. You just follow the road to the next town," Elisabeth explained. Frank confidently assured her that the men would take care of it.

The soldiers walked back to the barn discussing their plan. When they walked in, Frank informed everyone of the conversation they'd just had. He and Joseph planned to take a four-wheeler into town to reclaim the livestock that had been taken from the Drummond farm.

Kevin asked, "And how do you propose to do that?"

"Well, I can't see anybody stopping us," Joseph answered.

"And if they try?" Mike asked.

"Well, we've already demonstrated what we are capable of doing," Frank shot back.

Jan was the first to raise an objection. "Is it really worth it to kill someone over a cow?"

Frank, eager to deliver on his promise to Elisabeth, was resolute. "The Union Army stole it from these people and left them with nothing. I intend to do my first good deed for the day." Frank

"Besides," Mike cut in, "they don't even know who inflicted the devastating defeat on them. As far as they know, you two are aliens from another planet."

"Exactly," said Frank with confidence, "and we'll demonstrate to them that it was our crew who kicked their asses."

To ensure that Frank had thought through his plan, Kevin asked, "And how do you propose to do that?"

Frank had an answer ready. "I think a short burst on full auto will get their attention."

Kevin, reluctant to see another massacre take place so soon, cautioned him, "I don't think this is what I intended when I said we can alter history."

"We gotta start somewhere!" Frank shot back.

"It won't take long before everyone knows who we are, and then we won't have to prove ourselves anymore." Jan reasoned, "Is that what we're going to be all about?"

"He's got a point," said Mike. "If we intend to right the wrongs of history, we have to carry a big stick. All the important historical decisions were made with a stick. We're bound to upset a lot of people, and we have to be prepared to stand our ground."

Kevin felt the tension uptick and quickly replied, "Not for something as trivial as some livestock."

"Since when are theft and hunger trivial?" Frank fired right back. "You don't have to eat any of it if it is against your principles."

Mike immediately stepped in. "No need for that," he said. "We're all trying to put together the pieces of the same puzzle."

Frank and Joseph had clearly made up their minds, and the others determined that it wasn't worth the confrontation to try and stop them. It was, though, the first seed of doubt about how long they would all remain on the same team.

Four

While Frank and Joseph mounted the belt-fed M-249 machine guns on the four-wheelers, Jon volunteered to go with them. "I'll bring a radio so we can stay in communication with the rest of the team back at the house, otherwise known as HQ," Jon said with a smirk. He made a plan to call Tom on a set schedule and check on things. To keep the channel open, Tom would also leave his radio on until the group returned.

With that, the three once again asked Edwin for directions. Then Joseph said, "Look, Edwin, would you be interested in joining us and acting as our guide? We could use someone with your expertise in the surrounding land. Should be quite an adventure."

Edwin smiled at the prospect of helping his new friends as equals. "I'd sure like to accompany you folks."

The four men set off on the four-wheelers, not sure what they might find or who they might encounter. Joseph wasn't sure what would be more alarming, the two white men and two Black men together, or the steel horses that probably looked like creatures from Mars.

Edwin found the ride terrifying and exhilarating. Here he was riding through the country as a free man, and he was accompanied by three others who not only didn't seem to exhibit any fear of traveling with him, but even enjoyed his company as they zipped through the middle of battle-torn Virginia.

He couldn't help but think about how Joseph looked like him but was treated as an equal by his comrades. It gave Edwin great pleasure and filled him with an optimism he'd never known. With these kinds of friends, he wasn't scared of anything anymore, and that was a feeling he didn't want to end.

Edwin couldn't believe how fast they whizzed down the road on these iron beasts. When he was a boy, Edwin had been told to ride a former racehorse to test its speed. The thoroughbred was trained to outrun the competition at all costs. As horse and rider sailed around the makeshift track, Edwin was sure he'd never travel at a higher speed. Yes, here he was on a steel horse that maintained top speed without tiring.

After traveling another 20 minutes, the band of men encountered a large group of Union Cavalry in a cluster up ahead on the road. They downshifted the metal beasts so as not to spook the horses.

One of the Cavalry soldiers raised his hand with his palm up. Frank, driving the lead four-wheeler, stopped about 200 yards short of the horsemen to discuss what they were going to do.

"Guys," Frank said, "there is a house just off to the left of the road on a slight hill. The soldiers have obviously been using it as a headquarters. Look, there are tents and campfires scattered around. Over there are maybe 40 or 50 horses staked out 100 yards behind the house. Did you guys get a look at those uniforms?"

This was the moment for a critical decision. Frank got off his four-wheeler and walked purposefully ahead. Joseph and Jon instinctively covered him with the machine guns as Edwin stayed by the four-wheelers. The Cavalrymen who blocked the road seemed confused, yet resolute that they were not going to let anyone get past them.

Joseph turned to Jon, "Are those guys the rear guard for the Union Army that retreated after we gave them the old SF team smackdown?"

The four men looked at each other and without speaking knew they were in agreement. They were going to pass.

Joseph was the first to notice that some of the soldiers were bringing their weapons to the ready position. He looked back over his shoulder, yelled, "Warning shot!" and let loose with a five-second burst of machine gun bullets that punctured the air. Next, all hell broke wide open as the horses scattered in a panic, tossing their riders as they broke into a full gallop away from the uproar.

The sound of the barking machine gun spitting out 150 or more rounds was a terrible reminder of what the Union Army, and its steeds, had recently experienced at Sayler's Creek. The Union soldiers recognized that they were face to face with the source of the overwhelming defeat they had so recently experienced. With fear and submission hanging tangibly in the air, Frank boldly strode up to the Cavalry officer who had raised his hand to stop him.

"Let me be clear," he hissed. "We will not only be passing through here, but also coming back this way soon. See to it that none of your men attempts to stop us again. Is that understood?"

"Yes, sir," the lieutenant snapped back.

Frank turned to leave and then wheeled back around on his heels, adding, "Another thing. We will reclaim the livestock that was stolen from the Drummond farm." The lieutenant volunteered to ride ahead and round up the livestock in preparation for their return.

"You do that," Frank said. "We'll wait here for two hours and don't make us come looking for you."

With a smart "Yes, sir!" the lieutenant beat a hasty retreat.

Frank returned to the four-wheelers, high fiving Joseph, who said, "Good thinking. I never would have thought of that, but it scared the hell out of them."

"Can you blame them?" asked Jon. "After what they witnessed on the battlefield, they would have dropped their pants and bent over if you told them to. That approach worked because we are dealing with people who saw what we can do on the battlefield. Be aware that we might need another approach for those who didn't experience it firsthand."

"Well, I think we're good for a while then," Joseph said laughingly. "At least long enough to round up some grub."

Frank then explained that the lieutenant had ridden off to round up the livestock and should return in about two hours. "We might as well make a commo shot back to HQ to let them know all's well," he instructed. "Tell them we'll be back later with a herd of livestock, so they better get to mending those fences," he said with a grin.

Five

The four men returned late that evening with a herd of cattle, some pigs, and even a few chickens and turkeys that had been surrendered. They managed to tie the birds onto the four-wheelers and led all the rest of the animals on foot. In addition, Joseph had even enlisted some of the Union soldiers to help drive the livestock back. The rest of the team shared celebratory high-fives as Elisabeth beamed with joy. They had managed to bring back more animals than the soldiers had taken.

Mike asked, "How did everything go, team?"

The men relayed the story about Joseph unleashing a warning burst on the machine gun, which garnered cheers all around. For the first time since they had arrived, the mood felt light as they all laughed and congratulated one another on a job well done.

Joseph added, "Edwin here has even volunteered himself and Silas to butcher a cow in the morning."

"That's excellent. Thank you both," Kevin replied. "All of us will eat good tomorrow." Everyone was satisfied and they began settling in for the evening.

Soon, though, Mike interrupted the quiet to share his thoughts. "Men, I don't think we need to keep anyone up for guard duty anymore. I'm fairly certain we can leave all the sensors on and set them to alarm if anyone or anything approaches. Does anybody disagree or have any other thoughts?" he asked.

No one objected so he moved on to the next subject. "While you three were gone, some of us discussed our plight. Now that we have some meat to supplement our rations, we need to consider what we're going to do about money. We can sustain ourselves here at HQ, but we have no means of obtaining anything via the local economy, unless we use Joseph's technique," he mused. "For example, what are your suggestions for clothes and how to acquire them? What are we going to do about transportation? The four-wheelers will run out of fuel if we use them for extended travel because we initially planned only to use them around the base."

Jack stepped forward. "I saw some of the horses that the Cavalry rode. As you may know, the Union Army was known to have supplied their men with good horses. Let's send a team out and round up some of them," he suggested.

Frank added, "After the impression we made on them, I'm sure the lieutenant I spoke with would be glad to assist."

"We can't wait long," Jack cut in, "they're probably hightailing it back north right now. How about four of us head out in the morning and get this impromptu mission rolling?"

With no objections, they made plans for Frank, Joseph, Jon, and Jack to ride back into town at sunrise to round up some horses.

As the last slivers of light faded in the dark countryside, the men decided to turn in for the night. They set off for the barn, but Frank paused to glance backward at the main house. Elisabeth was holding court in a wooden rocking chair on the porch as she stared out into the night. Frank waited for the others to file into the stables, and he quietly looped back toward the porch. Elisabeth seemed lost in thought, her long auburn locks blowing gently in the breeze.

Frank tried to make a bit of noise as he approached so as not to startle her. When he was close enough, he whispered "Excuse me, Mrs. Drummond," he said in his deep Southern drawl.

She turned her head and smiled politely. "Thank you again, Mr. Holland, for helping reclaim our livestock. We have been on the verge of starvation, and we might not have made it without your generous assistance. We are eternally grateful."

He nodded his head and replied, "Please call me Frank, and the pleasure was all mine, ma'am. Well, what I mean is that we are all glad to help. You've been such a kind hostess letting us stay here while we..." His voice trailed off as he realized that he didn't know quite what they aimed to do.

Elisabeth gestured to the rocking chair on her right and watched as he approached with mild hesitation but eventually settled down into the weather-worn chair beside her as he rested his hands on his knees.

The two sat in silence for a few moments while Frank contemplated what to say next. He had not considered why he wanted to talk with her; he just knew that he wanted to get to know her better. It was a feeling he had, and he'd learned long ago to trust his instincts. Although some of the guys found her sophisticated and somewhat reserved, Frank felt quite comfortable in her presence. Perhaps it was that she was a refreshing departure from his buddies in the ODA, or maybe she was a reminder of the good country folks back home in Red Level, Alabama.

Frank had grown up there but later moved to Birmingham for an engineering job. He had not been back to visit the small town of his youth for more than five years. Not that it much mattered, as things seldom changed there, but he thought of it often. A new restaurant might be the only thing different in that small town that seemed eternally and refreshingly frozen in time. He decided to ask her if she had ever been as far south as Alabama.

No, Mr. Holland, er, Frank," she replied with a shy smile. "I was born in Richmond, where my father was the town doctor. I occasionally traveled with him to the surrounding counties as visited his patients, but I've never been outside Virginia."

"If I may ask, how do you find Alabama? Did you enjoy growing up in such a small town?" she asked.

His face lit up as he began to describe the small farm where he ran barefoot every day as he performed his chores. She listened attentively and asked thoughtful questions about his family and his life there. Her genteel manner and the lilt of her southern twang put him so at ease that he was surprised to discover they had been talking for hours. The conversation flowed effortlessly until Elisabeth slowly stood up.

"I have enjoyed our visiting time, Frank, but I really must retire for the night."

After she entered the house, Frank continued to rock in his chair for several more minutes, simply pondering their new reality and his feelings for such a pure soul. While he longed to return to the familiarity of home, he had begun to establish a genuine connection with the civilians who were housing the band of strangers with unfettered generosity. In return, he wanted to do whatever he could to help improve their lot in life and ensure that they—and Elisabeth, in particular—were properly cared for. As he headed off to bed, he resolved to protect their best interests when the team made plans to move forward. He had joined the army to serve, and in this new time and place, he had discovered a new cause worthy of defending.

The next morning, everyone was up early seemingly eager to get started with the day's agenda, but none earlier than Edwin and Silas. To make sure everyone was able to eat as soon as possible, Edwin and Silas had risen earlier than everyone else to butcher one of the cows. The Holstein was hanging by its back legs when Joseph approached. "May I offer my assistance to you gentlemen?"

Edwin enjoyed his time with Joseph, and he immediately replied, "Yes, sir."

Joseph smiled politely and put his hand on the older man's shoulder. "Edwin, I can assure you that it's not necessary to address me as 'sir.' While it might be hard to believe right now, in this country, all men are created equal."

"In fact," he continued, "You, sir, are my elder. Therefore, I will call *you* 'sir,' and you can call me 'Joseph.'"

A wide, beautiful smile spread across Edwin's face as he basked in the warmth and consideration. His family was unused to such kindness, and he wasn't quite sure what to think of the arrangement, but he wasn't going to argue. As they finished preparing the cow, Edwin mustered the courage to ask Joseph the all-important question. "How did you become a free man?"

Joseph had to think about that for a minute before he answered. "That, my friend, is a long story, and it is also the reason we're here. I promise you, very soon, all Black folks will be free."

Edwin and Silas smiled even though they had no idea how such a societal change would come to pass. Joseph's confidence gave them a reassurance that he was someone they ought to trust. The three of them finished butchering and started a fire to cook the meat. When Joseph saw Frank, Jon, and Jack making their way across the yard, he stood up to greet them. "Well, if it isn't the three musketeers," Joseph shouted to the trio.

"I'm more of a Snickers guy myself," Frank quipped.

Ignoring him, Joseph turned to Edwin and said, "Thank you, sir, for all that you are doing for us here. Your kindness will not be forgotten." Edwin just smiled and nodded his head. He vowed to himself then and there that he would do whatever Joseph asked—not because he had to, but because he wanted to. "Thank you, Mr....umm...thank you, Joseph," he managed.

"We'll see y'all when you get back." Joseph smiled in return and waved as he walked away. The four soldiers then hopped on their four-wheeled steel mounts and rode toward the rising sun in search of horses of a different color.

Six

The trip to town went off without a hitch. The quartet of soldiers managed to acquire a couple of dozen horses that the deceased Cavalry men no longer had use for and brought back twenty pack horses, as well as two wagons and mule teams. Even with such an impressive haul, they made it back in time for the huge feast. With the livestock safely ensconced in one of the Drummond paddocks, everyone was able to relax and enjoy the festivities. They ate their fill, and there was plenty left over, an unusual situation given the recent food shortages. Jan even brought out his guitar and serenaded the crowd while Frank danced with Elisabeth as the others cheered them on.

Later that night, the discussion returned to their plight and a brainstorming session to explore their available options. Kevin was still focused on the opportunity to inject themselves into the political scene and change the direction of the discussions that were undoubtedly taking place in both capitals.

"We have the ability to initiate and control peaceful negotiations between the North and South to avoid the disastrous consequences that resulted from the first conclusion," he said. Since Kevin was the undisputed authority on Civil War history, Jack knew that drawing the entire team into the fold on this subject was critical, so he prodded Kevin for more information.

"Can you give us some background on the dynamics between the two sides, Kevin? I took American History, but feels like it was about four decades ago," Jack quipped.

Kevin fancied himself a lifelong scholar and was visibly excited to give the others a quick lesson. "History tells us," he continued eagerly, "that at this point, support for the war is flagging in the North. Money is tight, and public resistance to the conflict is increasing. Lincoln is in a politically tight spot and keen on ending the fighting. With this recent defeat that we dealt the Union Army by happenstance, his options are fading even more. So, in a way, we've already made an impact on history."

Kevin had become downright professorial as the team trained its attention on him. He continued with the animated enthusiasm that only a history major could muster. "Lincoln is a pragmatic man who has publicly supported favorable conditions for the South in the event of surrender. I see an opportunity for us to intercede here. We know that Jefferson Davis is on the run, both literally and figuratively. We also know that the South is facing severe economic hardships due to the northern blockade of southern ports. We already saw that on a small scale with the issues the Drummond family has faced. With little manufacturing capability, the South can't sustain war much longer. Moreover, its people are weary, making the situation ripe for bilateral reconciliation." He paused briefly to allow the others to consider his words.

"OK, the professor is using words like 'moreover.' This must be serious," Frank cracked.

Mike, always looking for the bottom line, stepped in to ask for clarification. "What exactly do you hope to accomplish by playing diplomat?"

Kevin had his answer at the ready. "Neither side has any idea what happened when we arrived or why the tide of war has suddenly shifted. We can use that to dramatic effect to coerce Lincoln and Davis to sign a more equitable agreement between them: one that abolishes slavery, preserves states' rights, and most crucially, respects the rights of all humans." None of the men disagreed with that logic.

Kevin added, "If we are considering taking action, we must hasten to Washington since historically, Lincoln will be assassinated on April

15, 1865. That doesn't give us much time—only about seven days—to set this plan in motion."

It was Jon's turn to speak up. "Don't forget, we still have no way to buy supplies or fund our journey if we decide to strike out for Washington, DC. My suggestion is that we head for Deadwood and claim the gold that is there for the taking."

Jon had clearly brought up the topic to gain support from others willing to accompany him and a party of prospectors on a gold strike for the history books. It was obvious that the team had already bought into Kevin's proposal to reshape political relations, so the guys turned the discussion to the prospect of mounting an expedition to South Dakota.

"Remember, although our GPS doesn't work here, we still have the topographical map data on the laptops," Tom offered. "Just take a couple of solar chargers and an extra battery," he added.

"As you guys know, I'm a full-blooded Mohawk," Jon said. "I know the area well enough, and if we can get in the general vicinity, I can steer the prospectors close enough for them to discover the gold. With some of the explosives we have available, we could easily blast an exploratory mine." He stopped to let the group take it all in before continuing.

"I'm confident in saying that all we need is a dependable crew to take us up the Missouri River, which we all know is no small feat, but the payoff would be worth it."

Despite the challenges they would face, the team agreed to support the plan. After all, they would never back down from a challenge. They would strike out as soon as they finalized the details of personnel.

Then Tom spoke up, "I just want to point out that the team laptops are loaded with map data, but we won't be able to track the group as it travels, which, as you know, is standard protocol. Even so, the data may help provide important waypoints and landmarks."

It seemed the logical place to start was St. Louis, Missouri. However, getting to St. Louis was going to be an ordeal itself. Mike instinctively entered planning mode, his blue eyes gleaming with excitement. This was his forte. "Three of us can head to the east coast, find a ship bound for New Orleans, offer our services as security, and then take a steam-ship up the Mississippi River to St. Louis. Once there, we'll provision ourselves for the expedition up the Missouri River to Deadwood. We just need to decide how to pay for the supplies and manpower we will need."

As they sat around the fire that night, the sky was clear, and the stars were bright. No artificial light pierced the darkness. It was peaceful and lulled everyone into a complacent state. Had it not been for the intense planning still hanging over them, they could have dozed off peacefully without a care in the world. That, however, would have to wait because time, as they knew, would not. The men needed to get moving straightaway because their plan, and their lives, depended on it.

They reached a consensus that Mike, Jon, and Frank would depart as soon as possible for Deadwood via Baltimore. Meanwhile, Kevin and Joseph would accompany them as far as Washington, DC. Armed with the knowledge that Kevin had laid out earlier in the evening, he and Joseph would attempt to track down Lincoln and urge him to the bargaining table. They appealed to Jack to do likewise in seeking out Jefferson Davis to get him on board, using force if necessary. As for Jan and Tom, they had chosen to remain at HQ to tend to the wounded, maintain the camp, and monitor the team's radio communications. They knew that with their long-range antennas, they would be able to stay in touch with one another and coordinate their actions as events progressed.

Tom informed everyone, "I've drawn up a sitrep board to keep track of everyone's progress to help us here at HQ. Try your best to call in as often as possible so we can keep it updated. This way, we can stay informed no matter which one of us receives the radio call. Timewise, this should roll out in three phases. The Washington team is the first leg and the only one with an obvious deadline, April 14, 1985, the day Lincoln was, er, *is* shot. Next is the New Orleans jaunt, followed by the Deadwood trip which will likely take the longest amount of time. The only urgency with those two missions is that they need to reach their destination before anyone else gets the same idea."

Kevin added, "I just want to clarify that our plan is not to rewrite or erase history. It's to explore how and why things happened as they did, decode the ramifications of those decisions, and try to influence a better outcome for this country."

Satisfied with the progress they had made working as a team, Mike announced, "It looks like we've laid out an ambitious operation made up of three tactical missions. To clarify, our purpose is to preserve the peace and security of the United States, today and in the future. Let's all raise a glass to Operation Altered History!"

Everyone saluted the official kickoff of their plan and headed off to bed.

Dawn came early on that crisp April morning as the dew-covered landscape stretched as far as the eye could see. Everyone was wide awake and eager to get rolling. As the men prepped their gear, Edwin and Silas came ambling down the road to see them off.

"Greetings, all. Might Silas and I be of assistance?" Edwin asked.

Joseph smiled as he strode over to them. "You're welcome to help us pack."

As they stacked the packs in a pile, Edwin said, "We sure hope you fellas will be OK. Mrs. Drummond is mighty worried; I can tell you that."

"It will be fine," Joseph assured him. "It's a military operation. This is what we are trained to do."

"Yes, sir—er, Joseph," Edwin replied.

Joseph noted that Edwin and Silas were especially curious about the MREs they saw the men loading. He handed one to each of them, opening one himself as they observed. He gave them a nod indicating they should do likewise. It was as if the father and son were biting into Thanksgiving dinner as they tore open each packet and tasted the contents with such pure joy.

"Dee-licious!" Silas exclaimed with a smile.

The rest of the team watched in amusement as Frank commented, "I've never seen anyone so thrilled about eating vacuum-sealed food. Image if they tried a Hungry Man dinner!" The simple scene reminded everyone just how far food science had progressed in less than 150 years.

Traveling on horseback would allow them to use saddle bags, rather than the typical 55-pound rucksacks they were accustomed to. While they loaded their ammunition, spare batteries, radios, MREs, extra clothing, and sleeping bags, they relished the thought of not having to carry it all on their backs.

However, they soon realized that saddle bags and bed rolls had a much smaller capacity than their military packs. The men were discovering that although much had changed, some things were still the same; for example, their line of work was all about constant adaptation. They all knew that failure to adapt was failure to survive.

Tom's arrival interrupted the preparations. "Team, we have visitors approaching."

They all stopped to observe a horse-drawn carriage bouncing along the four-wheeler tracks that they had established while transporting their gear from the battlefield. The carriage was a rather elegant one, led by four fine horses, and the driver stopped a few hundred yards short of where they all stood. An elderly gentleman, smartly dressed in a dark suit and a top hat, descended the carriage steps, glancing curiously about the party assembled before him.

He began walking in their direction, and when he was within earshot, he waved and said good-naturedly, "Good day, gentlemen." Kevin reciprocated the greeting and stuck out his hand.

The distinguished gentleman shook it saying, "I'm Robert Winslow, and I've come here looking for my son. He is a captain in the Richmond garrison troops. I scoured the battlefield back there, searching among his comrades, and spoke to one who told me he was wounded and then evacuated by a troop of soldiers. I followed your tracks here, and I hope to recover his remains for a proper burial back in Richmond."

Kevin interjected, "Mr. Winslow, I just want to assure you that we were not the aggressors in the situation. Our goal was to defend ourselves and restore peace."

"I do understand," Mr. Winslow said. "This is a complex war and one that I don't pretend to fully understand. There is plenty of blame to go around. My only concern is my son's well-being."

After the man briefly described his son, Jan approached to introduce himself. "I'm Jan Stanton and I'm the medic treating the wounded. I think your son may be under my care, recuperating from a severe injury, but I believe he will not only survive but make a full recovery."

With that, they all walked to the barn. As soon as they entered, Mr. Winslow immediately recognized the man in the first bed on the right. An IV bag dangled on a makeshift stick, and bandages encircled the young man's head and chest. Mr. Winslow seemed startled, but Jan assured him that the young captain was just sleeping.

"He suffered a bullet wound to the chest and a concussion, but he's in stable condition. You're welcome to talk to him when he wakes up."

The older gentleman was awestruck, and the men could see tears welling in his eyes. "As I said, I'm from Richmond," he repeated, "and this is my son...Robert Winslow Jr. I feared him dead, and I can't thank you enough for the care you have rendered. I would like to take him home, but Richmond is in a state of siege since Lee retreated. Is it possible that I stay until such time as I can make other arrangements?" Mr. Winslow continued, "I have money to pay my way, as well as to compensate you for his care and any other needs that may arise." Slowly, Robert Jr. began to stir, and the men decided to step out to allow the father and son some privacy to reunite as Jan stood by.

Jack quickly pointed out, "Well, boys, there's an offer on the table to obtain some funding. I see no reason to refuse." Mike and Kevin pondered the situation momentarily and concluded there weren't any inherent security risks.

Mike spoke first. "Any objections?"

When there were none, they all breathed a sigh of relief. Then Mike stepped into the barn and asked Jan to join them briefly. Back outside, Mike informed him that they had decided to allow Mr. Winslow to stay while his son recuperated and that they would ask him to temporarily fund their outfit. Jan nodded his approval, noting that a source of cash flow was their plan's missing link.

When Robert Winslow was finished visiting with his son, Mike and Jack pulled him aside and laid out their proposition. In classic Mike fashion, he got straight to the point. "Mr. Winslow, we're heading to Richmond. It's a long story, but we have none of the local currency. If you're willing to advance us any amount of capital, we will see to it that your estate suffers no further damage once we arrive. We'll do so by putting an armed guard in place to secure the property."

Mr. Winslow was not certain who these men were or what their objectives might be, but he was a sharp individual. He could easily see that allying with them would be to his benefit, as their unorthodox rescue and medical treatment of his son had already demonstrated. He readily agreed and walked to his carriage. The coachman pulled out a satchel and handed it to Mr. Winslow who retrieved a wad of Confederate money.

As he handed it to Mike, he said, "I have more if you require it. Please see to it that everyone still in my home and employ are taken care of."

"You have my word," Mike replied. "Tom, can you take down the direction to Mr. Winslow's home?"

Mr. Winslow turned to Tom and continued, "It's just north of Richmond on the road to Fredericksburg. Anyone along the way can tell you which one." With that, he shook hands with Mike and Tom before returning to the carriage to retrieve his bag and settle in for his stay.

With this most recent development, the team reconvened. Everyone understood the significance of the happy coincidence that had just fallen into their laps. Almost as if it were meant to be.

Mike was first to point out the obvious. "Men, we have the missing piece here that will allow us to press on with Operation Altered History.

Mr. Winslow just handed me a stack of cash, and it's enough to get us started. Trouble is, it is Confederate money, so we'll have to find a way to exchange it after we leave the South. I think we can manage that, so I'd say we're ready to launch."

"I'll keep my eyes open for a Chase Bank," Frank cracked.

Jan suddenly interjected, "This may just be the start of our medical mission as more people hear about us and come looking for their loved ones. I've got no problem with running point as the senior medic. I will say, though, that Tom and I are going to need more help here than just the two of us." As everyone thought about it, they knew Jan was right. Mike considered and then asked for a volunteer to assist in running the HQ and medical operations.

Frank, not wanting to appear too eager, said, "Since Mike, Jon, and I are the only group of three, it's got to be one of us."

Mike was out because he would be leading one of the missions, and Jon was needed for the Deadwood leg of the operation. That left Frank, who was none too excited to stay behind to clean bedpans and stand watch. However, Frank agreed because he knew it made sense, and he had an ulterior motive. He would be able to stay close to the Drummond household and of course, to Elisabeth.

Each man had readily accepted his assignment and relished the challenges that awaited. The two heading to Deadwood knew they had a long, hard road ahead of them and that they would need all the luck and expertise they could muster.

Kevin and Joseph knew only the gist of what awaited them in Washington. What they were certain of was instilled in every Green Beret: diplomatic missions are far more difficult to predict and control than those on any battlefield. However, they were both trained and determined to execute their objective, despite the obstacles that undoubtedly lay in their path.

For their part, Jack and Dave would set out to find Jefferson Davis. He had fled Richmond, and if history was correct, his whereabouts were unknown. Kevin had remembered that he was captured in Georgia, so the two were to head that way. With the grace of God and a bit of good luck, they hoped to find him. Then, like Kevin and Joseph, diplomacy would be their primary mission, and that was certainly not what either of them had prepared for.

Everyone finished loading the horses with supplies as a cloud of uncertainty hung over the team. The men knew that dramatic changes would soon take place, and the civilians clearly sensed that even more were in store for them.

Not ones for sentimental farewells, the men said brief goodbyes, knowing they would be in radio contact throughout their travels. The civilians, however, had no grasp of what was happening, nor if they would ever see any of these men again. Edwin and his family were sad to see Joseph departing, as they had developed a fondness for him, along with a sense of security in his presence. Joseph realized their reluctance to say goodbye, so he hugged them all, giving his word that Tom, Jan, and Frank would take care of them in his absence. Witnessing the bond that they had quickly formed only served to solidify Joseph's resolve to accelerate progress when they reached Washington.

Mike and Jon decided to accompany Kevin and Joseph to Washington and then inquire about ships sailing to New Orleans, Louisiana. They all rode east toward Richmond, Virginia, where they would attempt to learn where Jefferson Davis was headed. They would then relay that information to Jack and Dave.

Kevin's knowledge of history was critical in helping them surmise that Davis had fled Richmond via train and was headed west toward Greensboro, North Carolina. There was only one track following that route, so if Jack and Dave could intercept that train, they could effectively capture Davis and force his hand at a diplomatic solution. Although there was one impending issue: Davis was known to have been fiercely resistant to surrender.

However, that was the old history, and there was a new sheriff in town with an elite squad of deputies. If Jack and Dave accomplished their mission, and if Kevin and Joseph were successful in gaining

Lincoln's ear, they felt good about their chances of reaching a peaceful end to the war.

They knew it would be challenging to enter Richmond, where the Confederate government had just departed, leaving the city in a state of lawlessness characterized by riots and general anarchy. To combat this, the men were counting on their reputation, as well as the overwhelming fire superiority they possessed. They knew that the big stick they carried was no guarantee of easy passage, but it certainly put the odds in their favor.

Seven

The road to Richmond was littered with remnants of the Confederate army's retreat. A defeated force since their withdrawal from the southern capital, the threadbare troops had made their way west on this same route just a few days earlier. Numerous skirmishes had occurred the entire way as Confederate rear guards engaged the advancing Union Forces. Confederate foot soldiers, along with their horses and wagons, had beat a hasty retreat upon the muddy, rutted track. Food was scarce, ammunition and supplies even more so, leaving little behind for the locals to scavenge. Union Army stragglers now made their way back on the same road that they had pursued the retreating Confederate forces not so long ago. Kevin remarked that it was a good thing they were on horseback since the road had never been traversed by a motorized vehicle. What was more, the fleeing troops had tried to demolish the road in a last-ditch effort to delay the pursuing Union Army.

Nevertheless, the four made good time and were in Jetersville, Virginia, in short order. There, they located the Richmond & Danville Railroad that ran from northeast to southwest, linking the two Virginia cities. This was the track Jefferson Davis took when he fled the seat of his crumbling government; the same one Jack and Dave would follow south to find him.

As they made their way east, the men encountered grim stares from everyone in their path. Whether fleeing locals or demoralized soldiers from either side, it didn't appear as though anyone wanted to confront the four strange horsemen. A stale haze of defeat hung over the entire landscape.

They followed the railroad tracks north for a few miles before again turning east. Stopping to check the map on Kevin's laptop, they estimated they were 35 five miles from Richmond. Their sore backsides convinced them to ride until early evening and then stop for the night. If they encountered no obstacles the following day, they would be in Richmond by afternoon. As they rode, they tried to envision what they would find when they got into town. In contrast with the depredation of Jetersville, the Virginia countryside was rather picturesque, as yet unblemished by telephone poles or billboards. The valleys were just starting to bloom as spring awakened the flowers and trees.

When the evening sky turned to dusk, Mike stopped by a grove of oak trees on a small knoll overlooking the road. "Men, I think we found a good place to stop for tonight. There's a creek over there to water the horses. Then we can drop their saddles and tie them over there in the grass. Let's keep one man up on a one-hour rotation. We'll grab some chow, sleep 'til sunrise, and then head for Richmond at daybreak."

The weary men, unaccustomed to traveling on horseback, ate in silence with only their thoughts and memories to reflect on. Although each man was focused on the situation at hand, they were all still trying to adjust to the shift in time and what it meant to them and their families. It seemed for now that the only way back to the future was through the past. They quickly fell asleep until each was awakened for guard duty. Posting security was their SOP, and fortunately, the watches were largely uneventful. Without headlights or flashlights, people's movements all but ceased at dark. The soldiers had night vision goggles in the event of a disturbance, in which case they could quickly tip the scales against anyone looking to cause trouble.

As soon as sunlight crept over the eastern sky, Jon arose from his guard post overlooking the road and quietly woke the others. No conversation was necessary as they methodically packed their gear, stuffed some food in their bellies, and saddled the horses. The men mounted up and rode in silence as they watched even more refugees head west, escaping the devastation that became more evident the closer they got to Richmond. The two-day ride was unremarkable since most of the Union Forces that they encountered were still either battle-scarred or had heard the stories of the formidable enemy their comrades had already encountered. It took just a short burst of automatic fire to force a meek surrender upon any dissenters, and it did not happen often. The team regarded all the retreating Union Forces with respect and a wary eye as they moved past. They kept their military bearing about them, intent on maintaining tactical measures to ensure that no one got cocky or attempted some misguided revenge. Fortunately, no one seemed ready to cross that line, and the group moved ahead without delay.

By noon, they approached Petersburg on the southern outskirts of Richmond. "This is where Robert E. Lee had set up his defense of Richmond," Kevin informed them.

The men soon realized that everyone with whom they crossed paths was closely observing them. The stares were unrelenting, and the four soldiers knew that the time would soon come when they would have to prove themselves.

In response to the suspicion in the air, Mike ordered, "Keep your head on a swivel and eyes open for trouble."

Those folks could hardly be blamed for their caution and curiosity: the four oddly dressed men must have looked like aliens. Knowing they possessed the upper hand—the metaphorical big stick—they rode on confidently with their jaws set tight and eyes focused straight ahead. They exuded confidence and superiority as they reached the first Union soldiers blocking the road. It was evident that these four men meant business. They were clearly bigger, healthier, and more self-assured than the battered soldiers and downtrodden civilians they had encountered.

Kevin addressed the Union soldiers first, announcing, "I need to see your commander."

The guard who appeared to be in charge asked who they were, and Kevin replied sharply, "Captain Kevin McKenzie, United States Army." The guard immediately snapped a salute and dispatched a fellow guard to summon the sergeant in charge. When the sergeant arrived, Kevin, in his most official voice, requested to speak with the commander. The Union troops did not know which unit this Captain McKenzie was from, but they dared not go against his orders.

Kevin then sought out and engaged the Union general that commanded the garrison. In the exchange, he left no doubt that he and his men were the force that the Union Army had encountered at Sayler's Creek. He also requested that the general send a messenger with them on their travels, notifying his higher-ups at headquarters that they were coming in peace to negotiate and meant no further harm to anyone unless they encountered resistance. The general agreed, arranging for a six-man military detail to escort them and facilitate movement through all Union lines.

Upon entering Richmond, the men were met with angry Union Forces that had just arrived, in addition to the hostile residents who were fed up with the war. The Union Army detail escorted them to the Winslow estate, where they found Union Forces using it as a camp. Kevin and Mike, accompanied by two of the Union escorts, went inside, while Joseph and Jon posted up outside to watch their surroundings and the horses.

The two men found the senior officer, a lieutenant, seated comfortably in a wingback chair and looking rather smug. It was obvious that the Union soldiers had ransacked the place, and Kevin and Mike weren't about to renege on their promise to look after Mr. Winslow's estate.

Kevin pondered his next move when Mike suddenly yelled, "On your feet!" The startled lieutenant jumped up as Kevin addressed him sternly. "I want this place cleaned up and your men and horses out of here immediately." Kevin stepped up within inches of the poor lieutenant, where his imposing size and manner instantly had the desired effect. Kevin then informed the lieutenant that he was charging him with cleaning, restoring, and safeguarding the estate from now on until he returned from Washington, DC.

The lieutenant meekly nodded his acceptance and set about instructing his men to start cleaning and preparing to move to the guesthouse and the barn.

That settled, Mike stepped out and asked Joseph and Jon to come inside. "We can spend the night here, guys. It's a short train ride to Washington," he said.

They returned outside and invited their army escorts to move in. Joseph and Jon then headed to the slave quarters to inform the occupants that they were free. The two knew that helping these folks along the post-freedom road would be a task to tackle once they reached Washington. In the meantime, they asked if anyone wanted to stay on as a paid caretaker and hired those choosing to remain. Joseph then led the new staff members and a couple of the Union soldiers to buy enough food to sustain the Winslow house. They needed to stock up until the team returned from Washington.

Everything was proceeding as planned. Mike's pessimist brain, however, knew that the lack of resistance would not last long. These war-weary masses were bringing dull knives to a gunfight, where Mike and his men were shooting fish in a barrel. He knew from experience that dealing with people in positions of power would be a different story altogether.

The other three seemed satisfied with the journey's first leg, and they paused to radio their progress to Tom at HQ. They were looking forward to a good night's rest because they, too, instinctively knew that the real work would begin at the next stop in DC.

Eight

Jack and Dave saddled their horses and loaded their rucksacks. They agreed to head south by way of the 12-mile trail and catch the Richmond & Danville train at Burkeville Junction. There, they would load the horses onto a cattle car and ride south, from which point they could make their way into North Carolina and pick up Davis' trail.

Tom coordinated the radio frequencies and arranged times to make commo shots back and forth, and Jack and Dave split their share of the money that Mr. Winslow had given the team. Their first priority was to buy some clothes as soon as they got to a decent-sized town. They waved goodbye and set off for Burkeville.

They skirted the battlefield as they made their way south, to avoid the carnage and scavengers. A considerable crowd combed through the remains to either recover the bodies of loved ones or to loot valuables from the dead soldiers and horses. It wasn't a matter of greed but survival.

"Not much we can do for anyone," Jack said, shaking his head.

"Yeah, it's pretty miserable," replied Dave. "By the way, what do you think the odds are we make it back home?" he mused. None of the team members had vocalized their feelings on this particular subject, partly because they had been consumed with their mission, but also because the uncertainty was unsettling.

As he often did before speaking, Jack paused first to consider his words. After a few moments of silence, he said, "Well, that depends on what you're calling 'home.' But knowing Tom, he'll have a theory before long." They rode on silently, mulling over their individual thoughts until they were close to town.

Jack and Dave trusted each other's instincts, but Jack knew that it bore repeating, "One of us stays focused on our surroundings at all times. We can't let our guard down for a second."

Dave gave a quick "roger that" in reply.

The two rode into town acutely aware of suspicious eyes from everyone they passed. "Until we find some other clothes, we're gonna stick out like flies in a rice bowl," Dave warned.

"Well, I'm not trading in these weapons for one of theirs no matter how much attention it attracts," Jack replied. "Let's stop at this dry goods store and see if we can find some clothes that'll help us blend in," he suggested. "You go first, and I'll stay out here and pull security."

Dave climbed down and tied up his horse while Jack did likewise. Jack stepped up on the wooden sidewalk to keep a keen eye on the approaching passersby. His rugged looks and aloof demeanor purposely discouraged anyone from engaging him in conversation, and that was just how he wanted it.

However, it did not prevent the stares that he garnered. The M-4 and the kit he wore ensured that he and Dave would be the center of attention no matter where they went or what they did. He felt as though the onlookers' red-hot stares were boring holes through him. He reasoned that the uneasiness he felt paled in comparison to the disquiet they created in these unarmed civilians and poorly outfitted soldiers. Rumors were assuredly flying among the townsfolk and the people who had fled Richmond by train when the city fell. The Union Army's unexpected loss at Sayler's Creek would undoubtedly stem the tide of people fleeing south to avoid the anticipated Union Army advance.

Everything was in a state of upheaval, and mistrust and suspicion were the order of the day. Dave came out of the store just then, wearing some slightly more discreet clothing and carrying extras.

"No offense, but you look like a greenhorn in your new duds," Jack immediately chided.

Dave sheepishly replied, "Not sure which one of us looks more out of place. But get in there and get your fashion makeover. You might want to get your hands manicured while you're at it," he joked.

"Oh, I will," Jack laughed.

Dave assumed Jack's guard post, keeping a watchful eye on the surroundings. He, too, noted that he was the focus of attention of all the townspeople. Like Jack, he resolved not to appear too friendly, discouraging any attempts at approach or conversation. Since Jack and Dave were both 6'2" and each weighed around 210 pounds, it was a simple matter for Jack to buy similar clothes. He quickly paid the store clerk and exited the store with purpose.

Both were eager to get moving, find the train station, and be on their way. The ticket master at the station eyed Jack warily when he stepped confidently to the window. "Two tickets and four horses to Danville," he stated, somewhat sharply. Not one for small talk, he added, "How long ago did President Davis come through here?"

His voice commanded respect, and the ticket master nervously stammered, "T-two days ago, s-sir." Then, as if eager to be rid of them, he quickly handed the travelers the papers necessary to board and instructed them where they could wait for the train. It was due to arrive in an hour, and he informed them that it would depart an hour after that. Jack tapped Dave on the shoulder, as he had been a few paces back facing the opposite direction to keep an eye on everything.

"Want to go to McDonald's and grab something to go?" Dave joked. "But hope you don't want a shake because that machine is always down!"

"Hell, yeah. I could put a hurtin' on a few Big Macs right about now, but I guess I'll settle for some beef jerky from that general store over there," Jack replied. "Anyway, Davis has got a two-day lead on us," he informed Dave. "We've got some ground to make up, and we have to find him quick." Dave nodded, and the two set off for the store across the street.

When the train arrived, they made sure the horses were taken care of, climbed aboard, and settled in for the 70-mile ride to Danville. That's where the track would run out and where, they hoped, Davis' time on the lam would, too.

Nine

Jan conducted his morning rounds, checking on all the patients while Elisabeth, Mattie, and her daughter Annie went about feeding them. Robert Winslow, who had volunteered to help in any way he could, brought water around to the beds. He was astonished at the level of care he witnessed. Several of the injured soldiers had suffered life-threatening wounds that during the Civil War would have certainly meant death. Doctors from that time were ill-equipped and medical procedures were crude. Jan, on the other hand, had medical knowledge, equipment, and supplies far superior to anything Robert had ever seen. He was in awe as he studied the injured and the treatment they received. All he could do was shake his head in disbelief.

Tom was in the Drummond house establishing a command post by organizing the remote monitoring screens alongside his laptop. His natural ability to understand the big picture and bring structure to it was on full display as he went about setting up his makeshift office. Frank had asked Edwin and Silas to carry in equipment as Tom requested it. The two were amazed at the sight of Tom's setup, complete with wires connecting the portable solar panels, now located on the roof.

"What kind of devilment is that?" Silas asked.

"Hush, now," his father said. "We put our trust in these folks and don't want to ask too many questions."

"Yes, sir," Silas said.

After the last load, Frank came in to see if Tom needed further assistance. Satisfied that they were finished, Frank sat down to discuss their next steps.

Frank volunteered, "With all the commotion going on—and more to come—we have neglected security. I know we have the sensors and monitors up, but we don't have the bodies to keep someone watching the comings and goings around the clock. I foresee that as a problem as more visitors arrive."

Tom replied, "You're right, and it will certainly get busier as word of the medical facilities here spreads. What do you suggest?"

"Well," Frank pondered, "I could give Edwin and Silas firearms training, and I could include any of the wounded who are capable enough to assist."

"That's not a bad idea," remarked Tom. "We've got spare weapons and plenty of ammo. Hell, we've even got extra uniforms if that would help intimidate anyone who wants to bow up to Edwin and Silas."

"I'll set up a range and get on it tomorrow," said Frank.

"I'm gonna stay near the command post as much as I can," remarked Tom, "and I'll coordinate with you or Jan if I can't be here."

"That'll work," replied Frank. "I'm going to check on Jan and see what I can do to help him."

He entered the barn and saw the medic reapplying a bandage to a patient's wounded leg with Robert carefully assisting at his side. He approached and admired the senior medic's handiwork. Although the whole team had received medical training, none had the level of expertise that Jan possessed. Special Forces medics underwent surgical training on top of rigorous medical and pharmaceutical instruction. Of course, Jan also had access to medical advances the folks in this century could only dream of.

Any observers were keenly aware that they were witnessing amazing feats of medicine, bordering on sorcery or the divine. As soon as a few of these patients were released, the word would spread quickly. Frank conferred with Jan about his plan to provide additional security and crowd control and inquired as to their plans to deal with the imminent influx of patients.

Jan answered, "I haven't given it much thought yet, but now that you bring it up, we certainly can't continue at this rate. The time is fast approaching that we're gonna have to move out of this barn to find more space. I'm just not sure how that fits in with the team's plan. Why don't we talk it over with Tom this evening? Meanwhile, I'm teaching Elisabeth, Mattie, and Annie how to assist as nurses, and they're all doing great so far."

Robert had been listening to the conversation and interjected, "I may be able to help. I can fund the building of a hospital here that might better suit your needs."

Jan's ears perked up at the thought, even though he realized such an endeavor might take a while. After all, none of the team knew how much time they had left there.

"How would you do that?" Frank asked.

"I'll hire people to build it, and we can run it as a business. Your medical knowledge and skills will attract people from all over the world. It can't miss," Robert proposed.

Appealing to Jan's ego was all it took for him to buy into the idea. "What do you say, Frank?"

"Let's talk it over with Tom," Frank answered, "but I think he'll be all for it."

As the afternoon wore on and Frank started setting up a range to teach the others how to shoot, he saw people approaching from the direction of the battlefield. He walked out and met them before they could get too close. As the civilians asked about locating survivors, he realized that he, Tom, and Jan could not implement their plans quickly enough.

It seemed that the tidal wave of visitors they had envisioned was already fast upon them. Not having had time to discuss any of it with Tom, he decided to escort them to the house and have him weigh in on the location. Frank told the visitors to wait on the front porch while he went inside to talk to the commo sergeant. He told Tom about the earlier discussion and Robert's volunteering to back the building of a medical facility.

Tom, an entrepreneur in his own right, liked the sound of it, immediately assuming the role of CEO. "It seems like a solid plan," he replied. "Why don't you get with Jan and draw up some plans, and I'll talk to Robert about getting the construction going as soon as possible?"

Just like that, they had made up their minds to move forward with establishing a surgical center. Tom knew there were a lot of moving pieces to orchestrate, but he was keen for the challenge. He set to work on his laptop, laying out the plan and the schedule for the project. Frank returned to the porch and collected the visitors who patiently awaited his return. He asked Edwin and Silas to help get everyone in a single-file line so they could walk to the barn and see if they knew anyone who was being treated inside.

Edwin entered and found Elisabeth. "Mrs. Drummond, we have many people outside looking for survivors. Would you come out and talk to them to see if you can help locate their kinsfolk before we parade people through the barn?"

"Of course," she said, "and I think it's time you called me Elisabeth." She quickly deposited a handful of bandages in the barrel Jan had instructed everyone to use for medical waste. She then asked Jan if she could bring visitors inside to determine if they had survivors being treated.

"As I've been telling everyone, germs are a serious issue. Make them wash thoroughly and then you can escort them in one at a time. If it's not too severe of an injury, they may be able to stay and visit a little while."

It took the rest of the afternoon to get to the visitors and successfully identify those who had family members in the ward. Everyone commented on the level of care their loved ones had received. The patients and their families would soon return home and repeat the tales of medical miracles taking place in the small barn outside of Amelia, Virginia.

Ten

While Joseph accompanied the party to buy food, Mike and Jon explored the port of Richmond to see if there was any chance of boarding a boat. The lieutenant told them that just south of town on the James River, it was common knowledge that blockade runners docked and unloaded supplies. It was a lucrative business run by pirates, and he recommended that they steer clear of that area. The Union Navy had orders to sink them on sight because the dangerous crews, usually comprised of unsavory characters, were smuggling contraband to the South.

Mike talked it over with the others before deciding that he and Jon would venture down to the docks and see for themselves. They asked two of the Union soldiers to accompany them to facilitate movement through the turbulent city streets. The four of them rode south to the outskirts of town, where Mike instructed the soldiers to wait until he and Jon returned. He knew that the soldiers' presence would spook the crews since they were wanted by the Union for providing supplies to the South.

They were three miles down the road when they arrived at a particularly raucous tavern. Mike decided to stop and investigate. Upon entrance, he discovered a large crowd. It was peculiar given that there was not a single horse tied up outside. Based on the accents he detected, he concluded that he had stumbled upon the international crews for the blockade runners. They were a rough-looking crowd, but Mike had a daunting presence of his own. His pistol and large knife were in plain sight, and he kept his right hand ready to draw at the first hint of trouble. He knew that their pistols were black powder and, thus, had a built-in delay as the hammer struck the flint and the black powder smoldered before igniting. As an expert pistol and rifle shot, Mike was confident he could outdraw and outshoot anyone in the place. Satisfied with his assessment, he scrutinized the crowd, his steely blue eyes glaring at anyone who dared to meet his gaze.

He ordered a beer and positioned himself at the corner of the bar. As he drank his ale, he finally zeroed in on a man he determined was in charge from the way the others gathered around and deferred to him.

Mike sauntered over and said curtly, "I think you and I have some business to discuss."

The man looked defiantly at Mike and said in a dialect that was hard to place, "Who the hell are you?"

"I'm Mike, and we need to talk. Right now." The domineering tone in his voice left no room for argument. When Mike stuck out his hand, the stranger reluctantly returned the gesture.

"Captain Pete," he said shortly.

They went to an empty corner table and sat down.

Mike decided to be blunt. "I need a fast boat to New Orleans."

"Well," Captain Pete said suspiciously, "I've got a fast boat that'll make it, but I've got a schedule to meet. I pick up a load of rum and sugar in Havana, Cuba, in a week. Don't have time for New Orleans," he said in broken English.

"I'm sure you could make time if it suited you," Mike pitched.

"And why would it suit me?" the shifty captain replied.

"Money and security," Mike answered.

"That's interesting...tell me more," Pete urged, his curiosity finally piqued.

"I can offer you whatever you need to make it profitable," Mike stated, "and I have no objection to stopping in Havana and picking up a load for you to sell in New Orleans."

"The Navy is guarding the Port of New Orleans. Going there is risky. I got no time for raids," Pete countered.

"And for that, I have a rifle capable of deterring any ship that might approach," Mike assured him.

"I'd like to see that," Captain Pete scoffed.

"You can and you will if you agree to the terms," Mike told him, adding, "it's just me and my partner."

After a moment of contemplation, the captain seemed satisfied with the offer. "That's $500 each," Pete stated matter-of-factly, "leaving at daybreak."

"We'll be here," Mike said. Then he stood up, and the two shook hands again before Mike walked outside.

He relayed to Jon his discussion and the agreement with the surly captain. "Do you trust him?" Jon asked warily.

"No, I don't," Mike conceded, "but he's our best shot to get there quickly. We'll just have to stay alert and at the ready."

"That's what we do best," Jon said.

With plans to press on, they mounted up and rode back to collect the two waiting soldiers who had escorted them to the waterfront.

Upon their return to the Winslow estate, they were met by Kevin and Joseph, who were keen to discuss the latest developments. Kevin told Mike and Jon that he and Joseph would depart on the 10 o'clock train the next morning. Mike likewise told Kevin and Joseph that he and Jon would board transportation of their own, a rumrunner boat bound first for Cuba and then New Orleans.

The four of them finalized their plans for the following day, and then each went about packing as necessary. Mike was glad he had thought to bring one of the .50 caliber sniper rifles for the outing. He also decided that it might be an ideal time to use the digital micro recorder that he had been issued in one of his intel schools. It was a recording device meant to be planted in a discreet area where sensitive subjects were being discussed, often with foreign counterparts. Mike would use it to covertly monitor their newfound ocean guides and then review the recordings in secret.

"It might come in handy with this crowd," Mike told Jon. "Also, be sure to charge up your night vision goggles and bring spares. We'll need those NVGs in the morning to make sure there are no surprises."

They would both take a heavily loaded rucksack, and Jon would have his M-5 medical aid kit in tow. It would be wise to have a variety of medical equipment and medicines that all SF medics considered essential. Mike was taking the .50 cal, as well as his M-4. They both carried pistols, a lot of ammo, and some spare batteries for the radio. They sacrificed the comfort of clothes and sleeping bags in favor of space for more necessary items.

Kevin and Joseph, for their parts, were able to pack a bit lighter for their diplomatic mission. Joseph asked one of the former slaves, a man named Julius, who had been the Winslow's butler, to be in charge and interact with the Union troops that remained housed in the outbuildings. He gave him some money and promised that one of them would return soon. He and Kevin then briefed all the staff who were to remain behind at the Winslow estate. With preparations for their departures in place, the men settled in for some sleep.

Mike and Jon were up at 3:00 a.m., and they quickly dressed and saddled their horses before strapping their gear on two pack horses. They donned their NVGs and set off for the dock to meet Captain Pete. They asked the two soldiers that had accompanied them the day before to retrieve the horses later in the day once they were aboard the ship and sailing southward. The streets were empty, and they rode without incident to the docks. They stopped about 300 yards short and panned the area using their NVGs for any suspicious activity or signs of an ambush. Seeing nothing of concern, they rode down to the dock and issued a hushed greeting to the captain, who was already waiting for them.

Captain Pete looked as though he had imbibed an inordinate amount of alcohol the night before, but he was eager to get sailing, so he had one of his men help them load their gear. Mike and Jon quickly hoisted the equipment up to the sailor and climbed aboard. Pete made the introductions to his crew of two, and Mike introduced himself and then Jon.

They exchanged hurried "hellos" as Captain Pete ordered them to shove off. They untied and poled the 40-foot vessel into the main current of the James before the swift current quickly pulled them downriver.

Kevin and Joseph, meanwhile, awoke to the smell of breakfast cooking, which prompted them to dress hurriedly and investigate the source. They found everyone at the outdoor kitchen, where they were handed two heaping plates of bacon, eggs, and biscuits, which they gulped down like they had just come off a hunger strike. They then arranged for Julius and one of the soldiers to ride with them to the train station so they could take the horses back.

Upon arrival at the station, Kevin and Joseph dismounted and bade the other two farewell. They entered the station and purchased two one-way tickets to Washington, DC, in a private coach. Although they preferred to maintain a low profile, they also understood that the Union general had telegraphed Washington to apprise the top brass of their arrival. As the train chugged forward, Kevin ditched all his US Army insignia. Introducing himself as a captain to gain entry into Richmond had been successful in preventing any violence; however, he didn't want to enter negotiations with generals, and possibly the president, as a mere captain.

The roughly 100-mile trip would put them in DC in the late afternoon due to the numerous stops the train would have to make. They were actually glad for the lengthy ride because it would give them time to transition into their new roles as statesmen.

Kevin turned to Joseph and reminded him, "We'll need to keep a keen eye out for each other. I'll need you to be my eyes and ears while I'm in discussions with these politicians." Joseph nodded his agreement. They were both forces to be reckoned with, but they were still just two men inside the country's powder keg of divisive emotions.

They both sat back in their seats and pondered the altered future they were about to create.

Eleven

Jack and Dave settled in their seats for what they hoped would be a quiet trip. That thought, however, was short-lived as two Confederate officers and two men in civilian clothes suddenly came down the aisle and took their seats directly behind them.

As they sat down, one of the men muttered "deserters or Yankees." Jack and Dave knew it was only a matter of time before the situation turned sour.

"We might as well settle this right here and now," Dave said.

"Agreed," said Jack. "I'll flip you for it."

"That's OK," Dave replied, "I'll give you the pleasure."

They stood up and Jack took two steps, putting him in the aisle directly next to the two officers. He glanced around to make sure there were no women or children within earshot before he said brazenly, "Is it any of your fucking business who we are?" His harsh glare and stern demeanor left no doubt that their feeble attempts to construct an answer had better yield the correct response.

Dave kept his hand close to his hip, ready to draw if anyone moved a muscle toward one of their flapped holsters.

"Sorry, sir," came the weak reply. "Just wondered who you were."

One of the civilians who had accompanied them down the aisle stood and offered his hand in apology. "My friends didn't mean any harm, and I hope you'll forgive us all. It's just that the war has worn everyone down, and we don't see many men in these who aren't part of the war effort for one side or the other. You two seem to be on a mission, and I can see that you're well-armed," he explained in a blatant attempt to deescalate the situation.

"It would appear that both of you can take care of yourselves in a scrape," he went on. "My friend was just thinking aloud and meant no harm. Again, please accept my apology on behalf of all of us and the Confederate States of America."

There was a pause as Jack stepped backward until he was beside Dave. They exchanged brief glances. When Dave shrugged, Jack took that as a sign that he was satisfied with the man's plea. Neither of them felt comfortable with the party being seated directly behind them, so Jack returned to the apologetic gentleman and asked if he might have a word.

"Of course, sir," he obliged.

"Would you mind, then, if I exchanged seats with the gentleman next to you?" Jack inquired.

"It would be my pleasure," the man replied. He then instructed his seatmate to move forward and switch seats with Jack.

"I know you wonder who we are, and I think I have some idea who you are," Jack began. "Since you apologized on behalf of the CSA, I assume you are a government official of some sort."

"I am indeed," said the man, "and my name is George Tindall. I am the chief of staff to President Davis."

"That's very interesting," remarked Jack, "because that is precisely who we wish to speak to."

"What is your business with him?" inquired Mr. Tindall.

"As you are well aware, someone inflicted a tremendous defeat upon the Union Forces at Sayler's Creek a few days ago," Jack began tactfully.

"I am aware," Mr. Tindall replied, "although I, nor anyone else, can explain how that happened."

"Let me explain it to you," Jack interjected, "because it was my soldiers who did that. If you wish for Lee's army to avoid a similar fate, then I suggest you communicate to President Davis that we need to speak." Mr. Tindall's collected expression promptly turned to one of apprehension. "Rest assured," Jack continued stone-faced, "that what happened to the Union Forces can just as easily happen to yours." Jack was never much for beating around the bush. It was safe to say that he had Mr. Tindall's full attention.

"We were just on our way to discuss the recent developments with President Davis. I think I can telegraph ahead when the train stops at Danville," Mr. Tindall said, now visibly shaken.

"You do that and be sure to tell President Davis that there is a time limit on my patience. If he runs and I have to come looking for him, he will not enjoy our meeting."

After coming to an understanding, the men turned to the topic of the Confederate strategy going forward. Jack asked about where the CSA was moving its headquarters and how long it would take to refit Lee's army.

"We both know that provisions and morale are in short supply for the Confederate army. How long do think you can sustain the war?" he pressed.

"Indeed, the situation is dire, and we fled Richmond after it was taken by Union forces," Mr. Tindall admitted. "But the defeat at Sayler's Creek has strengthened our resolve." He paused for a moment before continuing. "Just how big is your army, and how in the world did you defeat the Union troops so decisively?"

"We have an enormous force," Jack lied. "And we lost only one man in that battle. I guarantee that we will lose no more in the next engagement."

Mr. Tindall was clearly thinking about the gravity of his new acquaintance's words while Jack was hoping that his message had achieved its intended effect, which was to light a fire of urgency beneath President Davis. The rest of the train ride passed in silence as everyone contemplated their next moves. Jack remained in his seat next to Mr. Tindall to make sure that the Confederate officers didn't attempt to bushwhack him or Dave from behind.

When the train stopped in Danville, the entire group stood and exited in a single-file line. Mr. Tindall assured his entourage that everything was copacetic, and then asked that they wait for him in the restaurant across from the train station while he sent a telegram by Western Union. He told Jack that he would do as he had been instructed and wait for a reply before meeting them at the restaurant.

After about 10 minutes, George Tindall walked through the restaurant door. He took a seat across from Jack and announced, "President Davis has decided to meet with you to discuss the recent turn of events. In fact, he has agreed to meet us here to formulate our new strategy. I suggest we all get a room at the hotel and wait for his party to arrive."

Upon hearing that their strategy had proved surprisingly successful thus far, Jack and Dave relaxed slightly and enjoyed a hearty meal. Mr. Tindall dispatched his assistant to the hotel to secure reservations for the entire party, as well as the guests expected to arrive two days later.

"The arrival of President Davis will be quite an event for this town, and I'm sure they would like notice in order to make suitable plans," he stated.

"I'm sure his departure will be, too," Dave added under his breath.

"Well, gentlemen, it's been a pleasure, but we have to get going," Jack declared to the men at the table. "We'll be at the hotel should you need to discuss anything further."

He and Dave left the restaurant and walked out into the street, where they found the hotel just two doors down. They checked into adjoining rooms on the top floor of the four-story establishment before hauling up their gear. Then, they decided to take a stroll around town to stretch their legs and simultaneously get a feel for their surroundings. The two strapping strangers walking around town caused something of a stir among the townsfolk: the women in particular. Most of the men were serving in the Army, and that left a lot of war widows and single ladies eyeing them as they made their way through the streets. Jack and Dave were married, but they appreciated the attention all the same. They said nothing but could almost certainly read each other's thoughts.

Jack interrupted their fleeting daydreams, "We need to radio HQ and update Kevin on our situation."

"OK," Dave replied, "I think we should arrive in DC in just a few days...hopefully with President Davis."

"Sounds reasonable to me," Jack agreed. "You want to make the commo shot and let them know?"

Dave said, "Sure, I'll take the radio up to the hotel roof and set it up."

Jack offered to pull security at the rooftop access door for the duration of the comms exchange. When the radio update was complete, they retired to their rooms for the night.

The next morning, they awoke as the sun pierced through the thin, dusty, lace curtains. At breakfast, Dave said, "We've still got another day until Davis arrives. What are we gonna do, and how do you feel about the gear stored in our rooms?"

"Not a lot of options to store our stuff," Jack said shrugging, "but I'll have a talk with the manager and put a scare into him."

Neither of the men was a drinker or a card player so the saloon offered little enticement. A hot bath, a haircut, and a shave on the other hand sounded great, so they decided to take turns keeping an eye out for any sign of trouble.

They passed the day that way and met at dusk to discuss plans for transporting President Davis to Washington, DC. "He's going whether he likes it or not," Jack stated emphatically. "It's just a matter of how comfortable he wants to be on the train ride there. I just need you to cover my back closely," he told Dave. "Now let's get some sleep and come out firing on all cylinders tomorrow."

Twelve

The pace quickly picked up at headquarters as more civilians arrived, inquiring either about survivors or how to get loved ones treated for various illnesses and injuries. Plans were coming together for the construction of a small hospital, while the team also conducted medical and weapons training for its new recruits. On top of that, Tom was busy maintaining a command post to monitor the movements and schedules of the two-man teams that were currently orchestrating their own missions. It was hectic, but the three found it exhilarating to be hard at work. They thrived on achieving difficult objectives, but it also served to keep their minds preoccupied with their purpose rather than fixated on the lives they had left behind.

Access to Tom's command post was restricted to the three of them for security reasons. Frank and Jan were engaged in their own work, but they periodically checked in to see how everything was going.

"Everyone's on track and there are no hiccups so far," Tom was glad to tell them when they stopped in one day at noon on their way to get something to eat. "How's the training going?" he asked.

Jan replied first. "The ladies are doing great, and Mr. Winslow is turning into quite a capable assistant. Before long, he'll be able to act independently without my constant supervision. He gets along fine with the women, and there seems to be no animosity between him and Mattie or Annie. I've talked to him about how we are abolishing slavery, and he recognizes the injustice done to African Americans and wants to be part of the solution. He plans to further his medical knowledge and then take a leadership role in mending the literal and figurative wounds that the North and South have inflicted upon each other."

Tom and Frank nodded their approval. "I guess that means we can count on his son sticking around, too. That's good because we can use the help," Frank said.

Jan made the point that he was going to need a lot of assistance with the cleaning, cooking, medical prepping, and sanitizing.

Tom summed it up, "We're all going to need a lot of help. There's plenty of work to be done before we can bring many more people on board here. We need housing and food, water, and hygiene facilities for starters." As they chewed on their MREs, the food issue sunk in for all of them.

After they finished eating, Jan returned to the ward, as the barn had come to be known. Upon entering, he saw Elisabeth sobbing. He approached her and asked what the matter was.

She looked and him with tear-stained cheeks. "One of the recovering patients had his family visiting, and the young man's father grew loud and indignant about not wanting any slaves caring for his son, at which point, he ordered Mattie and Annie out." She stopped for a moment to catch her breath. "Robert had been eating so there was no one to step in and help. Mattie and Annie were out back, and I didn't know what to do."

Jan set his jaw, and his face took on a hardened look that she had never seen from the typically calm, compassionate medic. She reflexively stepped back. Jan assured her, "Don't worry. Go get Mattie and Annie and show me who this man is. I'd like them to hear what I'm going to say so there will be no doubt in their minds where everyone stands on this issue."

Elisabeth pointed to the man sitting by the last bed on the right and then stepped out to bring Mattie and Annie back inside. As soon as they shut the door and gathered around the bed, Jan launched into a speech that no one present would ever forget.

"You are all here as guests of mine, and I will tell you one thing: If you would like to remain here, you had better remember that there are no slaves here nor in all of the United States any longer. My teammates are seeing to that right now. In the meantime, this is a free zone, and everyone will be treated as such."

He then stepped to the foot of the bed where the disruptive father sat and looked the elder man square in the eye. "If there is anyone here who isn't comfortable with that, be he a patient or a visitor, I will personally throw you out, drag your ass back to where I found you, and let the buzzards care for you. Is that understood?" Jan took another step forward and towered over the man who had dared to offend Mattie and Annie. "Is that understood by *everyone*?" he barked.

When he was satisfied that there was consent throughout the ward, he ordered the man to apologize to Mattie and Annie.

The ornery southern codger replied, "I'll be damned if I ever apologize to a couple of no-good slav—"

Before he had even finished his sentence, Jan sprang into action. With lightning-quick reflexes, he hit the man with a straight right directly to the nose, causing him to topple like a sack of potatoes. Jan bent over and, with little effort, picked him up and slung him across his shoulder in a modified fireman's carry. Before he turned to dispose of his unconscious burden, he addressed the man's son, who was in the bed staring up at the melee in disbelief.

"Are you good with the rules here, or should I put you over my other shoulder?" he sneered.

"Yes, sir!" the weakened soldier spat out with no hesitation. "I concur with your ideals."

"If that's the case, you're welcome to stay, and the ladies will take fine care of you," Jan declared with finality. The three women stared at him in shock, almost as though he were an alien. He stepped past them with a polite "excuse me," and was pleased to see looks of pride beginning to spread across their faces. "Sorry about that," he added as he walked outside.

Jan dunked the old man's limp body in the water trough, awakening him with a jolt. The man started to object as he slowly rose to his feet until he was standing face to face once again with the imposing 6-foot medic. He quickly realized how Jan dwarfed him and suddenly seemed to regain his memory of the outcome of their first tangle.

"Get your racist ass on that horse of yours and don't come back until you change your attitude...and your heart," Jan told him sternly. "Your son is in good hands, and he will be recovered soon," he added. "With the help of those wonderful women who are graciously volunteering to care for him."

As the man rode off, Jan reflected on his behavior. He wondered if he had made the right decision, and if it would spur a change of heart in the old man and others who heard the tale. It was also possible that this encounter would serve to harden his resolve against newly freed African Americans. He knew that the team was in uncharted waters, and that any decisions they made wouldn't fit neatly into all situations. Furthermore, he grasped the unfortunate reality that no one could foresee the impact that today's actions would have on tomorrow...that every decision had unexpected consequences. He remained pensive as he went back inside and found the three ladies dutifully tending to their patients as if nothing had happened. He couldn't help but notice that Mattie and Annie seemed to be standing a bit more squarely and holding their heads a little higher.

He smiled to himself as he sighed and said to no one in particular, "We've got a long way to go."

Meanwhile, Tom and Frank had been meeting with Mr. Winslow to figure out how he would gain access to his money. "It's in the Bank of Richmond," he explained, "but I fear going there to withdraw it. It was mob rule when I left, and I'm not sure if it's safe. Hell, I'm not even sure if they can cover my withdrawal."

Tom assured him that if one of the team accompanied him, his safety would be all but guaranteed. "I can't guarantee the money will be there, but I promise you will be safe. Are you comfortable with that arrangement?" Tom asked.

Robert considered it before replying tentatively, "I guess so. But who will go with me?"

Frank spoke up right away. "Tom, if you agree, I'll take Mr. Winslow on a four-wheeler, and we can be back in a few hours."

Tom answered, "It's sort of dicey just sending you with no backup."

"What other options do we have?" Frank countered. "Plus, it will be exciting to play the role of a Pinkerton guard," he joked.

"OK. How about you get Robert and Silas up to speed on the M-4, and the four of you can ride to Jetersville. Leave your horses at the livery stable and catch the train to Richmond," Tom proposed. "You can then go to the estate to check on things. After you stop at the bank and make the withdrawal, you can return the same way. Kevin left some soldiers stationed at Mr. Winslow's place in case you need some more bodies while you're carrying the money. You can make that call once you assess the situation there," he said sensibly.

"That's not a bad idea," Frank agreed. "I'll take those guys out shooting right away and see how quickly they catch on. Then I'll schedule a departure and keep everyone informed."

"Sounds like a good plan," Tom nodded, "and we'll bring Jan up to speed this evening at chow time."

Just like that, the men at HQ were back on track and ready to push forward with their mission. They knew that at headquarters they were only fighting small, individual battles for justice; however, they also knew that small battles led to winning a war.

Thirteen

Mike and Jon stowed their gear below deck in a small storehouse where they were told they would sleep. It was about 8 feet by 8 feet with a heavy wooden door that opened inward, further shrinking the space. It was also dark, dank, and dingy from years of apparent neglect.

"Oh, well, we're only sleeping in it...we've slept in worse," Jon commented.

"Yeah, you're right. Let's go topside and see what's up," Mike said.

They made their way on deck and tried to drum up small talk with the crew. They got scarcely a nod from any of them, so they turned to one another.

That's when Jon said, "I've got a little experience sailing, albeit on a smaller boat." He then asked Mike if he knew how to sail.

Mike answered, "My wife and I lived aboard a catamaran for two years, and we sailed around the Caribbean. Sailing is sailing, though: It's just a matter of being familiar with the sails you have on board."

"That's good," said Jon quietly, "because we may have to sail this baby ourselves judging by the looks they're giving us. They're like hungry sharks circling the water. And I think we're the chum!"

"I get that feeling, too," Mike agreed. "If it comes to that, I think I can handle this boat. I just need to see what charts he has. I'm familiar with the Atlantic coast but not the Gulf of Mexico."

Mike made his way to the ship's wheel, where Captain Pete was at the helm. He studied the bridge intently, looking for a possible place to stash his recorder. "How long until we hit the Atlantic?" he asked.

"Oh, a day or so," Pete responded dismissively, as though the question annoyed him.

"How do you manage to navigate to Cuba?" Mike inquired, genuinely curious as to the answer.

"That's quite a trip," he conceded. Pete tapped the side of his head, indicating that he did it from memory. Discovering that they had no charts made Mike even more apprehensive. He also remembered that Pete said he didn't normally make runs to New Orleans.

He thought to himself, *he's either foolishly unconcerned about navigating unfamiliar waters or he doesn't plan on going there. A lot can happen between here and Cuba.*

The cruise down to the mouth of the James River was smooth, but Mike knew that once they entered the Chesapeake Bay and then hit the Atlantic, it would get rougher. During his sailing days, Mike enjoyed the luxury of up-to-date weather forecasts and high-quality instrumentation. They certainly wouldn't have any of that, not to mention any radio contact with harbor masters or other ships to anticipate weather conditions during the journey.

Mike returned to the bow of the ship where Jon was daydreaming. He tapped Jon on the shoulder and said, "Let's see if we can discreetly make a commo shot to HQ and Kevin before we get too far out. I'll grab the radio and go to the stern. Hopefully, no one will pay attention if you stay here on the bow and keep them occupied. Maybe you could give them some medical attention. That's always appreciated and will keep them engaged. See if you can determine a good spot to bury my recorder, too, will you?"

Mike went below and dug out the radio and antenna, as well as Jon's M-5 bag. He tossed the med bag to Jon as he made his way astern to make contact with HQ.

Jon unzipped his aid bag to display his surgical tools, which he stored in elastic keepers for easy access. The two crew members were immediately intrigued, and they shuffled forward to gawk at the foreign hardware. Jon removed each item carefully and wiped it down before replacing it with another. He pretended to immerse himself in the charade, but he could sense their curiosity. Even the captain was intrigued, although he was unable to leave the helm. Jon decided to draw them in further by demonstrating each piece of equipment and then holding it aloft for everyone to see. He grabbed a pair of hemostats and opened and closed them a couple of times. Pete gestured for him to bring them closer for inspection. Jon walked over and demonstrated how to use the tool before handing it to the captain. The crew had become completely engrossed in the game of show-and-tell that Jon was conducting. He kept it up until he saw Mike stow the radio and antenna and return them below deck. He quickly wrapped up his demonstration by carefully replacing all of his equipment, thanking them for their time, and then disappeared below to talk to Mike.

"I noticed there's not much of an opportunity to place the recorder at the helm, but I've got a plan," Jon announced.

"Let's hear it," Mike replied.

"I noticed Pete has a cut on his head. It's a long shot, but I could bandage his wound and wrap the recorder up inside the bandage. I'll numb it up with lidocaine so he doesn't feel it and explain that it will help with the healing. Then I'll give him some antidepressants, and he'll think it's all working. Later, I'll recheck the bandage and we should be able to listen to his conversations with the crew."

"Not a bad idea," Mike allowed, "since they were enthralled by your medical magic show. They'd buy anything you're selling right now."

With that, Jon returned to the helm and pointed at the cut on Pete's head, indicating that he could take a look at it. Pete cautiously turned his head toward Jon and submitted to the medical procedure. Jon cleaned and disinfected the wound before applying the anesthetic to numb the area. He then showed Pete the small recorder and explained that it would help his cut heal. Fortunately, it didn't weigh much, and Jon hoped the anesthesia and the antidepressant would keep him from becoming annoyed with it. Pete grinned as Jon returned below deck to stash his med bag and tell Mike they were in business.

"Why don't you go talk to Pete and stir up some conversation about our plans? That might entice him to open up to his crew once you leave," Jon suggested. Mike nodded, knowing just what to say to trigger a conversation that would divulge the captain's intentions.

Mike approached the helm with a stern look on his face and then addressed Pete in a firm voice. "How are you going to sail to New Orleans without any charts and no knowledge of the area?"

Pete shot back incredulously, "Leave that to the captain."

Mike quickly retorted, "That's what I'm afraid of, Captain," a hint of disdain in his voice. "You better get us there, and you better be quick like we discussed. We made a deal."

Mike cast him a menacing look and then left him to stew in his thoughts, mulling over the last threatening words the blue-eyed bully had left him with. The crew, curious about the awkward exchange they had just witnessed, asked the captain if everything was OK. He grumbled halfheartedly "yes" and then told the younger deckhand to go below and fix something for them to eat. He then resumed the conversation with his other crewman, an older man with leathery, weathered skin and a faint scar that held a secret of its own.

"What is it?" he asked the captain.

"Just a little trouble with the taller one. He keeps squawking about how we're gonna get to New Orleans without any charts," Pete griped.

"Well, how *are* we?" the mate asked.

"We're not," Pete snarled. "As soon as these two landlubbers get seasick, we'll slit their throats and feed 'em to the sharks. We'll snatch their money and fancy gadgets and get back to our schedule," he said as he laughed so hard that he started coughing until one of the guys patted him on his back.

Mike and Jon witnessed the conversation from the stern and knew instinctively that it had not been a pleasant one. When it was over, one of the mates shot them a wicked glance, further confirming their suspicions that something sinister was afoot.

"Better recover that recorder sooner rather than later," Mike muttered.

"I'll do it before dark," Jon replied.

They had a hunch that something was up, so they quickly began to mentally prepare themselves for a rumble on the high seas.

Fourteen

The train whistle screamed out a warning as it approached while the steward walked down the aisle, announcing the next stop at Washington. Kevin and Joseph looked at each other, took deep breaths, and Kevin sighed, "Here we go."

When the train ground to a jerky halt, they gathered their bags and headed for the station. It was immediately apparent that a small crowd anticipated their arrival: the assembled army officers anxiously eyed the disembarking passengers and zeroed in on the two as they approached. The two men stood out like sore thumbs.

The senior officer was a colonel and he simply asked, "Captain McKenzie?"

Kevin and Joseph had prepared themselves for this situation but still had to fight back the urge to say "Yes, sir." The habit was ingrained in them, and it would be hard to break. It wasn't that they minded extending military courtesy to these officers. They just simply could not afford to cede any amount of authority to the other side when it came to negotiations.

"That's correct," replied Kevin.

The first order of business was to clear up the confusion created by the telegram stating that "Captain McKenzie was on the way." Kevin addressed it straight away.

"I used my old rank from the US Army to gain trust and entry into the Union lines. I am no longer in the military." His explanation seemed to satisfy the colonel for the time being.

"We're here to gain an audience with President Lincoln," he said in as official a voice as he could. "Can you arrange that?" he added.

"Well, he's a very busy man due to the recent developments down in Virginia. I'll have to see how soon you can get in to see him, but he is expecting you because of the urgent nature of the telegram we received," the colonel informed him.

Kevin was rapidly gaining confidence in his newfound role, so he pushed his luck a little further. "See to it forthwith, Colonel." When the officer responded with a sharp "Yes, sir!" Kevin and Joseph knew they had everyone's attention.

"If we can make a similar impression on Lincoln, we'll be off to a good start," Joseph said quietly.

They had agreed on the train that Kevin would be the primary spokesman, but that Joseph should feel free to add any discussion points to demonstrate that he was an equal.

With that in mind, Joseph asked, "Where is our hotel?" He was purposely testing the waters to see how much attention their arrival had generated. The colonel said that a carriage was outside to take them to the famed Willard's City Hotel at the intersection of 14th Street and Pennsylvania Avenue, where two rooms had been prepared.

"President Lincoln insists that you be his guests while here in Washington. The carriage will drop you off at the hotel, and I'll send over a courier with news of when the president will meet with you. Will you both be attending the meeting?"

"Of course," Kevin insisted.

"Understood. I will make arrangements for the two of you. Your escorts will see to your safe arrival at the hotel, and I shall be in contact as soon as word comes down from the president," the colonel said before departing.

After he had settled in, Joseph met up in Kevin's room to discuss the news they had just received.

"I guess we're the talk of the town already," Joseph stated.

"Looks that way," Kevin replied. "Now we just need to live up to those expectations." He went on, "With the Union defeat in Virginia, Lincoln is desperate. He must see us as a potential solution; otherwise, he wouldn't make himself available during such a time of turmoil and uncertainty."

Joseph smiled as he listened.

"What's that grin about?" Kevin asked.

"I can just hear the excitement in your voice. I can see it on your face."

Kevin grinned at his friend. "I can't explain what it's like to be in the middle of such an historic event, something I've read about and studied for years. It just feels surreal. It's better than a front row seat at a Charlie Parker jazz show."

Joseph nodded. "Hey, you're about to meet Lincoln, maybe Parker is next! Who knows?"

"OK, OK, get out of here and get some shuteye," Kevin said.

The two decided to dine in the hotel restaurant that evening. They came to a decision after no small debate. Joseph had joked that he wanted to order from Domino's, but Kevin wasn't putting up with his foolishness.

"I think it will be many years before they have pizza delivery, much less in 30 minutes or less," said Kevin.

"Very funny, but I know that you want some now that I mentioned it!" They laughed at their present situation and tried to enjoy the hand life had dealt them. They ate in the stately dining room, where well-dressed strangers seemed to watch their every move. They had grown accustomed to being scrutinized, so they immersed themselves in the delicious meal and focused on their conversation instead of the onlookers that surrounded them.

Just a few blocks away at the White House, the president received a briefing from his staff. In attendance were the vice president and several cabinet members, as well as a group of congressmen and senators. The question that hung heavily in the room was finally voiced by President Lincoln himself.

"Who are these two men, and where are they from?"

"Mr. President, I met them at the train station, and I cannot determine their country of origin from their accents, but it's none that I've heard before. No one has any idea who possesses the capability to inflict the devastation that we have heard occurred at Sayler's Creek, and those men were part of the unit responsible. Your guess is as good as anyone's at this point," said the colonel who had welcomed the men to town.

The president frowned, his gaunt face showing the ravages of presidential stress. He did not relish the thought of negotiating with two strangers who seemed to be a mystery to everyone. "Are you convinced that they are responsible for the army's defeat?" the president asked pointedly.

"In the absence of any other explanation, yes, sir," the colonel answered.

"Then set up a meeting with all those currently present for 10:00 tomorrow. I want everyone to hear the same discussion so that we are all of the same understanding," President Lincoln instructed.

With that, the meeting concluded, and the participants huddled in small groups of lawmakers, interspersed with White House staff. Small talk and speculation were all over the board.

Finally, Vice President Johnson spoke up. "Gentlemen, we will not solve any issues tonight. Let's adjourn until morning when we again attempt to settle this." Everyone got the message and exited, but hushed rumors continued to fly.

A courier soon arrived at the hotel with a message to be delivered to Kevin and Joseph's rooms. Joseph answered the knock on his door and accepted the letter that was handwritten on thick onion-skin paper. After reading it, he went to Kevin's door. "I got one, too," he said, holding up a letter of his own.

"Looks like we're on stage at 10:00 tomorrow morning, buddy. Be sure to get some sleep. I got a feeling we're both gonna need it," Joseph announced.

Kevin returned to his bed and plopped down to reflect on where he was and how he had gotten there. "A week ago, I was in Afghanistan in charge of ten men and a small outpost. Now, I'm in the capital of the United States, preparing to meet the 16th president of the United States to discuss the future of this great country," he thought to himself. "No pressure," he reassured himself, only half-joking.

In the morning Kevin was up early and getting dressed when Joseph rapped on his door. "You ready in there?" he heard from the hallway.

"Let's do this," Kevin exclaimed.

"I need something to eat first," Joseph answered without hesitation.

"Let's go grab some chow, then."

They ate in somber thought, interrupted only when the maître d' approached and informed them, "Gentlemen, your carriage has arrived."

"Finish your breakfast," Kevin cut in. "We'll be fashionably late."

Joseph shrugged and they proceeded to eat every bite. When they stood and walked to the door, they found several soldiers awaiting them. The senior officer greeted the men and motioned toward the carriage, where one of the soldiers opened the door for them to step in. Unlike the travel they had recently come to rely on, the carriage ride to the White House was over in a few short minutes. There, the men were hailed by an even larger crowd of soldiers and civilians.

They stepped from the carriage and were escorted into the White House with all the pomp and circumstance of royal dignitaries. They were humbled as they stepped into the president's office, which by that time was filled to capacity with cabinet members and legislators. Their escort led them directly to the president, who extended his hand and said in a gravelly voice, "Welcome to the White House."

It was a surreal moment, made even more so by the president's imposing 6-foot-4 stature. The men had yet to encounter anyone who stood taller than they, and Lincoln's quiet, yet fierce, demeanor intensified the moment. Kevin could barely contain himself. Inside, he was an utter disaster as he tried to wrestle with the fact that he was meeting one of his historical heroes, a man who, while not perfect, accomplished some amazing things during his relatively short tenure.

President Lincoln introduced everyone in the room and then paused before declaring, "I will allow you to introduce yourselves, gentlemen."

Kevin took a mental deep breath and boomed, "I'm Kevin McKenzie and this is Joseph Strong. We are from North Carolina, but we are strong supporters of the Union. In fact, we are here to ensure the preservation of it, as well as to secure states' rights and individual liberty for every human in the United States. We will stand as defenders of life, liberty, and the pursuit of happiness 'til our last breaths."

He paused momentarily as everyone in the room remained stock-still, every eye trained upon the two men. He continued, "I'm sure everyone wonders what happened at the Battle of Sayler's Creek. I can only assure you that it was unintentional. My unit was attacked, and we responded as soldiers are trained to do. Nevertheless, I am giving notice that, as of this moment, anyone who does not stand with us stands against us and will be dealt with just as harshly. Jefferson Davis is on his way here as we speak, and he will be informed of this, same as you."

President Lincoln raised his hand. "We will be glad to discuss with all of you our intentions while we wait for Mr. Davis," he assured him.

"Perhaps, Mr. President, you can advise as to how you would like to proceed with negotiations," Kevin suggested.

President Lincoln explained that he wanted to meet privately with Kevin and Joseph and that perhaps they could meet with Congress and then the Senate later in the day. The crowd left the office to arrange a special assembly of Congress and the Senate so that Kevin could address the full membership.

When everyone else had left the room, Kevin spoke first. "Mr. President, I assure you that Mr. Strong and I possess the capability to punish the opposition, and that we share the same values that you do. We will work with you to ensure that the United States stands firm as a nation and as a model for human rights for the rest of the world. Understand this, though: Although the South is tragically misguided in continuing slavery, the path ahead must be forgiveness and solidarity. There are those who seek to punish the South, and we will not stand for that. As we see it, there are some war crimes committed by the Union that are to be forgiven, too. General Sherman and others targeted civilians as they burned and pillaged their way through the southern states. I will not dwell on the past but focus on the future. My hope is that you share that sentiment and can use your influence to convince the legislature to join us on that path. As I have said, I will use everything at my disposal to defeat any armed opposition."

The president nodded his head, almost imperceptibly, but said nothing. Kevin and Joseph extended their hands in turn to shake the hand of one of the most influential and respected presidents in US history. Joseph paused briefly as he looked the president straight in the eye, filled with admiration and emotion. He knew that the groundwork they would lay together would radically change the course of future history, and it moved him deeply.

Kevin, too, had a sense that they were on the verge of earthshaking change. They bowed their heads out of respect and then bade him farewell as they silently took their departure.

Fifteen

The Special Forces duo strode out into the crisp April morning and headed down the cobblestone street. The town was already bustling in anticipation of President Davis' arrival. They decided it was time to review their options for capturing him. The presence of so many people discouraged them from simply abducting Davis and absconding with him. No, they would somehow have to persuade him to join them voluntarily. Kevin had advised them that Davis was known as a smart and reasonable man who, of course, was also fiercely loyal to the South.

"Well," Jack rationalized, "we'll just have to appeal to his sense of reason." They didn't have much time to think it over because President Davis' arrival was announced, accompanied by loud cheers and applause, as the noble riders flanked his well-appointed stagecoach.

George Tindall greeted Jefferson Davis as he descended from his coach, and the two of them stepped aside for a brief conversation in private. George then headed over to the sidewalk where Jack and Dave observed the crowd. "President Davis will meet with you privately after he gives a speech," George told them. "We will reconvene at the Danville prison, where he is scheduled to meet with the warden to check on the conditions and treatment of the Union prisoners in the facility." Jack and Dave exchanged quizzical looks. "You can expect no interference there," George added.

Dave asked for directions so that the two could travel on foot to avoid the festivities taking place in the streets. They set off at a brisk pace and were surprised to arrive only a short time later. The warden granted them access after Dave informed him that they were to meet with President Davis. The warden nodded, welcoming them to wait for his arrival.

In the meantime, Jack and Dave elected to walk the grounds and observe the treatment of the prisoners for themselves. Clearly, the prison had been neglected, and the inmates equally so—they were malnourished and filthy. Jack surmised that the reason President Davis had scheduled to come here was that just a few days ago, he had expected the prison to fall into Union hands. He would have wanted to know how poor the conditions were to gauge how much effort the North would put into arresting him. Now that the situation had changed, he was going to use it as a political event.

When the stagecoach arrived with its attendant escorts on horseback, President Davis made a grand show of his arrival. Jack commented to Dave under his breath, "I bet he wasn't this cocky when he left Richmond."

"I can guarantee that he wasn't," Dave replied, a hint of disdain in his voice.

"Well, we'll just have to feed him a big helping of humble pie and hope he sees the light," Jack stated.

When the speech and prison inspection were finished, George sidled up to President Davis and gestured to the two strangers. "These are the gentlemen I spoke to you about, Mr. President."

The men introduced themselves, and the party proceeded to the warden's small, shabby office. The prison was a large stone structure, and this was the only private room in it.

Jack, in his usual manner, got straight to the point. "President Davis, we know who you are, so allow me to tell you a little about us. I'm Jack Morrison and this is Dave Woods. We're from North Carolina, but we are staunch supporters of the United States. It is our mission to ensure the survival of the country as a whole—a single nation, undivided. It was our army that defeated the Union Forces at Sayler's Creek. That was unintentional. While we saved General Lee from a certain surrender, rest assured that we will use that same overpowering force against the Confederacy if it continues to engage in hostilities. We are prepared to escort you to Washington, where we will guarantee your safety and allow you to negotiate from a position of strength while you still can. Our only conditions are as follows: slavery will be abolished, states' rights shall be preserved, and there will be no retaliatory measures imposed on the South."

"If you are truly committed to the South and wish to preserve it and the lives of you and your army, you will heed my advice and accompany us to Washington. Otherwise, consider that you are declaring war against me and my army. And that is something you would do well to take under advisement after consulting any of the officers who witnessed the Battle of Sayler's Creek. I'll give you the rest of the day to consider my proposal. We'll await your decision at the hotel and plan to proceed on the nine o'clock train tomorrow. Should you decline my offer, I suggest you get on your horse immediately and ride as fast and as far as you can until you reach the ocean and then keep on going. We will find you, and then you won't be going to Washington under such generous terms. Good luck, and may God guide you in your decision."

With the conclusion of his monologue, Jack and Dave left the warden's office and walked back to the hotel. As they sat down to eat in the dining room, Dave asked, "What do you think the odds are he comes with us?"

"Voluntarily, you mean?" Jack corrected him. Dave nodded in the affirmative. "I can't rightly say. We'll just have to wait and see if he chooses the easy way or the interesting way," Jack mused. "Now, let's eat and then get ready to catch the train to Washington in the morning."

The messenger arrived at his door at 10 o'clock that night and handed Jack a note. "George and I will meet you at the train station in the morning," signed President Jefferson Davis. Jack decided to wait until the next day to tell Dave.

At breakfast, he gave Dave the fortunate news.

"That's great news! Why didn't you tell me right away?" Dave asked.

"I thought you'd sleep better dreaming about hunting him down rather than taking a long train ride," Jack said with a smile.

"You know me too well. That was exactly what I thought we'd be doing this morning, so I even prepared a checklist of supplies for us to take on the pursuit," Dave admitted, grinning and exposing his dimples.

"Bring it along so you can study it on the ride," Jack said laughingly. "Meantime, we have a date at the train station for a nine o'clock departure."

The train ride was rather monotonous and uncomfortable, not the glamorous affair one might imagine with dapper gentlemen serving coffee and tea. But that was OK because the men were able to use it as an opportunity to get to know Jefferson Davis. They wanted to understand what kind of man he was and what motivated him every day. If Kevin had been there, he could have probably listed everything about the man including what he ate for breakfast, but this time, they would figure it out on their own.

During the arduous train ride, Jack and Dave concluded that President Davis was indeed a reasonable man who was likely caught up in the politics of the situation. At the time, he was probably the best man for the job, and with a little coaxing, the people were able to convince him to lead as president. Once he was in, the sheer momentum that war creates with its wins and losses likely swept him up in the action...and kept him there.

It was refreshing to hear him concede that he was willing to grant slaves their freedom. That was a huge step for a man charged with preserving the traditions of the Old South, no matter how painful and unjust. To sway his constituents to his side, he needed support in dealing with the wealthy plantation owners. They were the bread and butter of the Confederacy's financial support, and it was they who truly controlled politics at the local level, in their home states.

Jack reassured the president that his men would strike a deal guaranteeing that federal aid would flow to the South to assist in the postwar transition. Davis, it turned out, was not so different from anyone else:

All he wanted was to safeguard his own survival and come out of the conflict with his dignity.

Fortunately, this was a language the Green Berets spoke because it happened to be universal. They simply had to do so in a manner that made everyone involved want to listen—and more importantly—comply.

Sixteen

Frank was surprised to learn that neither Edwin nor Silas had fired a gun before, much less one as advanced as the M-4. "I would have thought you fellas would have at least done some hunting or chased off a Yankee with a rifle," Frank said.

"No, sir," said Edwin. "Folks around here don't take kindly to giving guns to menfolk like us. That is, until today," he said with a wide grin.

"Well then," said Frank, "this is your lucky day. Both of you get to feel the raw power of a firearm. It's gonna change your life. I guarantee it!"

"We won't let you down," Silas said softly.

"I know you won't. Now, some say 'shoot first, aim later,' but that's a bunch of horseshit. If you don't hit the target, all you've done is make a bunch of noise."

"Mr. Frank, I'm kinda nervous," said Silas.

"Yes, young man, I could tell. You're over here sweating bullets!"

The men were silent at first and Edwin said, "How did he do that?"

"I'm just messing with you guys. That's a saying from the futu—well, never mind. It's just a funny thing to say. Anyhoo, let's get started."

"Pa, he talks kind of funny," Silas said.

"Listen up, son. We might just learn something."

Next, Frank took great care in showing them how to get comfortable with the rifle, starting with breaking it down and putting it back together. Then it was time for the fun part; they would try to hit the makeshift shooting range.

"Where does the gunpowder go?" Edwin asked as seriously as a night owl.

"Edwin, my friend, there's no need for that with these babies! Just you watch."

As Frank showed them how to handle the gun, they quickly grasped the fundamentals. With no previous shooting history, they didn't have any bad habits to break. In fact, they were model students, respectful of the firepower but not afraid to open it up and empty the chamber when the time came.

Although Robert had hunted many times, he had limited experience maintaining firearms, but he adapted well to Frank's method of shooting. After two days of training, Frank was confident in the ability of his students, and he smiled with pride as they wielded their weapons like pros. Now, it was just a matter of their working as a team in a stressful situation. The four of them, each armed with M-4s at their highest rate of fire, presented a formidable front against most any opposition they might encounter. At that point, Frank felt confident about having to leave the next morning. Edwin and Silas demonstrated a newfound sense of confidence after the weapons training and expressed an interest in learning to shoot the pistol that Frank and the other team members always wore.

"We'll get to that soon enough," Frank promised.

Tom kept busy running the operation and tracking the rest of the team while Jan was overwhelmed managing the ever-growing ward. Patients were recovering satisfactorily, and many had either been picked up by relatives or were able to leave on their own. The trouble was, as soon as one left, another was waiting for the bed. There was a constant flow of prospective patients angling to be admitted into what they were calling "the miracle ward."

Tom and Jan's schedule precluded much time to analyze each day's activities, and they both slipped into their own routines. One evening when they sat down to eat, Tom broached the subject of the hospital building that he had been working on.

"Jan, I'm wondering if this is the right location for a hospital."

"What do you mean?" the medic asked. "We are busy as can be and there's no sign of it letting up."

"I understand that, but it might be more strategic to locate it in town or somewhere that is served by a railroad to facilitate transportation in and out. It would be nice for us, as well as patients and visitors," Tom stated.

"To be honest, I haven't given that any thought. I've been so busy," Jan answered. "However, you make an excellent point. We shouldn't be complacent and just stay here because it's where we started."

Tom asked, "On that note, would you be comfortable running the place by yourself while Frank takes Edwin, Silas, and Robert to Richmond? There might also be time for me to hop on the four-wheeler and scout possible locations to build an awesome hospital."

Jan said, "Since Robert Winslow Jr. is up and walking, he is capable of assisting me. There are also the three nurses who deal with most of the routine needs of the patients, which has lightened my load a little more. I don't think it should be a problem. How long do you think you'll be gone?" he asked.

"I'll only be out for the day. Planning to ride south to Burkeville and scope it out, and maybe farther east to Blackstone. Either way, it's not much of a ride on a four-wheeler," Tom replied.

"I think we can handle that," Jan answered.

"Good, then I'll gear up and grab a radio, and I'll plan on leaving in the morning at the same time Frank does," Tom decided. "I'll keep the radio on should you need me to get back here in a hurry, and I'll keep you informed of my location."

With plans in place for the next few days, everyone prepared for his own upcoming mission. Tom conducted a more in-depth map study on his laptop, relying on the information that Jack and Dave had relayed on their way south to Burkeville. He felt comfortable enough traveling solo if he took his M-4 and pistol. He wouldn't be going too far.

Word of his team's lethal capabilities had undoubtedly filtered through the surrounding towns, and he was confident there wouldn't be trouble. Another reason for his outing was to meet and mingle with the townspeople. Thus far, his interactions had been limited to just his team members, the help they had recruited, and some occasional visitors. His only reservation was about the four-wheeler. He wasn't a big rider and didn't have much experience on one. Tom was a brain, though, and knew he could figure it out.

Jan, on the other hand, was looking forward to a slower pace for a little while. Easing up on the patient intake would give him time to inventory his supplies, figure out what he needed, and determine how long he could get by without more provisions. Bandages weren't much of an issue, but medicine was a real problem. He trained his nurses on how to save needles for sterilization and reuse, but he needed to figure out how to sterilize IV bags and mix IV fluids if the ward was to remain operational.

The two parties set off at dawn the next day. Tom was hoping for a relaxing day of sightseeing around the neighboring areas and maybe even stopping for a cold beer. Frank, however, had a hunch that his crew might encounter trouble somewhere along their route, and he was soon proven correct.

First, the four men dismounted, left their horses and tack at the livery stable, and walked to the train station. As soon as they arrived, Frank stepped up to the ticket master, and two men began to approach, while another three waited a few yards back.

They cornered Robert Winslow and spat out, "Those two can't carry guns here," pointing at Edwin and Silas.

Silas, with mounting confidence, stepped in front of them and challenged, "Why don't you try to take them?" Edwin shot him a stern look but said nothing.

The two strangers were utterly taken aback, unaccustomed to being challenged by a young Black man. They looked at each other as if deciding how to respond.

"We need to teach this boy a lesson," the first one said.

Frank, having witnessed the encounter from the start, decided to hang back and see how the young man would handle the aggressors. As a matter of precaution, Frank stepped behind Edwin to reassure him that there was backup if needed. At 18, Silas was not a boy at all but a man, and it was never more apparent as when the squared up his solid frame and prepared for a confrontation.

After quickly eyeing Frank and his solid steel friend, the two strangers had second thoughts. They stepped back meekly and one of them said in disgust, "You ought to teach him some respect."

"Why don't I have him teach *you* some respect?" Frank fired back.

They turned away and grumbled, "Damn Yankees..."

That was enough for Frank, and he took a few quick steps in front of them and stopped. "You'd better be talking about the Broadway play or the musical supergroup led by Tommy Shaw of Styx fame," he boomed.

When the men looked at each other in confusion, Frank zeroed in on the older one first. He quickly used his martial arts skills to deliver a fist strike to the solar plexus and a side kick to the kidney, immediately dropping the man and leaving him screaming in agony.

Frank then looked at Silas. "Do you want to teach this bozo a lesson?"

Despite not knowing what a bozo was, Silas eagerly obliged by grabbing the other man, throwing him on the ground, and pummeling him with a series of punches. The defeated man commenced to apologizing nonstop, like a skipping record. Frank watched with interest to see how Silas would react. It would tell him a lot about the young man.

Silas was caught up in the moment and continued wailing on the pathetic fellow for a few moments before stopping just as abruptly as he had begun. He then quietly stood up, offered the man his hand in assistance, and helped him to his feet. Frank was pleased that Silas was neither cocky nor remorseful. "Perfect," he thought. "Just the kind of soldier I need watching my back." They then boarded the train without further incident, sincerely hoping it would stay that way.

Tom rode at a moderate 25 mph pace and soon found himself in the tranquil town of Burkeville. Understandably, the people were awe-struck by the sight of him on the steel machine. He parked in what he assumed to be the center of town and climbed off with an audience watching his every move. He went for a walk to get a look at the quaint town. It was in the flatter region of Virginia, east of the Appalachian mountains, in a part of the state he was unfamiliar with. In his former life, Tom had traveled extensively in the DC area and along the I-95 corridor, not to mention the nearby Appalachians, but he had never seen this part of Virginia.

After he was satisfied that he had sufficiently explored the humble burg, he decided to continue on to Blackstone, which was another 15 miles to the east along the Southside RR tracks. He climbed on the four-wheeler and hit the electric start. The machine roared to life, much to the astonishment of the crowd that had gathered to watch him. He quickly accelerated down the dirt street and followed the train tracks all the way to Blackstone. There, he stopped in front of a saloon in the middle of town. It didn't appear to be open at such an early hour, but he went in anyway.

He encountered a man that he supposed was the owner. "Barkeep, mind if I get a cold beer?"

The man put down his cloth and stopped his chores to address the interloper. "Well, it's a might bit early, but I'll do what I can do." Then he disappeared into the back room and soon returned with a large mug of beer.

Tom savored his first swallow and then asked, "Is there a doctor in this town?"

"Not since the war broke out," the barman replied. "Not much of anything left since the damned war started. Most of the men are off fighting, and everything that was here has been plundered by one side or the other," he lamented. "I'm barely staying in business myself. The only way I manage to stay afloat is to offer free drinks to whoever is in charge of our little town at the moment. From the looks of it, right now that would be you," he said with resignation.

Wanting to dispel the notion that he was there to take advantage of the man, Tom pulled out a wad of cash and paid the man handsomely for the beer. The proprietor accepted it gratefully and thanked Tom profusely.

Tom nodded and asked, "Is there any land for sale around here?"

"Look around you," the owner declared. "Everything is for sale...and cheap!"

"I'm just looking for 40 acres or so close to town," Tom stated. "And let me give you some advice: don't be so eager to sell your place just yet. Big things are about to happen here. That's a promise."

Seventeen

As Jon checked the bandage on Captain Pete's head, he said, "By the way, my buddy Mike is feeling sick, so he went down to the sleeping quarters. I'll go check on Mike as soon as I get you patched up."

When Pete seemed satisfied, Jon went about caring for the head wound and then excused himself to go below, the recorder tucked in his pocket. He handed it to Mike, who plugged in his earbuds and started listening. Since it was a voice-activated device, it only recorded when there was conversation. Jon kept a lookout near the door while Mike listened intently. It soon became readily apparent by the sudden change in Mike's demeanor that something was going on.

He ripped the earbuds out and handed them to Jon, announcing angrily, "Listen to *this* shit!" Jon took his turn with the device as Mike watched the door.

When Jon handed the recorder back to Mike, he asked stoically, "So what do we do now?"

"I'll go kill them all," Mike growled.

"Why don't we wait until we get out in the ocean?" Jon suggested. He knew that Mike was an impulsive operator, and Jon wanted to be sure they didn't execute a half-baked plan. "He said they'd wait until we were seasick. I told him that you were feeling ill to explain why I didn't stick around with him. We should be out in the Atlantic tonight, and we can both feign seasickness and wait for them to act. My conscience would be clear then," Jon proposed, as he paced slowly back and forth.

"I'll agree to that plan for one night, but that's it. I'd rather not get caught by surprise and have that pirate bastard cut my throat," Mike snapped.

"Besides, wouldn't it be better to throw them in the ocean than the bay?" Jon reasoned.

Mike shrugged and then nodded in agreement. "I can feel the chop steadily increasing, which means we're hitting open water now," he said. "Wait an hour or so, then go on deck and tell him we're both really sick. From that point, we can keep an eye on the door. I imagine they'll wait until dark, and that will work in our favor. As soon as the door opens, one of us can hit them with a SureFire light in the eyes to temporarily blind them while we see if they've got a weapon in their hand. If so, it's game on." Mike set his jaw, and his bright blue eyes turned cold as ice.

"Aye, aye, Captain Mike," Jon dutifully replied. Mike shot him a sideways glance. "Well, you *will* be Captain Mike if that happens," Jon pointed out.

"Yeah, I can't wait for that," was Mike's sarcastic reply. "Now grab something to stuff down your gullet, sailor. You've got first watch when you get back from telling him that we're sick and staying in for the night. Meanwhile, I'll go hang over the side of the ship and act like I'm throwing up and retching, and you can do the same on your way back. Make it convincing because I don't want to wait long for them to show up. If our plan works, I'll have to go to the helm immediately, and I want to be well-rested for when the time comes," Mike ordered.

Jon returned a short while later, and they set the plan in motion. Mike would sleep with a pistol while Jon kept an eye on the door with a SureFire flashlight in one hand and his SIG 226 pistol in the other. Two hours later, just as Jon was thinking about waking Mike up for his shift, the door hinges creaked slightly. Jon instantly focused all his senses.

As it opened slowly, a body stepped over the threshold. Quick as a flash, Jon hit the button on the back of the SureFire, shooting a glaring beam of light into the intruder's eyes. The man was stunned, frozen in his tracks, but it was too late. As soon as Jon saw the large knife in the man's right hand, he fired a two-round burst center mass, and the assailant crumpled on the spot. Mike was up on his feet in half a second, and he and Jon sprinted out the door in search of the remaining two partners in crime. They discovered Captain Pete at the helm, breathing heavily with a panicked look on his face as they advanced on him. Mike wasted no time taking him out with a double tap to the head. He quickly dragged the captain's limp body to the side of the boat and tossed him over.

"Where's the other one?" he shouted.

"He's in his rack asleep," Jon yelled back.

"Get him on deck," Mike commanded. "I'll throw his ass overboard, too."

Jon escorted the young sailor to the helm, where Mike was now standing at the wheel of the ship. The young mate looked lost and confused. He asked groggily, "Hey, uh, where is Captain Pete?"

"He's swimming with the sharks just like your other pal. They just tried to kill us," Mike snarled. "So, it's time for you to face the music, deckhand. What the hell did you know about this?"

The kid was trembling in fear as he spoke, "Sir, I swear I didn't have no part of that plan or any other one. They never included me in on things because they said I was too young. They didn't think I could keep my mouth shut. You got to believe me, sir!"

Mike and Jon conferred quietly and decided the kid was telling the truth.

Mike turned back to face the quivering youth and announced, "OK, kid, we believe your story, but you'd better not be lying or else you'll regret it. I can promise you that. Now," Mike barked, "you have two choices: jump overboard and join your friends as shark chum or stay on as a crewmember. If you choose to stay, I'll pay you and let you decide your future once we get to New Orleans. Keep in mind, son, that I'm now the captain of this ship, and I will crush you in a heartbeat if you try any funny business from here on out."

The kid nodded vigorously, indicating full understanding of the taller man's decree. He replied timidly, "I've only been with Captain Pete a year, and the crew never really trusted me. But I trust you two, and I'd like to stay aboard. I can man the helm and keep a heading. I'll gladly take whatever the pay is you're offering." He paused to take a breath, as though he were convincing himself that he had made the right decision. When he spoke again, he was less fearful. "My name's Tad."

"Hi, Tad. I'm Mike and this is Jon," the de facto captain replied. "I want you to stay up with me as a lookout on the helm until daylight. Jon, why don't you try to get some sleep? It's gonna be in short supply for a while."

Jon retreated below deck and rested fitfully as he rehashed the night's events in his head. He tried to reconcile how they were going to navigate the boat and sail all the way to New Orleans. He trusted Mike, but he also knew that they were up against some tough odds, and the sea was an unpredictable mistress. Anything could happen.

Up on deck, Mike and Tad guided the boat through the moonlit night as they passed the Outer Banks of North Carolina. Mike told Tad to keep an eye out for obstructions. He also instructed Tad to hang 30 feet of rope overboard with a weight attached to it so they would know if they were getting close to shallow water.

The two of them manned the boat until the dazzling orange sun slowly rose over the Atlantic Ocean, greeting the men with fair winds and calm waters, making it a perfect day for sailing. Mike decided to keep heading south to take advantage of the ideal conditions. He yelled for Tad. "Why don't you go wake up Jon and then get some sleep? We're going to ride this good weather for as long as we can."

Soon, Jon was on deck. "I had the strangest dream that we were sailing to New Orleans with a crew that had never been there before." He laughed good-naturedly, and Mike cracked a small smile.

"Take the wheel for a while, bud, so I can grab some shuteye," Mike declared, now in full captain mode. "Just hold the same heading. We're far enough offshore to avoid any shoals or hazards. I'll be sleeping on that pile of sails right there. Wake me up if you need me," he directed. He then walked over to the stack of tattered canvas and collapsed into a deep slumber.

Jon held the ship's compass on the 190-degree heading as Mike had instructed and enjoyed the peace and quiet for a few hours. He watched the gentle waves crash against the side of the boat as the sun continued its daily climb across the sky. He was jolted out of the trance when he heard Mike stomping along the deck behind him.

"Morning, Jon! I'm so hungry it feels like a claw is gnawing at my empty belly!"

"OK, I get the point. I'm hungry, too! Why don't you take the helm so I can wake up Tad, locate some fishing gear, and catch some breakfast?"

In no time at all, the three men were feasting on fresh fish, and plenty of it. For Mike and Jon, it was a welcome change from the MREs they had subsisted on lately. The group was making good time, and Mike estimated that if their luck held out, they would round the tip of Florida and enter the Gulf of Mexico in about three days. The sunny weather, plentiful fishing, and calm waters worked together to make the next three days fly by without incident. On the morning of the fourth day, the southern tip of Florida gave way to the west as the vast Gulf of Mexico loomed large before them. Mike consulted the map on his laptop and estimated a heading to take them directly to the mouth of the Mississippi.

"From now on," he declared, "two men on and one man below deck until we reach New Orleans. Keep up the commo shots, too. We can string up the antenna in the rigging and just leave it mounted. That should simplify making comms."

They sailed on in the gentle, warmer waters of the Gulf and settled into a routine. For the first time in a while, Mike and Jon felt that they could relax a bit. They took in the tranquil views as they ate and joked, the wind pushing them ever closer to the Crescent City.

Eighteen

Jack and Dave's arrival in Washington was quiet and seemingly inconsequential. It was not heralded the way Kevin and Joseph's had been —no fanfare or welcoming delegation—but that was just fine with the two low-key men. Dave had actually arranged via radio for them to stay in a different hotel to avoid drawing any undue attention to the arrival of the President of the Confederate States of America.

Jack, Dave, George Tindall, and President Davis grabbed their luggage and caught a wagon to the hotel. They checked in using assumed names to maintain anonymity. For further secrecy, they agreed to avoid contact with Kevin and Joseph in public due to the attention those two had begun to attract. Jack radioed Kevin with their hotel and room numbers in the hopes that they could arrange a clandestine meeting the following day with only President Lincoln, President Davis, and the four team members in attendance.

Kevin was insistent that there be no distractions at the initial introduction. He used his remaining time that evening to scout out a discreet meeting spot. He had trouble finding a place that was out of the public eye and wouldn't draw an audience. Suddenly, he had a novel idea: they would use the livery stable. It was clean, yet inconspicuous. He also reasoned that the environment would level the playing field as much as possible, which would (theoretically) speed up the negotiation process. After all, this was just the initial conference, and he didn't want either man to have an advantage. Kevin paid the owner of the stable to allow him to use it without interruption. He and Joseph would stand on either side of President Lincoln while Jack and Dave did the same with

President Davis. He radioed Jack and briefed him on the arrangements, and they agreed to meet at the stable at 10:00 the next morning.

Lincoln and Davis were understandably apprehensive about meeting each other. The Civil War had been bitterly fought with many casualties on both sides, and the feelings of animosity were mutual. In addition, Jack had informed the team that the men had a complicated history. It was said that Davis appointed two men to the Confederate Secret Service (CSS) as they continued to engage in acts of terrorism. This included the Lincoln kidnapping conspiracy that began taking shape in the fall of 1864, led by a man named John Wilkes Booth. The ultimate goal was to use the President of the US as leverage to free Confederate soldiers.

While the plot fell apart in March of 1865, John Surrat, a Confederate spy participating in the kidnapping plot, met with Jefferson Davis and the Confederate Attorney General in Richmond. On April 10, a Confederate explosives expert was arrested for plotting to blow up the White House.

Kevin and Jack had done their best to prepare the team for what was to come historically so that their actions could be measured accordingly. If they planned to alter history, they had to understand the existing timeline and their place in it. Knowing that they were surrounded by talk of explosions and kidnapping plots, it was difficult to determine who to trust and who to approach more cautiously. So, it made sense that the two leaders did not have even a respectful professional relationship. Lincoln was most assuredly informed of the Confederate subterfuge in its various forms; thus, he was likely not anxious to welcome Davis to the White House. That gesture would have given credence and acknowledgment to Davis's presidency, something Lincoln wanted to avoid at all costs.

While it's said that they never met personally, on February 3, 1865, Lincoln and his Secretary of State William Seward did meet with three Confederate officials to discuss an end to the Civil War. That conference took place on neutral ground on a boat in the Hampton Roads area of Virginia. However, the issue was that officials representing the Confederate States of America were not in a position to accept any other settlement but southern independence. That was a deal-breaker for Lincoln, thus the war continued for another two months, and the Lincoln-Davis faceoff never happened...that is, until now.

Given those bits of history, whether rumored or confirmed, it was important that the four men be aware of the delicate relationship between Lincoln and Davis, and the political dance required to allow each to maintain their dignity and values. The team understood that any successful negotiation required an agreement of three elements: identifying the common ground (an end to the Civil War), then clarifying what each side wanted. Lincoln had expressed in his second inauguration speech, just one month before the war ended, that he wanted "lasting peace among ourselves" with "malice toward none."

On the other side, Davis justified the southern rebellion saying the North was becoming more powerful and populous, which meant controlling the affairs of the nation regardless of the values specific to the South, including the institution of slavery. The question was, how could they change history for the better by possibly saving Lincoln's life, and still ensuring that history wasn't permanently altered? Or should they not do anything to stop the assassination and let the chips fall where they may? For now, they would concentrate on the meeting. While it may or may not have happened historically, it was a small change that if done discreetly, would likely have little historical impact, unless, of course, they reached a form of détente, which was unlikely.

Everyone from both parties spent a restless night in anticipation of the next day's events. Jack and Dave had a relatively easy time escorting President Davis to the stable without detection because few people were aware he was even in town. Kevin and Joseph, on the other hand, had quite the challenge convincing President Lincoln's staff that they were just going for a short walk, and then getting Mr. Lincoln's distinctive lanky frame into a horse stable without drawing attention. Fortunately, he decided to forgo the stovepipe hat, which made the task that much easier. Surprisingly, when he was dressed casually, he looked like any number of unremarkable men from the country paying a visit to the nation's capital.

Jack and Dave arrived first with President Davis and were both in awe when President Lincoln walked in, flanked by Kevin and Joseph. They managed to keep a lid on their feelings and also refrained from acknowledging their team members. While the historical importance of the meeting was at the forefront of their minds, they preferred to leave the moment to the two leaders as they met for the first time. There was a moment of hesitation as both commanders-in-chief allowed the reality of the situation to sink in. This was going to be neither a political event nor a formal debate, leaving nothing but brass tacks for the heads of state to address. What Kevin had envisioned was the two presidents standing face to face, no crowd or advisers in sight. For his part, he would not interfere unless it became absolutely necessary.

The two men silently sized one another up. Lincoln was expressionless and unaffected. Davis seemed a shade uncomfortable but took pains to set those feelings aside lest they be mistaken for weakness. Finally, President Lincoln extended his hand to President Davis and gave a formal introduction. They shook hands forcefully as each man carefully measured the other. Each was equally determined not to blink.

President Davis said, "Mr. Lincoln, I have come here to discuss the consequences of the recent Battle of Sayler's Creek. I have been informed by my escorts that they played a key role in the defeat of Union Forces there. If I were not convinced that this was the truth, I can assure you, I would not be here."

Lincoln paused thoughtfully as he considered his response. When he replied, he was stone-faced and deliberate. "Mr. Davis, I, too, have been told by my escorts that they were responsible for the tragic loss at Sayler's Creek. The sudden defeat of our army there has dealt us a crushing blow." A look of remorse flashed across his face, but it was gone only a second later, just as quickly replaced with a solemn expression. He went on, "This...turn of events has forced me to reconsider the

Union strategy. I know, too, that Lee's army is still retreating and very close to defeat. He cannot withstand another sustained war campaign. The South is weary, and we are both desperate for an end to this miserable war."

Jefferson Davis softly replied, "Mr. Lincoln, you are correct. Neither side can continue suffering as we have for the last few years, but we have not given up just yet. What do you propose as a solution that might satisfy both of us and our constituents?"

As one who had honed his negotiating skills while in office, Lincoln knew at that point that he had gained the upper hand. In his most presidential tone, he proclaimed, "It is my unwavering trust in these gentlemen that has led me here to engage with you. They are men of integrity with a noble devotion to one United States of America. Let us set forth an equitable compromise that you and I can take to our respective representatives. We must convince them of the fairness of this agreement, along with the necessity of supporting it. There has been too much bloodshed and destruction. Whatever coercion brought us here, let us be guided by our own principles to negotiate in good faith for the benefit of all the people we represent."

Then, it was President Davis' turn to choose his words with care. He quickly recalled the talking points that Jack and Dave had forced him to repeat ad nauseam on their train ride. As though he were putting an internal demon to rest, he took a deep breath and answered, "Mr. President, I assure you that I am committed to fully transparent negotiations that will free the slaves, preserve the Union, and bring healing and prosperity to this great country of ours. I agree that the time for unity is upon us. We now need only to convince our legislatures to support our efforts. I know not what challenges you face in accomplishing this, but as for me, it shall be a daunting task."

President Lincoln said, "We can, and we *must* accept the formidable challenge. I am confident that with the assistance of these brave and wise men who have led us here, we shall rise to the occasion." He continued, "I offer you all the hospitality of the White House for the duration of your stay here in Washington. You, Mr. Tindall, and our escorts are my invited guests at the presidential residence for as long as you shall remain here."

"I will consider your generous offer in partnership with my companions," Davis answered respectfully.

President Lincoln then turned and introduced himself to Jack and Dave, heartily shaking both of their hands. President Davis took advantage of the opportunity to do likewise with Kevin and Joseph. It was not until then that the four teammates and friends greeted one another and spoke among themselves. As the resident Civil War buff, Jack could barely contain his excitement as two key historical figures he'd studied for years were not only standing in front of him but actually shaking his hand!

Kevin gave them all a brief smile and said, "Good job, fellas." Anything more was unnecessary, for they all realized what a watershed moment this was. As they prepared to depart, Kevin turned to address Lincoln. "Mr. President, we should be getting back before there is too much concern over your whereabouts." He glanced over his shoulder and mouthed softly to Jack and Dave, "Stay in touch," and they quickly departed.

Jack looked at the gentleman whose time as a head of state was rapidly expiring. He knew that Davis would be reluctant to bow out of his position of power. He was, after all, only human. When Jack spoke, his words were terse.

"Good job sticking to the script, President Davis. If you continue to play your cards right and toe the line that we've drawn for you, there just might be some mercy down the road. I don't need to remind you what can happen if you step one foot off course...do I?"

Jefferson Davis shook his head vehemently. "No, that won't be necessary, Mr. Morrison. We all seem to be in agreement," he assured his imposing attendant. "Now, come, let us set off for the White House, gentlemen," Davis announced emphatically. "I am sure there will be much planning and drinking ahead of us, and I, for one, am looking forward to a delicious meal."

Jack and Dave nodded and then started for the door. They were anxious to get the bureaucratic antics out of the way so everyone could move forward with the new future...whatever that might be.

Nineteen

Tom wasted no time getting back to HQ, which he did without a hitch. He found Jan at the ward working diligently to sterilize hypodermic needles. He hurriedly pulled Jan aside and said with excitement, "There's a great little town not too far from here, and the railroad runs right through it! It looks like the perfect site for our future medical facilities. I'd like to head over and look at it when Frank gets back."

Jan nodded and mumbled, "And when's that going to be?"

"Probably not for a few more days, but I'm going to proceed with plans to relocate us if you're good with it," Tom answered.

"As you wish," Jan acquiesced. "It makes no difference to me, other than the matter of getting supplies in and out. It sounds as if this new place is more accessible," he voiced, if only halfheartedly.

Satisfied that he had secured the support of another team member, Tom shifted into high gear with plans to purchase land in Blackstone. He wanted to set the wheels in motion for Robert Winslow to arrange the first phase of construction as soon as he returned from Richmond. Tom was an idea man. All he needed was a plan and some capital and he could sell snowballs in Antarctica. He scheduled a series of meetings with Jan to discuss the requirements and a design that would fulfill their individual visions. Jan used the knowledge and experience he had gained serving in hospitals to sketch some rudimentary drawings for Tom.

After seeing the first set of sketches, Tom said, "Jan, you're not thinking on a big enough scale. We should aim to become a major research facility. Imagine yourself as the head physician of the Mayo Clinic of our time and create that idea here! This place can easily become the world's premier surgical center. Think about it: This is not only an opportunity to bring mankind into the future of medicine and improve their quality of life but also to launch a wildly successful business venture."

"Never thought of it that way," Jan joked. "I'm just a simple country doctor."

"Well, country's coming to town, so load up your bags. We're moving to Beverly Hills, Jethro!" Tom exclaimed. "And stop being so humble!"

"That's *Dr.* Jethro to you," Jan shot back good-naturedly.

"As you wish. I'm just a simple venture capitalist and international businessman," Tom smirked.

"Like Travis Tritt, I smell T-R-O-U-B-L-E," Jan teased.

Tom laughed and said, "When the crew gets back, I'll have Frank put some blueprints together. Then I'll talk to Robert Winslow about starting construction as soon as we buy the land in Blackstone. Meanwhile, I'll go do a radio check and get an update on their progress."

Once he was able to make radio contact, Frank informed Tom that they had arrived in Richmond and that all was well at the plantation. "We're planning to hit up the Bank of Richmond in the morning and withdraw a large sum of money. After that, we'll immediately board the train back. We should arrive by tomorrow evening. I'll keep you posted every step of the way."

Frank then accompanied Robert as he went around the plantation, shaking hands and congratulating each of the former slaves who had chosen to stay on as paid staff members. He also advised them that he would transfer to them the title of the plantation, leaving Julius as the custodian of the small fortune he planned to bestow upon them. He expressed his wishes that they would continue to run the plantation as a business outfit, but that was completely their decision to make. He assured them that they had the knowledge among them to do so.

"You just need to cooperate with one another, and you'll be successful. For starters, you can begin by charging these soldiers to stay here," Mr. Winslow counseled Julius.

Silent tears of joy and gratitude rolled down the workers' faces, no matter how much they tried to hide them. Frank was proud of Robert and told him he was honored to have witnessed such a noble and generous gesture.

"It brings me more pleasure than it does all of them collectively," Robert promised.

"You're a good man, Mr. Winslow. Don't worry about them, either. We'll come back and check on them periodically," Frank assured him.

"I'd like that," Robert said with a smile.

"Well, we'd love to stay," Frank announced, "but we've got other fish to fry. We've got to pack up Mr. Winslow's belongings and personal effects and get them loaded on the wagon." Julius and two others helped their new benefactor pack and load everything he wished to take. Turns out it wasn't much, just a couple of suitcases filled with clothes and books. He left all the furnishings for the new owners. Edwin and Silas were particularly moved by Mr. Winslow's incredible act of kindness. They kept a close eye on him as he helped load his possessions and shook hands with his steward once more. The father and son stood up straight with their heads held high, serving as a reminder to all those present that the times, they were a-changin' as Bob Dylan said. They all slept that night with a deep sense of satisfaction and awoke the next morning eager to get started on the next leg of their adventure.

After breakfast, they saddled their horses, and the small caravan set off for Richmond. Their arrival at the train station drew plenty of attention, so Frank handed Edwin some cash and asked him to buy the train tickets. Edwin, now brimming with newfound confidence, stepped up and handled the transaction.

"Get used to it," Frank said. "You are an example to everyone watching." Edwin beamed at the thought. "Now, let's all go to the bank, but be sure to keep your eyes open," Frank cautioned.

Robert entered the bank and made a complete withdrawal of his fortune, which caused a bit of a stir among the staff. The president of the bank soon approached him and asked if there was a problem.

Robert assured him that everything was fine and that he was simply preparing to relocate. He explained that he had gifted his plantation to the former slaves who had worked on it and asked that the president continue to serve them in their financial dealings. He had left Julius a considerable sum of money, along with instructions to open an account in their names.

"I'm counting on you to assist them, William. I *will* be back to ensure that my orders were carried out," he pledged.

"Yes, sir, Mr. Winslow. I'll see to it personally," the president agreed.

"I should hope so, as it is my expectation," Robert replied sharply. Then, with a handshake, he bade his longtime friend and banker goodbye.

The small party made its way back to the train station just in time to hear the conductor yelling, "All aboard!" They hurriedly stepped on and took their seats, keeping a wary eye on their fellow passengers since the large amount of money they transported was plenty of motive for robbery. Frank hoped that their alert postures and menacing attitudes would discourage any attempt to interfere with them, but he remained vigilant all the while.

Thankfully, the train ride was smooth, and they reached Jetersville by early afternoon. At that point, Silas felt confident enough to go to the livery stable alone and get the horses. He saddled them all and led them to the train station where the other three hastily mounted and then started toward HQ. They relaxed a little since they were in the home stretch. They were sure that everyone within miles was now aware of who they were and how big of a stick they carried.

Twenty

Mike, Jon, and Tad sailed into the Port of New Orleans only to be greeted by the city's oppressive heat. Mike had just finished studying the conditions of the Mississippi River and decided that the best course of action was to continue upriver to St. Louis. The wharf teemed with boats whose cargoes were being unloaded by throngs of men, mostly African American, working shirtless as the sun beat down.

Jon commented, "I guess New Orleans isn't 'The Big Easy' yet."

"Hardly!" Mike scoffed. "Can you believe people settled in these miserable lands before the days of air conditioning? No wonder it only cost the government four cents an acre."

Jon snickered and said, "Those early settlers thought we Native Americans were dim-witted savages, but soon, they realized we had all the good land for a reason. Then they pushed our asses into god-forsaken territory kinda like this!" He was good-natured and forward focused, which did not conflict with his Native American heritage and pride. He accepted that to transgress was to be human. He also knew that evolving meant righting the wrongs of those past transgressions, and that was now the team's primary mission.

They managed to pull the boat into an empty slip, only to be met by a fat little man who was sweating profusely and yelling, "You can't dock there!"

Mike jumped ashore and stood face to face with the portly character. "Settle down, buddy. We won't be here long." The man scowled in protest, but Mike's daunting size and icy glare soon put an end to his objections.

Just then, a paddle wheel riverboat blew its steam whistle and landed in a nearby berth. "Where is that boat headed?" he asked.

"St. Louis. It leaves in an hour," he replied.

"Thanks. We'll be out of your way in 15 minutes," Mike assured him. He stepped back on board and hurriedly informed Jon of his plan to take the riverboat to St. Louis. "Grab your gear and let's get over there," he urged.

"What are we going to do with the boat?" Jon inquired.

"You mean Tad's boat?" Mike replied. "Hey, Tad, this boat is yours, by the way," he mentioned offhandedly. The young man was stunned but had no time to question or object. He simply offered his thanks as Mike and Jon hastily finished packing their gear and offloaded it on the dock.

They noticed four Black men watching them, obviously waiting to unload the boat that was next to pull into the slip.

"Want a job?" Mike asked them without explanation.

They looked confused and unsure of how to answer this stranger. They all turned to the same heavy foreman, who was now shuffling toward the small gathering of men.

"Get back to work!" he barked at the four unloaders. "These men work for me. If any of y'all have other ideas or give me any problems, I'll send you back to Haiti!" The four dock workers turned around reluctantly and started walking away.

Mike quickly outpaced them and asked again, "Want a job?" The four screwed up their faces, trying in earnest to size him up and decide what to do. Mike continued, "I can use the four of you to help haul our gear to that paddle wheeler over there, and then we'll all board it for St. Louis. We're going on an expedition, and I need some strong, hardworking, trustworthy men to go along. Pay's good and you'll be free men from this moment on."

Mike sensed their hesitation and added, "Don't worry about him or anyone else. I'll take care of that." The four exchanged glances and shrugged. Mike and Jon offered their outstretched hands and introduced themselves. "That settles that. Now let's get our gear over there and hope we still have time to snag some new clothes for all of you," Mike announced. Then Jon accompanied them to the haberdashery while Mike booked passage for six to St. Louis.

The six men walked up the boat ramp, where the boarding agent collected their tickets and directed Mike and Jon to the left and the other four to the right. Mike stepped up to the boarding agent and said firmly, "They're with us."

"I know, sir, but slaves are quartered separately," the agent protested.

Mike's face stiffened as he steeled himself for the encounter. "Let me set you straight on a couple of things, pal. First off, they're not slaves. Second, the Civil War is over, and they are staying in the same accommodations as we are since that's what I purchased for them."

The agent knew better than to argue, so he let them pass without another word and went to alert the boat's captain.

They were assigned three rooms, and Mike and Jon chose the middle one. They dropped their gear, and Mike went to ensure that the new employees were settling in. The captain strode confidently up to Mike in the hallway and informed him that "those four negroes" were not able to stay on this deck.

Mike responded matter-of-factly, "They are staying right where they are, and they will be dining with us at every meal for the duration of the trip. There are not enough soldiers in the army to change that. If you think differently, send them this way before we depart. If you and I are in agreement, then let's get going. Let me also be the first to inform you that the Civil War is over, and slavery has been abolished."

The captain quickly learned that challenging Mike was not in his best interest, and his face turned ashen as his confidence evaporated instantly. The captain struggled to reconcile his grasp on the new reality that now towered over him. Finally, he nodded sheepishly and then scampered to the helm to prepare for departure.

Mike shouted after him, "And if there's anyone on board who disagrees, send them my way."

The paddle wheeler pushed off, steaming its way to the far-off destination of St. Louis. Mike and Jon would have preferred a relaxing trip, but neither was naïve enough to think that they would escape scrutiny as a result of the status they had conferred upon their travel companions.

As if it needed to be said, Mike reminded Jon, "We better stay alert and always remain armed. When we eat, we'll sit on opposite sides of the table so no one can approach unnoticed."

Jon agreed and then said, "I can put the recorder in the wheelhouse to monitor whether there was any talk of confronting them. After all, it worked with Captain Pete."

"We can try that. Right now, we've got time to do some map study and finish planning our trip," Mike pointed out. "When we get to St. Louis, I suggest we try to hire an experienced guide to take us up the Missouri River and find some prospectors to help with panning and digging for the gold," he proposed.

Jon concurred, then recommended that they spend some time practicing with the small drone they had brought along. "Neither of us paid a whole lot of attention during the class, and we're both gonna need practice if we hope to use it and not lose it," he suggested.

"Good idea. We can practice from the deck, and that will allow us to scout ahead as well," Mike added.

With a preliminary plan in place, the men prepared themselves for the first meal of the voyage. Jon summoned their travel companions and escorted them to the showers. He encouraged them to get cleaned up since they had come directly from their hot, sweaty work on the dock. He then shared some deodorant with them.

"Sir, what is this? Ladies' perfume?"

Jon smiled at them. "Oh, no, it's, uh, it's a new invention. It's called deodorant. It will make you smell good and feel great. Give it a try."

After providing a little more instruction, he then returned to his room to get ready. Dressing for dinner meant that both men would check their SIG 226s and stash an extra magazine in their pants pockets.

All six of the men proceeded to the dining room, where they immediately garnered unwanted attention and numerous stares from the diners already assembled. Jon leaned over to the guys and said, "Just relax because you are all ticketed passengers who belong here, same as everyone else. You're just as good as these bozos, and you smell great!" Of course, that was easier said than done since none of them had ever experienced a dining room situation like this.

Mike did not care a wit how anyone glared at the unusual band of men. He casually asked, "Can we have a table for six?" His icy cold stare left no doubt that he expected his request to be granted. The maître d' led them to a table near the back of the room, and they took their seats after Mike and Jon sat with their backs to the wall.

Jon steered the conversation toward introductions and getting acquainted with one other. One of the four men spoke up first. "I am Jacob, and this is Emmanuel, Stevenson, and Samuel. We are all in our 20s, with me being the oldest of the bunch. I made it my mission to watch out for these hardworking men. We are all just trying to earn an honest living."

They were a cheerful group, and they seemed excited about the opportunity before them. Mike said, "Just remember that you are welcome to call me Mike, and this is Jon."

Jacob cleared his throat and said, "Thank you, Mike, and you too, Jon. First off, we much appreciate the fancy new clothes. These would cost us a week's wages. If it's not too direct, can I ask how we will be paid? I assume it won't be entirely in clothing."

Mike chuckled, "I like a man with a sense of humor. You will earn $10 a day and have your food and supplies provided. We will also make sure to get anything you fellas need," he said, showing them for the first time that he could be kind and easygoing.

Everyone thoroughly enjoyed the meal and after a night of conversation, all returned to their rooms. Mike and Jon unpacked the drone and pored over the manual in preparation for its maiden flight the next day.

As the many sunrises faded to sunsets, the men continued this routine for most of the trip—the group sharing all their meals together, Mike and Jon took turns with the drone and charged the spare batteries with their portable solar panel, and the entire group of men walked around the ship to see the ever-changing sights passing by.

Mike and Jon eventually became skilled enough at flying the drone that they were able to launch it from the top deck and cut a circular pattern around the boat. They knew that this would be a tremendous scouting asset on their trip up the Missouri. While Mike experimented with the drone's range, Jon was on the foredeck as they drew near the port of Memphis, Tennessee. Mike steered the drone back, packed it up, and then went to talk to Jon.

"Why don't you take the four of them into town and buy them books so they can start learning how to read?" he advised. Jon readily agreed, as he was eager to set foot on dry land and see some new scenery. Mike would take the opportunity to explore the town on his own. "Take a radio!" he yelled back to Jon as he went to grab some money from the room.

Jon accompanied the four new expedition members down the gangplank, and they walked up the bank of the landing. They all beheld the town of Memphis, and Jon thought about the basketball, barbeque, and blues that would become its claim to fame over the next 100 years. The city was a key transportation hub due to its location on the Mississippi and the recently completed railroad depot. The Union had defeated Confederate forces there in June of 1862 before seizing the town. Since then, it has also become a major smuggling center for moving goods between the North and South.

Jon noticed some guns being bought and sold at a nearby shop, and he went in to see what was available. He spotted some of the new Sharps rifles and decided on a whim to buy four of them. He also got four Colt 1860 revolvers and a large cache of ammo in both calibers. He handed the weapons out amidst great cheers and excitement before they went in search of a leather goods store to be fitted for belts and holsters. After that, they scoured the main street for a place to buy some reading primers.

When they all reconvened at the dock, Mike was surprised to see the four men walking up the gangplank, each fully armed with a rifle in one arm and a stack of books in the other.

"Going to get interesting pretty soon," he murmured to no one in particular.

Jon heard him and grinned mischievously. "Couldn't pass up a good deal," he exclaimed. "Besides, they're gonna need to learn how to shoot sooner or later."

"Yeah, it'll probably be more useful than reading in the short term," Mike nodded in agreement.

"We can conduct weapons training on the back of the boat," Jon proposed.

"Good idea," Mike said, "and reading lessons on the front of the boat."

As they made their way up the Mississippi, they did indeed follow that training schedule. Mike and Jon continued to practice with the drone, so their days were filled with activity and thus, passed rather quickly. As training progressed, the four future frontiersmen soon became excellent shots. The Sharps was a .50 caliber rifle with a range of several hundred yards. The men became adept with the Colt pistols, too, and repeatedly rehearsed drawing from their holsters. As St. Louis loomed ahead, the six were determined to be prepared for the rough-and-tumble city known as the Gateway to the West.

Twenty-One

Coordinating a large-scale political roundtable proved to be more cumbersome and demanding than anyone had foreseen, except, perhaps, Jefferson Davis. The realization that this would not be a speedy process had begun to sink in for the four members of the ODA. Patience wasn't in ample supply among men in their line of work, but their dedication served as fuel for their efforts. As such, they resigned themselves to supporting the diplomatic efforts. Kevin and Joseph spearheaded the discussions, using persuasion when they could and resorting to coercion and threats when gentler tactics failed, knowing all the while that they were getting much closer to April 14.

The days dragged by, and Jack and Dave looked longingly to the west, wondering what adventures and opportunities beckoned them there. They sat up nights discussing what other possibilities might exist. It wasn't that they had a lack of interest in changing the political landscape of the United States for all generations to come. Just the opposite: They simply knew that Kevin and Joseph were better suited to that particular calling. There had to be another avenue the adventuresome duo could take to benefit mankind while making the most of this time-shifting experience.

One evening, it came to Jack as suddenly and clearly as the bright full moon overhead. "Oil," he blurted out. Dave gave him a quizzical look as Jack continued, "Oil, my friend. I got an associate degree from Nicholls State in Thibodaux, Louisiana, while I worked offshore in the oil drilling industry. We learned that drilling for oil began around 1865 in Texas, and that the first substantial oil discovery happened at Spindletop, Texas, in 1901. If we went down there and sought out the ones doing the drilling, we could hasten that discovery by some 35 years."

"How would we know where to drill?" Dave asked. "I don't know the first thing about that industry."

"The Spindletop well was drilled on top of a mound that contained a salt dome, and it's just southeast of Beaumont. That will be easy to find. It's locating the folks who are drilling now that might pose a challenge," Jack explained. "But think of what we could do with that commodity, knowledge, and wealth."

They discussed it further, the ins and outs of what it might mean, and the impact it would have on the future, their future. They considered what it would require to successfully drill, capture, and refine the raw petroleum into a usable product. Dave was admittedly out of his depth on this one, but he had full confidence in Jack's knowledge and initiative.

"I have the basic knowledge of the procedures for all of those steps," Jack said, "but we're talking about taking old technology and applying it to what I learned about modern equipment."

One evening while they were eating dinner with Kevin and Joseph, Jack broached the subject. "We want to run an idea by you guys. Dave and I have been thinking about going to Texas to strike oil. The goal is to forge a responsible path ahead into the industrial age."

Dave joined in to further articulate their idea. "We hope to use the profits for the good of the country, with everyone benefiting instead of a few large companies."

"We will definitely need industry assistance. And we're not talking about nationalizing the oil resources," Jack reassured, "just using some of the proceeds for education and assistance. We'll also take a resource conservation approach from the start."

Kevin leaned in a bit; his interest aroused. "You know," he mused, "this may dovetail quite nicely with what Joseph and I are engaged in here in Washington. We've been debating what solutions and incentives we have to offer states for abolishing slavery. Simply freeing those hardworking folks does not solve the problem of what is to become of them in the future. As we are aware, the strategy we're familiar with didn't work out so well. Maybe this is our chance to change that, to make a real difference for so many people."

Joseph picked up the narrative and ran with it. "I think that the average American will accept the freed African Americans if we can help eliminate the pain that was brought on by the divisive period of reconstruction. With money from the gold strike and this oil discovery you're proposing, we can fund education. We can help agriculture move into the machine age. We can demonstrate the ability of machines to replace the vast numbers of workers that these plantation owners have relied on to produce their crops."

Everyone nodded in agreement. Joseph, clearly passionate about the initiative, went on ardently, "The education effort can be a multi-pronged approach, focusing simultaneously on traditional education and vocational training for the inevitable skilled labor that will need to accompany the developing technology. If we don't educate and as-similate those folks, we will merely relegate them to the same fate that history has shown to be a dismal failure."

"I think we can all agree on that," Kevin said.

He turned to Jack to probe him further about the oil drilling proposition. "What do you two have in mind, and when do you plan to start? More importantly, when do you anticipate having results?" Kevin questioned, his gears fully turning now.

Jack, who never brought up an idea that was half-cocked, had an answer at the ready. "We'll take the train back to HQ—which, by the way, we heard they are relocating to Blackstone, Virginia—drop some of our gear, and then continue on the train to Memphis. From there, we'll go by boat to the Texas coast and begin to carefully put the plan in motion."

"That sounds like a solid path to success. Sorry, we've been so busy I forgot to mention the move to Blackstone," Kevin said.

"No problem," Jack replied. "We've been in contact with HQ, along with Mike and Jon. Sounds like they're making progress, too."

"Yeah, everyone is so caught up in their own journey that we forget there are other moving parts. It's good to be reminded to reinforce that each of our endeavors is linked to the others and the ultimate outcome of our presence here," Kevin preached.

"Well, then," Jack suggested before Kevin could start waxing philosophical, "Dave and I will contact Tom and see if he'll arrange to meet us in Blackstone, and we'll continue from there."

The men stood up and bade each other farewell with a man hug each, leaving as usual, with just the few words, "Stay in touch."

Joseph turned to Kevin and said, "I wish I were going with them."

"Me, too," Kevin said wistfully. "But as it stands, we're needed here for a while to nurse this compromise along until it's complete...for as long as that may take." Kevin rolled his eyes and sighed, "We both know the wheels of government turn only when force is applied, and even then, they turn ever so slowly."

"Thanks for the inspirational sermon," Joseph said, his voice dripping with sarcasm.

Kevin and Joseph, who were Type-A operators through and through, longed for the rush of a high-stakes exploratory adventure. They knew that their work in the nation's capital was vital in a different way, and they soon returned to the day-to-day frustration of dealing with self-righteous politicians and greedy lobbyists.

For their parts, Jack and Dave boarded a southbound train the following morning. They arranged to stop off in Richmond and check on the welfare of everyone at the new people's plantation. With another set of irons in the fire, the team members were beginning to see a clearer, brighter future on the horizon.

Twenty-Two

Frank, Edwin, Silas, and Robert arrived back at HQ and found Tom in a flurry of activity. He was clearly distracted by his work but quickly welcomed them back and then returned to his business.

"So, what's with moving to Blackstone?" Frank blurted out.

"I didn't have time to explain on the radio, but Jan and I decided that with our new hospital venture kicking off, we need to be more centrally located and have more access to the railway for supplies and visitors."

"Thanks for including everyone in that decision," Frank shot back, the edge in his voice razor-sharp.

"What difference does it make to you?" Tom asked him.

"I'm not saying it does, but I would've liked to have had my input considered," Frank declared in his trademark drawl. He continued to wrestle with his concerns as he went to unsaddle and cool down his horse. As he headed to the barn, Elisabeth walked out of the ward, ran up to him, threw her arms around him, and kissed him gently on the lips. Frank was struck not only by her forwardness, but also by the joy he felt at being reunited with her. He hugged her tightly and began kissing her passionately.

They remained in each other's arms until Jan peered out the door and yelled, "Get a room!"

Elisabeth pulled back quickly. "Why, I'm not sure what got into me. I assure you I would never act in such a manner. I do hope you can forgive my unladylike behavior."

"Oh, 'Lisbeth, you have nothing to apologize for. If I've learned anything in these last few weeks, it's that we have to seize the moment and take happiness where we find it. I'm so glad to know how you feel."

It wasn't until that very minute that Frank realized he was developing strong feelings for Elisabeth, and then the thought of relocating to Blackstone came back to taunt him. He decided not to mention it to her for the time being and instead just savored the embrace. Jan walked out and shook hands with Frank before relaying the recent happenings at HQ. He admitted that things had been incredibly busy, although they had fortunately avoided any trouble in Frank's absence.

"Good, then you won't need me or Elisabeth for a while," Frank said with a mischievous grin.

"I'll try to manage," Jan retorted.

Tom rounded up Robert as soon as the older gentleman had finished watering his horse and stowing his saddlebags. "Robert, I've got some ideas to discuss with you when you've got a few moments."

He ushered Robert Winslow into the HQ command post so as to impress him and curry favor, the anticipated financier of Tom's grand project. Robert was duly interested and offered no resistance when asked to help fund the new site in Blackstone.

"Good. Then you and I can head there tomorrow and set the wheels in motion!" Tom exclaimed. "We can take the funds to buy a parcel of land and then start making arrangements for construction. Jan and I have made a list of the necessary requirements, and Frank can get the blueprints drawn up pretty quickly. If you can initiate contact with some builders, we can start construction within a week or so. I've already put in a preliminary lumber order to be delivered by train since that takes a while."

Robert's head was spinning from the cavalcade of information coming at him, but he remained cooperative and agreed to accompany Tom as soon as he said the word "go."

Jan said, "How about if we take Tom and Frank with us to Blackstone? We can use the four-wheelers to save time and leave in a couple of days. That will give me time to make sure my patients are comfortable under the nurses' care. Frank already told me that he is confident that Edwin and Silas can handle any security issues that might crop up. In addition, he showed Elisabeth how to call them on the radio if necessary. He assured her he could be back in less than an hour in an emergency."

"Sounds like your troop has everything under control, just as I have come to expect. I look forward to helping with this new venture."

In the two days that followed, Jan kept busy tending to his patients and planning the medical aspects of the new facility, while Tom remained occupied with the business and logistics of the venture, and Frank's thoughts focused on his feelings for Elisabeth.

As with most things Tom undertook, he assumed control of the planning for the Blackstone trip as seriously and meticulously as his status board updates. For example, he had the four-wheelers packed with extra ammo, just in case. Although he hoped they would have some cold beer and a home-cooked meal while they were out, he brought water and MREs as a backup. Frank briefed Edwin and Silas, instructing them to notify Elisabeth if they needed to contact him. Jan left specific instructions for the nurses to follow in their care of the patients in the ward.

Tom led the way on his four-wheeler with Robert as his passenger, while Frank drove the other with Jan on the back. On the 25-mile ride, Frank recognized the tobacco growing in some small fields along the way, and it sparked an idea. They arrived in Blackstone in time to have breakfast at the restaurant where Tom and Robert had conferred about who owned the land they wanted to purchase. As the men ate, the sheriff walked in and Robert greeted him cordially.

"You are welcome to join us, Sheriff," Robert said graciously. "We would be honored if you would be good enough to spare us a few minutes of your time."

The sheriff accepted and found a seat. "Thank you, gentlemen. By way of introduction to those of you I've not met, I'm Sheriff Wyatt Boone."

Tom took the lead since it was largely his plan. "Sheriff, we are hoping you can help us secure some land for our project."

"As a matter of fact, there's a lot of land for sale around these parts," Sheriff Boone responded. "Pretty cheap, too," he added. "Lots of people have died in the war, and what with the uncertainty of the future with the slaves being freed, there may not be enough people to work the fields. That's causing some of the owners to sell off their land," the sheriff went on.

"We're interested in buying, and if you would be so kind as to show us around, I'd be glad to make it worth your while," Tom declared. "But first, let's finish our breakfast," he added.

"Much obliged. Where are you folks from?" Sheriff Boone asked.

"The three of us hail from North Carolina, and Mr. Winslow here is from Richmond. We are interested in some acreage close to town, as well as any plantations that might be up for sale," Frank interjected. Tom thought to himself, *where did this plantation business come from?* but dismissed it and made a mental note to follow up later.

After they had eaten, the sheriff led them on a tour of the small town, where they saw that there was plenty of available land, including several plots that would be suitable for their purposes.

Robert asked, "Sheriff Boone, what might 40 acres cost in your lovely town?"

"Well, I expect a dollar, maybe two an acre," the sheriff replied casually.

The answer shocked Tom, Jan, and Frank, but did not seem to surprise Robert in the least, or perhaps that was his business demeanor.

Encouraged by that figure, Frank asked, "How much for a plantation *outside* of town, sir?"

"Oh, I expect the price of land is lower in the remote areas, so less than a dollar an acre would probably do it. Of course, you'd have to negotiate over the house, though. I know of a couple of nice places where the owners passed on, and their widows may be interested in selling. I can introduce you to them this afternoon if you like."

Frank said, "I speak for all of us when I say that we would very much like that and as soon as possible."

"I could tell right off that you men know exactly what you want. I'll ride out there with you as soon as we're done here," the sheriff said.

Tom, Jan, and Robert talked over how much land they needed, and which parcel they preferred. After visiting several locations, they ultimately decided to buy 40 acres right on the edge of town.

"I'd advise you to pay a visit to our mayor's office to locate the landowners. They will have the proper records," Sheriff Boone said.

The foursome found the mayor's office not too far away from the diner. The mayor was there and welcomed the group warmly.

"As you can imagine, we are always glad to assist those wishing to invest in our small town. I will help you track down the owners myself. Then you will need to go to the county seat in Nottoway to record a sale if you are able to make a purchase."

The men waited patiently as the mayor and his assistant diligently shuffled through various papers behind the desk. "Ah, here it is," the mayor exclaimed. "You will likely find the owner at the saloon this evening. That may be an opportune time to discuss your offer."

Tom suggested, "Let's just head over to the saloon now and pound a few well-earned beers while we wait. We might as well start contributing to the local economy of our future hospital."

"This town has no idea that this state-of-the-art facility is about to put them on the map!" Jan exclaimed.

Frank, for his part, was still focused on seeing the plantations he had mentioned. "I'm ready to ride out and take a look at a few properties."

The sheriff agreed, "However, if I may, I'd suggest that you saddle up on a horse instead of the iron wagon you men have been riding around in. A horse will not only be able to travel the often-overgrown terrain, but it will also create less commotion that could frighten some of the owners."

"OK, I'm game," Frank said. "Now, where could I procure a horse?"

The sheriff led him to the town stable where he borrowed a horse, compliments of the sheriff. They saddled up and rode side by side to visit one of the nearby plantations.

As the horses trotted up the dirt strip leading to the front of the main house, Frank noted that the large stone structure looked solid but neglected, just as the sheriff had mentioned. He supposed it made sense, given that the owner had been killed in the war. The two climbed off their horses at the front steps, where they were met by an elderly lady who was clearly trying to hang onto her property with dwindling success.

"Mrs. Baker, how are you, ma'am?"

"I can assure you I am as well as a woman in my predicament can be, Sheriff."

"I have no doubt about that. Well, I hate to bother you, but this gentleman, Mr. Holland, is interested in possibly purchasing your lovely property, so I brought him out here to look it over," the sheriff said respectfully. She smiled faintly.

Frank asked, "Ma'am, how much land is there?"

She responded softly, "Why, there are two sections that include the house, a barn, and the fieldhand quarters."

Frank knew that a section was 640 acres, so he did some quick math. With little forethought, he found himself offering her $2,000 on the spot.

She almost fell over but caught herself, smiled, and said, "Mr. Holland, that is quite generous based on the state of the property. As you know, Sheriff, I've done my best, but it's just too much for a woman like me to handle on my own."

"Yes, Mrs. Baker, I know it is."

"Yes, well, with that being said, I would be honored to sell Split Oak Plantation to you on one condition."

"And what would that be, ma'am?" asked Frank.

"That you treat her with the respect and tenderness that you would a prize filly or bumper crop of tobacco. She's served our family well for many years, and I would only leave her in the hands of someone of like-mindedness. You do understand, don't you?"

"Yes, ma'am, I certainly do, and I can assure you she will be in good hands. I give you my word."

"Very well, then. Congratulations on your new home," she said wistfully.

Frank was now going to be the proud owner of his very own plantation. He had big plans for the future; he just had to figure out how to finance them. He promised her that he would be back soon to close the deal, and the men set off in the direction of the saloon.

When they strolled inside, they found Tom and Robert sitting at a beat-up wooden round top, deep in discussion with an elderly gentleman in a dusty cowboy hat. Frank plopped down at the other table, next to Jan, ordered a beer, chugged it, and promptly ordered another one. When the negotiations at the other table drew to a close, the three participants stood, shook hands, and then walked over to Jan and Frank.

Tom said, "A round for everyone! We're celebrating tonight! In fact, I'd like to propose a toast."

"To the future!" he trumpeted as he hoisted his glass and subsequently downed it. "To the future" the others echoed as Frank took advantage of the moment to ask Robert how things had gone with the landowner.

"He agreed to sell the 40 acres, as well as a couple more tracts on the edge of town if you're interested. We have to get them surveyed and then come back to close on the sale over in Nottoway. It may take a week or so to complete the transaction, though," Robert detailed.

Frank then inquired, with all the courage and certainty he could muster, "Mr. Winslow, if I may be so bold, can I ask to borrow $2,000 to buy a plantation? My plan is to raise tobacco, and I'll use the four-wheelers to pull the plows. I'll be the only tobacco farmer currently in business since the others won't have any fieldhands." He paused to survey Robert's face, but the old man's expression was impossible to read.

Frank went on, "I should be able to pay you back with interest in a couple of years, maybe sooner if things go well. There's a big house that everyone can stay in while we're building the hospital...also, y'know, while everyone decides what they're going to do and where they're going to live."

He took another breath as he awaited Robert's response. Finally, after what felt like hours, Robert gave his short reply.

"Of course."

Frank stood up and loudly exclaimed, "I propose a toast to Robert for making this all possible. Now drink up and let's get back to HQ before dark. We wouldn't want to get a DWI on the way home," he joked.

Twenty-Three

The paddle wheeler steamed into St. Louis, the city known as the Gateway to the West, but of course, it was absent the iconic Gateway Arch, which wouldn't make its debut until 1963, some 100 years later. It was a bustling city used as a launch site for wagon trains heading west and pioneers making their way up the Missouri River to points north. The adventurous spirit permeated the air as desperate men hustled around, scraping together supplies, horses, and wagons to continue their westward migration. The lure of the 1849 gold strike in California was still palpable as prospectors snatched up mining tools and equipment in hopes of discovering the next big strike. It added up to a Wild West atmosphere with two distinct groups: those adventurers headed west in search of treasure and those that made a living selling the goods and materials to the brave dreamers.

The huge steamboat pulled broadside to the wharf and was tied up in just moments. The gangplank was lowered, and passengers started disembarking, at which point they were immediately assailed by numerous merchants hawking their wares and a raucous crowd assembled to greet the newly arrived travelers, many with the hopes of lifting a wallet full of cash or slipping a bracelet off a distracted widow.

Mike and Jon had all the guys gather their gear and wait until the crowd of passengers had cleared the deck, soon to be relieved of most of the money they had brought to stake their adventures.

The six men carried most of their gear and paid the eager porters to transport the rest. Their determined and confident attitudes discouraged most of the pushy vendors, and they went ashore without incident. Mike and Jon had decided to find rooms near the waterfront to stow the gear. They would leave Jon and two of the new crew members to guard the equipment while Mike and the other two wandered the waterfront in search of prospectors who were headed west to look for gold. They walked around, keeping their eyes and ears open until they spotted a man loading several mules with mining tools and provisions. Mike circled his target. The man appeared to be in his 50s with a scruffy beard and a dirty straw hat pulled low over his eyes. *A loner*, Mike surmised, as he drew up next to one of the mules and addressed the bearded man.

"None of my business, but which way you headed?"

"You're right about that," the stranger growled, "and don't touch my mule."

"I wouldn't dare, but if you're headed up the Missouri, we might be able to travel upriver together. I can see you're gonna need a ride on a riverboat, and we're gonna need some help and a few of these nice mules you got," Mike pointed out.

The grizzled prospector considered the offer but didn't respond. He spat out some tobacco, and spittle dribbled down his chin and onto his beard. He continued loading a mule and then mumbled, "How far you going?"

Mike replied, "Into South Dakota."

The prospector raised his eyebrows. "That's serious Indian country up there. You sure you know what you're getting into?" the man asked.

"We can take care of ourselves, but what I need is an experienced prospector to help us find our treasure. We even have a map," Mike explained.

"Let me see it," the old man demanded.

"Not unless you sign on with us as a partner, and then, only when we get there," Mike negotiated.

"Well, I suppose we could ride upriver together," the prospector muttered. "But how do I know you're not some kind of con man?"

"I guess you're going to have to take your chances, but I can promise that you won't be sorry." Mike stepped forward and offered his hand to shake. "Let me introduce you to two more members of our crew. This is Jacob, and over here is Samuel." The old man nodded, extended his hand, and shook both of theirs.

Mike addressed him again, "I think we'll need some more supplies to find the gold and then mine it."

"You seem pretty confident there for a greenhorn," the old timer said skeptically.

"I am, and if you stay on with us and help, I promise you a greater reward than you ever thought possible. All you've got to do is become a member of my crew and show us how to mine the gold when we get there. Other than that, I just need you to show me what to buy here and help find a boat for hire to take us up the Missouri."

"Mister," the prospector replied with the slightest hint of a smile, "I'm Otis, and we standing out here jawin'? Let's get busy. Spring is here and we're already late."

Mike liked the surly prospector and was glad to have found an experienced miner that he felt he could trust, at least for now. They bought some more mules and more mining equipment, then loaded down the animals for the journey ahead. Then they all led the pack train back to where Jon, Stevenson, and Emmanuel waited. Mike made introductions all around, and then he and Otis set out to find a boat for rent.

Otis used his connections on the riverfront to steer them to a vessel that was captained by a similarly grizzled old man who was missing most of his teeth. Otis and the captain seemed to have a shared connection as they laughed and regaled over old memories until Mike got visibly antsy. Otis finally got to the point. "Looky here, Captain. We need good transport and a captain with the know-how to take us upriver to South Dakota. What you think about them apples?"

"It can be done, but that's a long, dangerous journey. It'll cost you...not just money, but maybe even your lives," the old captain said matter-of-factly.

Mike cut in. "We're prepared to do both. Now when can we leave?"

"Soon as you get all the supplies on board," came the sharp reply.

Mike liked this guy more by the minute. "It's settled then. My name's Mike," he announced.

"I ain't looking for a girlfriend, but I'm always ready to set sail. If you must know, I'm Cap'n Rogers," the old man responded in a gravelly voice.

"Pleasure, I think. We'll be back soon," he assured Captain Rogers as he turned on his heels in the direction of their waiting party.

Mike and Otis went back to collect everyone, along with the gear and supplies, before heading over to the riverfront to upload the cargo on the shallow draft steamship that bobbed up and down in the water. It was the same type of vessel that was designed to supply the trading posts on the far reaches of the Missouri and bring back furs from the trappers who had settled in the vast expanse after Lewis and Clark's expedition in 1803. As soon as the men hustled everything on board, the captain was good for his word, and they shoved off immediately.

Jon Silverheels had studied the mighty Missouri River in school. He knew that it fed into the Mississippi River just north of St. Louis, where it continued northwest to its source in Montana. The snowmelt fed the rough water, while the unpredictable Native Americans and the lack of civilization beyond Kansas City guaranteed them a challenging ride up the river.

Mike, for his part, was unfazed, and Jon was brimming with excitement. The thought of visiting South Dakota a century and a half prior to the raucous Sturgis rallies he had frequented was going to be an adventure for the ages—not to mention the possibility of discovering a fortune in gold. It would also be his humanitarian mission to liaise with the Native Americans, carrying the torch of fairness and peace on behalf of his tribal ancestors.

They made Kansas City in good time, and they took on fresh food and water before steeling themselves for the long journey northward. The next stop for resupply came at the newly established town of Sioux City, Iowa.

There, they bought more provisions, and as they paid the shopkeeper, he barked, "You Injuns load these on the boat!"

Every member of Mike's crew witnessed the scene, which reeked of hostility. Jon's radar went off immediately, and he boldly stepped up and berated the owner for his offensive treatment of his hired hands. Jon then turned to the two young men.

"Do you speak English? Do you want a job? We need help traveling upriver." They expressed their desire with eager nods. If they didn't speak English, they apparently understood it.

With a cold glare, Mike instructed the store owner to lead him to their stuff, and he quickly collected their meager belongings and brought them on board. None of the townspeople who had gathered to watch the scene thought twice about challenging the tough-looking crew, whose members were increasing in number.

"All aboard," Captain Rogers said. "Let's get out of this shithole!"

They shoved off to resume their river trek, with Mike and Jacob keeping an eye on the banks of the river with their rifles at the ready. They saved introductions until they were well clear of town. Once they had put a few miles behind them, Jon cautiously addressed the two newcomers.

"I didn't catch your names, and how the hell did you end up working for that jackass?" Jon's jet-black hair and tan skin created an instant kinship between him and the two young men, whom he surmised were in their late teens. He estimated they were both about 5'10" and around a buck-sixty soaking wet. After a quick medical assessment, Jon was happy to report that they appeared healthy and fit.

"I am Eagle Feather, and this is my brother, Gray Wolf. We were kidnapped when our village was attacked. Our family and most of our tribe were killed when the settlers came. We were very young, and the settlers took us and raised us in their ways. They called us George and Richard. If it's OK with you, we would like to be called by our real names. The other names never felt comfortable for us. We have been away from our people and speak English much better than the Sioux language. Our people who survived fled west, and we have seen very few of them since. We thank you and will help you, but I must tell you that we want to join our people if we can find them," the older youth said.

"No doubt you have grown suspicious of the settlers, and you have every reason to feel that way." Jon allowed.

The two brothers nodded in unison.

He went on. "You have every right to rejoin your tribe, and we will support your wish when that time comes. I give you my word." He extended his hand to each young man in turn, and just like that, their fraternal pact was sealed.

The untamed river fed by the melting spring snow occasionally relented and offered them a calm stretch to relax. On those occasions, they tried to shoot a passing buffalo or mule deer so they could then go ashore to butcher and cook it. When they were successful, the wild meat fed everyone amply and lifted their spirits. Eagle Feather and Gray Wolf were keen to learn how to shoot the fancy firearms, explaining that they had never been allowed to handle a gun.

Mike readily agreed to the task. He took his time and exhibited more patience than usual as he introduced the two young men to the fundamentals of shooting. They obediently followed his instructions and soon became skilled shots. Not only that, but it also helped pass the time as they slowly made their way upriver.

Their youth and enthusiasm became a refreshing addition to the long days on the river, where the fickle weather made for long days and fitful nights. Somehow, everyone maintained a positive attitude despite the often-miserable conditions.

Mike and Jon took the journey in stride, knowing that if things worked out, the ends would more than justify the means. Although their nights were filled with recurring feelings of anger over losing touch with their own families, they decided to keep a razor-sharp focus on the future. Things were looking up for the scrappy crew, that is, if they could make it to Deadwood.

Twenty-Four

The frustration and monotony in Washington dragged on for Kevin and Joseph. The days and nights passed with seemingly little progress, and a standard routine emerged. A delegate from one state or another would take the floor to voice their complaints about how their state or the interests of some business or industry there were not being addressed. Many shared the same fundamental concerns, yet no one was willing to compromise. However, there was one aspect that Kevin thoroughly enjoyed. He delighted in being direct with the politicians, readily dismissing their lobbying efforts to line their own pockets, as well as those of their supporters.

Kevin and Joseph both harbored a deep, abiding distrust of lawmakers, and this experience did nothing but reinforce that belief. Their constant attempts to thwart Lincoln and Davis' efforts were almost enough to cause Kevin to grab some of them by the scruff of the neck and read them their rights. President Lincoln, for his part, urged patience, and Kevin and Joseph reluctantly acquiesced. As the days wore on, the two spent much of their time considering what they deemed shortcomings in the US Government that they hoped to reform as ambassadors from the future. Of course, at the forefront of everything they did was the ominous event that would take place on April 14. They couldn't share what they knew, and who would believe them anyway? The fact was that they had an unyielding deadline to meet. The negotiations needed to conclude before the transgression at Ford's Theater that would shift the course of US history forever.

Fighting hard to stay focused, the men formulated plans to revamp education and human rights. They also felt that a thorough cleansing of the legal system was in order. Both knew what a challenge that would prove to be since Washington was already overrun by lawyers with their own agendas, those committed to keeping their professions at the top of the halls of power in the United States. Lincoln himself was a lawyer, like most of the men walking around sporting fine suits on the cobblestone streets of the capital city. It struck Kevin how things were so different from modern-day life, yet still very much the same.

Despite the fact that they lacked running water and electricity, the people of the time operated under similar conditions as the folks of his own generation: they generally believed they were doing what was good and righteous; they learned to do what they could get away with; the vast majority were sheep; and they rarely saw the wolves among them. Time in Special Forces had primed Kevin and Joseph for the sheepdog existence, and the two of them knew well what a herd mentality could do to the best of intentions.

They used the idle hours between the endless meetings to devise an effective approach. The two men had amassed quite an array of ideas to improve the state of the nation; the more difficult challenge would be to present their platform in a way that was compelling to their audience. They resisted the urge to just cram the proposals down the lawmakers' throats and tell them to swallow. After all, they needed these people to return home and enact the measures of change.

The amount of inertia that political leaders had to overcome to accomplish anything in Washington gradually cultivated a begrudging respect in Kevin and Joseph. Although they did not enjoy the inner workings of the political scene, they recognized that it was a necessary evil—one in which they would rather be operating the gigantic machine than watching it churn out dictates.

As time marched on, Kevin stayed in touch with the other team members and HQ via radio to keep abreast of everyone's progress. He envied his brothers who had embarked on cross-country treks, using their SF training and skills to rewrite the history books. He had to remind himself that he was, quite possibly, shaping up to be the most influential person of the age.

He could just hear Mike's razzing tone in his head. "You wanted to be the captain, sir. Well, here you are. Is it everything you hoped for?"

Yeah, Kevin thought to himself, *everything and more. Heavy lies the crown, I guess.*

Twenty-Five

Headquarters was abuzz with anticipation when Tom, Jan, Frank, and Robert returned from their exploratory trip that evening. Those who had remained found the idea of relocating to Blackstone exciting, even if they weren't sure what it would mean to their way of life. The prevailing mood soon turned feverish as everyone prepared individually for the move.

Tom was in his element as the orchestrator of such a large-scale and complex project. He juggled the delivery of materials and skilled labor to build the hospital while refining his business plan to recruit leading doctors and scientists in medical research to join the staff. He was a resourceful fellow but coordinating the construction of a medical research facility in postwar Virginia was a tall order, even for the accomplished businessman.

Jan, ever the pragmatist, maintained focus on the medical considerations of the new venture. While Tom was enthralled with the concept of building a hospital the caliber of the modern-day Mayo Clinic, Jan brooded over how he would manage to carry out the practice from day to day. For example, how would he cultivate a stock of sterile medical supplies? What would he do about instruments and pharmaceuticals? He was a miracle worker to the people who flocked to the ward for treatment, but he knew that he was only as good as the treatment options at his disposal.

Frank was hard at work putting his engineering abilities into practice, and it felt good to be in a key role. Although he had enjoyed conducting shooting lessons, he longed to take charge of...something, namely, his own destiny. He became immersed in drawing designs for the hospital buildings with Jan's input. He also spent a lot of time formulating ideas for his fledgling tobacco farm. No matter what he was doing, Elisabeth always seemed to creep into his thoughts. *How does she fit into the picture?* he wondered constantly. *In fact, how do I fit into this rapidly unfolding new reality?* He had plenty of questions but a dearth of answers.

Edwin and Mattie also felt uncertain about what was to come. After all, they hadn't been consulted about the move to Blackstone, but they trusted that they would be included in the transition. For one thing, Mattie and Annie had become so adept in their nursing roles that Jan trusted their knowledge and skills unequivocally. They were both developing into first-class caregivers and would soon surpass the level of expertise held by most doctors of the day.

Edwin, for his part, shined as he managed the comings and goings at HQ in light of Tom's mounting workload. His quiet confidence coupled with an unflappable demeanor made him the obvious choice for Tom to appoint as manager when the time came. Silas stayed busy, dutifully helping his father, although what he really wanted was to become a doctor. He had acted as Jan's surgical assistant on more than one occasion, and he found the art of medicine fascinating. He asked Jan how he could become a doctor, to which Jan had no suitable response. Certainly, some level of advanced education was in order, but Jan also knew that he could train Silas far more extensively than anyone at the medical schools of the era. Unfortunately, Jan simply didn't have the time or the accommodations at the moment; hopefully, though, that would change soon.

Elisabeth was capable in her own right, and she had a gentle, yet steady presence in the operation. Even so, she was unsure of her place in the future that loomed on the horizon. Everyone was thrilled about moving to a larger estate with untold possibilities, but for Elisabeth, it meant leaving her family's land and everything that she had called home for decades. Saying goodbye to the last place she had seen her husband alive would be a painful reality to confront. To further complicate the situation, she knew she was developing feelings for Frank, and she desperately hoped that they were mutual. Elisabeth maintained her graceful composure while tending to her patients in the ward and helping the others prepare for the move, but on the inside, doubts and anxieties swirled in her mind.

Robert Winslow had developed a friendship with Tom, and as a result, frequently confided in him about his concerns regarding the long-term plans for the hospital. Tom assured him that this would be an unqualified success for which Robert would be handsomely rewarded due to his investment. Robert was a man of integrity. After witnessing the humanity that the team members had extended to a growing number of strangers, particularly those on the fringes of society, he had made his intentions clear.

"I have already achieved financial success, and the goal now is to share my wealth and blessings with my fellow man. I have learned a lot from being around you gentlemen, and I wish to assist you in my own small way. Since my wife passed, I have searched for a mission to dedicate myself to for however much time God may grant me on this earth. You and your friends have inspired me to devote the remainder of my life to serving my Lord and country."

Tom felt moved by the kind old man's words. "Thank you from the bottom of my heart for making all of this possible, and for contributing your energies, time, and of course, money to the cause. It means everything to all of us."

With preparations for construction humming along, Tom made arrangements to return to Blackstone and close the deal for the land. Frank would accompany him to complete the purchase of the plantation with the loan from Mr. Winslow. Just as soon as patients recovered and left the current facility, new ones arrived seeking the services of the "miracle doctor" they had heard about.

Jan did his best to provide them with the finest care, but he was becoming increasingly frustrated with the dwindling inventory of adequate supplies, challenges with sterilization, and the fact that he was the only doctor available.

One afternoon, in a conversation with Tom and Frank, he said, "It's all fine and well that we have blueprints for this deal and someone's name to put on a plaque in the entryway, but what about the medicine and treatment that it's centered around? We've got to have medicine to dispense, laundry facilities, sterilization capability, and a sanitary kitchen. Not to mention a fully trained staff. There's only so much I can do. What are your big ideas for that?"

Tom realized that Jan was on edge and his head started spinning with possible solutions. Problem-solving is what he did best. "I'll see what we can put together," Tom assured him.

"Why don't we buy more land and train some of the local people to run the supporting businesses that we'll need?" Frank piped up. "We can start up schools and vocational training for anyone who needs a job, including freed African Americans. As far as I can see, we're going to need a lot of trained employees for our outfit, and the resulting industries that'll spring up will require many more."

He had clearly put a good deal of thought into how they would fire up the engines of this massive enterprise on a practical level. Jan was duly impressed and grateful that Frank had been considering solutions to what he viewed as their greatest dilemma. Solving those issues, or at least addressing them, would allow Jan to shift his focus back to medicine.

"Just what I need, more stuff to coordinate," Tom sighed with a mischievous smile.

"Oh, come on," Jan taunted him, "you know you're just itching to add more to your portfolio. Now go ahead and do your market research while I keep the patients alive. You work your magic, and I'll work mine."

Tom laughed good-naturedly and said, "Alright, Doctor, just keep wrapping those bandages, and I'll try to keep the lights on."

Twenty-Six

Jack radioed HQ and arranged to meet Tom and Frank at the train station in Blackstone, Virginia. Not wanting to chance getting roped into the goings-on at HQ, he informed Tom that he and Dave would only be stopping for supplies. He had drawn up a short picklist requesting ammo, batteries, and a few other essential items from HQ. Tom agreed, and they decided to rendezvous at the station the morning after next. Jack and Dave said their goodbyes to the DC crew and then took a carriage to the depot, where they boarded the southbound train and settled in.

"It's gonna be a long ride," Dave sighed.

"You ought to be excited about heading home," Jack quipped.

"So that's what we're calling 'home' now, huh? Somehow, I don't think I'll recognize anything or anyone," Dave retorted, "and I doubt Collierville even exists."

"So, you can't recommend any good restaurants or night spots in Memphis?" Jack kidded. Dave rolled his eyes in mock annoyance. "Just as well, we're on a tight schedule," Jack added.

The train wended its way southwest and after several stops, it slowed once again in Blackstone. Tom and Frank met their comrades on the boardwalk at the station with two rucksacks and two aviator kit bags full of supplies in tow. The four team members greeted each other with genuine fondness and used the layover to catch up on things.

"Keep a close eye on this rucksack," Tom instructed. "It's got a lot of money in it. I threw an anti-tamper device in there to let you know if anybody handles the bag after you've secured it and set the alarm," he added.

"Thanks a lot," Dave responded, grateful for Tom's masterful planning.

All too quickly, the conductor called for boarding, and Jack and Dave shook Tom and Frank's hands before stepping onto the train.

"Good luck and safe travels!" Frank shouted over the roaring steam engine. The train blew its whistle, and just like that, the locomotive chugged its way out of the station, taking the Texas-bound boys toward Memphis.

"Not a lot of stops between here and Memphis," Dave commented. "We should be there tomorrow."

They decided to sleep in shifts due to concerns over the money and irreplaceable equipment they carried.

The night passed quickly, punctuated by only a couple of stops, and they arrived in Memphis the next afternoon. Jack hired a buckboard to haul their gear while Dave stayed back to keep an eye on it. They directed the driver to take them to the riverboat landing, where they purchased two tickets to New Orleans aboard the riverboat *Sultana*. The two hastily boarded and secured their gear in their shared stateroom.

Jack agreed to stay on board so Dave could go ashore and explore his hometown circa 150 years earlier. He paused briefly as he thought about his home, where his wife and kids anxiously awaited an update from him sometime in the distant future. He missed them terribly, but they had all adapted to the long absences that were part and parcel of his line of work. As Dave wandered the unfamiliar streets, he felt no pangs of the nostalgia he had expected. Thus, he quickly decided he had seen enough and reboarded the riverboat, heading to the room to meet Jack.

The two had been on many a trip together, and their camaraderie, as well as their similar ways of thinking, meant they were usually on the same page. It was useful for planning, and it eliminated quite a few unnecessary disagreements. Jack despised those. They decided to keep the money with them at all times, tucked inside the satchel where Tom had placed it. They secured their gear, and they felt confident that once underway, no one would mess with the guns or ammo.

"Hell, they wouldn't even know what they were looking at," Dave cracked. "In any case," he went on, "I'll stay in the room until we get underway."

"OK, I'll bring you something to eat," offered Jack, "but no promises that it'll be a heaping plate of Memphis-style ribs." He flashed Dave a grin and set off for the dining quarters.

The grand paddle-wheeled steamship blew its steam whistle, indicating departure time, and slowly rumbled out into the middle of the Mississippi to begin its journey downriver. The river was at extreme flood level in the spring of 1865, and the huge paddlewheel churned into the swift current, allowing the steamship to make excellent headway. Jack and Dave had resolved to blend in with the other passengers while they attempted to make contact with any fellow travelers who might be of assistance. Most of the other passengers were well off, as evidenced by their attire and air of confidence. As Jack went in search of the dining quarters, Dave decided to use the time to mingle and catch up on the news of the day, which would allow him to gauge the attitudes of his fellow shipmates.

The next day, Jack and Dave took seats on the starboard side of the ship and watched as Arkansas drifted by. They listened for regional accents as people walked past or seated themselves in the vicinity. As they finished lunch, a steward paced the decks announcing that they would dock at the port of Vicksburg in an hour. Jack and Dave walked over to the handrail on the port side to watch their approach into the city. They saw a huge crowd awaiting the *Sultana*'s arrival.

After the ship lowered the gangway and passengers prepared to disembark, four masked men on horseback suddenly appeared amid a cloud of dust. They rode up the gangplank in a clamor of hooves and gunfire, shooting their pistols in the air and shouting for everyone to raise their hands.

"This is a stickup!" yelled the apparent leader of the outlaws. "Hand over your money and jewelry and you won't get hurt," he ordered. "If we see anyone's arms drop, we'll kill you," he bellowed.

Jack nodded, and Dave whispered, "I'll take the first two, on my call."

With their hands still in the air, they proceeded slowly, Dave waiting to give the signal until he was sure they both had a clear line of fire. "Now!" he whispered steadily, and in an instant, he and Jack had drawn their pistols.

Quick as a flash, all four riders were dispatched with gunshots to the head. Jack and Dave re-holstered their SIGs and calmly returned to the handrail on the port side of the ship.

The witnesses, both onboard and ashore, stood silent and frozen in a state of shock. No one seemed quite sure what to do. At last, some of the passengers began exiting the ship cautiously, and the sheriff strolled up the gangway, pausing to ask several people, "Who shot them?"

The swiftness of Jack and Dave's action, coupled with the ensuing confusion, left most of the passengers at a total loss as to what to do. The sheriff dispatched one of his deputies to gather a few prisoners to haul the bodies to the undertaker. He continued interviewing witnesses until he found one that was able to identify the two men who had shot the robbers. A bespectacled man gestured toward Jack and Dave, at which point the sheriff started making his way toward them. They eyed the approaching lawman warily.

The sheriff sauntered up next to Jack and asked cautiously, "Did you two shoot those four men?"

Jack hesitated momentarily before responding with a modest, "Yes, sir."

"I need you to come with me to the station to make a statement," the sheriff said matter-of-factly.

"We're not getting off this boat," Jack replied firmly.

Just as things were about to heat up, a bearded man in his 50s stepped forward and said, "Sheriff, if you don't mind, I witnessed the whole thing, and I just overheard your conversation. Let me introduce myself. I'm Elisha Root, and I'd be glad to make a statement on behalf of these two gentlemen. I can assure you that the four men were armed and came aboard guns a-blazin', threatening to kill anyone who lowered their hands. These two heroes shot all four of them tout suite! In an excellent display of marksmanship, I might add," the man proclaimed.

The sheriff, unblinking and nonplussed, regarded him with indifference.

"I will have my assistant write the statement immediately so as not to hold up our departure any more than necessary," the gentleman went on.

"And just who exactly are you, Mr. Root?" the sheriff asked dryly.

"Elisha Root, president of Colt Manufacturing, the company that makes the fine pistol you're wearing on your hip. If you're so inclined to accept my offer, I can see to it that you receive a new one from one of my staff." The sheriff glanced around surreptitiously, and when he felt certain that no one else had heard the exchange, he readily agreed. "I'll have that statement delivered to you at the foot of the gangway right away, Sheriff," Mr. Root assured him.

The sheriff seemed satisfied and as he turned to leave, the self-assured businessman approached Jack and Dave to introduce himself. "Mr. Root," he announced with an outstretched hand. "That was some fine shooting there, gentlemen. I want to thank you for averting that crisis."

Jack and Dave had heard the man's introduction to the sheriff and were well aware of the preeminence of Colt, the supplier of the finest pistols in existence at the time.

"Pleased to meet you," Jack said politely, offering his name and his hand to shake, after which Dave followed suit.

"Might I offer you both employment with Colt? That was the finest display of shooting that I have ever witnessed, and I am very curious about your pistols. I have never seen anything that looks or shoots like that."

As the two had much bigger irons in the fire, Jack quickly nixed the topic of their sidearms and aimed the conversation at Mr. Root's purpose for being on board.

"I'm headed to Austin, Texas, to finalize a deal with the Texas Rangers. We're developing a new pistol for them," Mr. Root responded with the air of a man who was accustomed to getting his way. His three-piece suit was smartly tailored, and his gold pocket watch glinted in the sunlight. In spite of their appreciation for his intervention with the sheriff, the two men were eager to take their leave of him. Dave thanked Mr. Root for interceding on their behalf and invited him to dine with them later that evening before they hastily excused themselves.

The three men took their meals together for the remainder of the voyage, during which Mr. Root periodically brought up Jack and Dave's pistols. Despite being repeatedly rebuffed, he was insistent that they accept his offer to work for Colt Manufacturing, an opportunity almost anyone would accept in an instant.

They imagined their buddies' reactions when they radioed their next update: "We met the president of Colt, and he asked us to work for him. He's on his way to sign a deal with the Texas Rangers, and we told him to kick rocks."

Some of the other team members surely would have had different ideas, but Jack and Dave had already made up their minds to strike "black gold." No, they were just fine as they were. However, from then on, they decided that concealed carry was their best option.

Twenty-Seven

The trip up the Missouri River into the Dakota Territory was a pleasure for Mike because of his love for big game hunting. He was spellbound by the droves of elk, mule deer, and buffalo watering peacefully on the banks of the river. He had been teaching Eagle Feather and Gray Wolf how to shoot, and he used the appearance of a solitary older buffalo on a sandbar to ask Eagle Feather if he would like to take a turn at it.

Eagle Feather hesitated until Mike assured him that they would recover the carcass and butcher it, leaving no waste behind. Convinced that the animal would be put to good use, Eagle Feather skillfully aimed and fired, dropping the huge creature instantly. Captain Rogers steered the boat as close as he could without running aground. Mike, Eagle Feather, Gray Wolf, and Samuel then jumped into the shallow water and went ashore to gut the buffalo and then tie a rope to it so the others could pull it aboard.

They ate their fill that evening and dried the rest of the meat as jerky. Everyone sat around nursing overfull stomachs when the conversation turned to the purpose of the expedition.

"How much farther you think we have to go?" Jon asked Captain Rogers.

"Shouldn't be too much, just up the river a piece to Ft. Pierre, and if the clouds hold off tonight with this moon lighting the way, we might be able to reach it. That's the last place to get any remaining supplies you might need. After that, we'll hit the Cheyenne River a little farther north, and we'll follow that west until we can't go anymore. After *that*, you're on your own," Captain Rogers said bluntly.

"Got any idea if there are any others up here trapping or prospecting?" Mike quizzed him.

"Me?" he scoffed, "I never step off the boat. There are savages out there, and I value my life. There've been several folks come up here, but I can't tell you if they're alive or dead now. You folks seem like you're prepared, though, so I look forward to doing business with you in the future...and of course, getting my ree-ward!"

Mike gave him a confident nod and said, "You get us there, and we'll definitely keep you busy shuttling supplies upriver to us. We're going to need men and materials straightaway."

The crusty captain smiled wryly. He had ferried many a man who fancied himself a prospector along this river, and they were always full of piss and vinegar before they arrived. *Maybe these folks are different,* he thought to himself. *And if they're not, well, that's none of my business.*

Mike and Jon knew from the map data on their laptop that the Cheyenne River would fork into the Belle Fourche River, which they would follow as far as the shallow draft steamboat would take them. They estimated it would only be a short hike down to Deadwood from there. They would have to dead reckon to find the junction of the Deadwood and Whitewood Creeks, but once there, they would set up a camp to run their operation.

That night, the two of them stayed up with Captain Rogers to act as lookouts for sandbars and shoals on the dark river. The sky was crystal clear, unsullied by artificial light, and for the two soldiers, it was a phenomenon they had seldom experienced in their modern-day lives. They marveled at the peace and simplicity present in those brief moments. Their thoughts drifted like the rolling current, from where they had been to where they were headed.

Captain Rogers startled them both at the first crack of dawn when he yelled out, "Ft. Pierre, dead ahead!"

He steered the boat to a makeshift dock and blew the steam whistle. A bearded man stumbled outside in long underwear, cussing them loudly for waking him up. At that time, Ft. Pierre was just a small trading post that served trappers in that isolated part of the country. Hard to believe it would be another 24 years before South Dakota achieved statehood with this remote little outpost designated as its capital.

As such, the choice of supplies was scant, and Mike hurriedly grabbed some coffee and flour. He and Jon exchanged a few words with the old man, passing along the news that the Civil War was over, and slavery had been abolished.

"We'll be bringing more supplies and men up this way soon, so you can expect more traffic up and down the river," Mike explained to the cantankerous storekeeper.

"Fine, but stuff a rag in that whistle next time," he griped.

Captain Rogers, true to his word, never stepped off the boat. As he backed out into the river, he gave a long blast on the whistle, grumbling, "Grouchy old bastard oughta be thankful for the business."

They steamed on westward, and the solitude resumed, nary a trace of man or machine for many miles. Mike paid close attention to their progress since all he had was a modern-day map to estimate where they would put ashore and begin their journey south to Deadwood. If he was right—and luck was on their side—it would be no more than a day's walk between the two points. With no landmarks other than the rivers and streams on the map, deciding where to stop was going to be a crapshoot.

As Mike and Jon sat on the bow talking, Eagle Feather and Gray Wolf approached apprehensively, pointing to the south bank of the river and mumbling. Mike swiveled in the direction they pointed and saw a small band of Native Americans on horseback, observing their approaching vessel from atop a small rise. He hoisted his binoculars up for a closer look.

"Ten of them, no rifles," he said quietly. "No threat."

Gray Wolf beat his fist against his chest, "My people," he pronounced.

Mike knew instinctively that the tribe would assume that Gray Wolf and Eagle Feather had been captured and were being held against their will. They would be followed until they stopped, and then they would probably face an attack, launched in an attempt to free the two young men.

"We might as well stop now and explain our situation. Let them see that we mean no ill will and that the young men are not prisoners," Mike sighed.

Captain Rogers was hesitant, to say the least, but Mike insisted that the tribal cohort had no firearms. Furthermore, he reassured the captain that if there were trouble, it would be over in a matter of seconds. He did not foresee any problems, and he was doing his damnedest to calm the old man's nerves.

Mike decided that he, Gray Wolf, and Eagle Feather would go ashore and engage with the men on horseback. Mike concealed his pistol and instructed Jon to open fire immediately if a scuffle broke out. As the three walked south toward the lookout point, Mike spotted one of the Native Americans approaching on his horse, almost dead silent but in a non-threatening posture. Mike detected a softness in the man's eyes as he got close enough to have a good look at Gray Wolf and Eagle Feather.

The man dismounted his horse and cautiously uttered a few phrases in his native tongue. When the two men responded, the man's expression turned warm, and he gave them each a hearty bear hug. In the conversation that followed, Mike sensed there was a connection among the three. Although he could understand nothing, he discerned that Gray Wolf was reassuring the man that he and his brother were OK. The exchange lasted several minutes, but finally, Gray Wolf turned to Mike and promised him that there would be no trouble. These were members of the Sioux tribe, and they were grateful to Mike and Jon for rescuing the two young braves.

"As a show of thanks, my people will help you in any way they can. They will follow along the river and make sure you reach your destination safely," Gray Wolf translated.

"And you, what will you two do?" Mike probed, genuinely curious what the brothers would decide to do going forward.

"We will ride with our people from now on, but we will always be here for you," Gray Wolf responded.

Mike nodded his understanding. "We would like to have a sit-down with your chief, but you can tell him that many more white people will come this way. He doesn't need to fear them, for Jon and I will keep the peace and ensure that no one encroaches on his land or harms his tribe."

Gray Wolf turned to the elder to relay Mike's message, after which they both nodded and bowed their heads in a gesture of respect. Mike was now satisfied that there would be no trouble from the Sioux; if only he could feel as confident about the rogue settlers headed this way from back east.

After the three were back on board the boat, Eagle Feather and Gray Wolf grabbed their belongings and gave everyone heartfelt hugs before waving goodbye. Then, Mike pulled Jon aside and debriefed him on the meeting that had just taken place on shore.

"Let's get on the radio with Kevin and see if he can influence President Lincoln to set aside this area as a protected reservation for Native Americans," Jon proposed.

"I'm pretty sure that occurred at some point but was quickly violated once gold was discovered. If we can get a treaty spelling it out now, then we can enforce it for the natives, and also sign an agreement with them to share the wealth. We can help them establish schools and medical facilities and teach them to protect themselves from the onslaught of westward migration," he added.

Jon was getting visibly excited. He knew that it was in moments like this where the rubber meets the road—where they would effect positive change starting with one simple decision and it would have a major historical impact. The thought of altering Native American relations in such a momentous manner gave him a rush of pride for his heritage and his people.

Mike replied, "I'll see if we can get Gray Wolf to arrange a meeting with the chief when we get ashore. I am going to suggest that in return for allowing us to mine and ship the gold, we split it 50/50. As soon as we hear back from Kevin, we'll be able to guarantee that no settlers will come to take their land. If they're amenable to it, we can train the tribe to mine and manage its own resources. This will minimize the need to import workers and thus, the chances of violence and disturbance."

"Let's call Kevin now," Jon suggested, "because you know how things work in DC. They'll probably need a couple of weeks just to show up and sign their names."

Mike rolled his eyes, knowing all too well what the passage of a treaty might entail. That was Kevin's job, though: to get it passed with or without force, using the big stick if diplomacy failed to do the job.

Twenty-Eight

Kevin heard the radio squelch and was surprised to hear Mike's voice come through the speaker.

"Hey, Kevin, just calling to touch base with you and let you know we're getting close to Deadwood. I also need a favor. You, being the historian, may be able to sort something out for us. I'm hoping you can convince President Lincoln to grant ownership of the Black Hills to the Sioux."

Kevin replied right away, "There was, in fact, a treaty signed sometime after the war that granted exactly that, but the discovery of gold essentially shredded the agreement."

"Well, with your influence and all Lincoln has on his plate, you should be able to just slip this in the pile of papers on his desk and get it signed unnoticed." Mike was being completely serious, and Kevin knew it. "And since everyone in Washington thinks it's a wasteland out here, there shouldn't be any objections," Mike wisecracked.

"Easy for you to say," Kevin shot back, "when you're out there riding the range, having yourself a grand adventure."

"You're exactly where every officer wants to end up, resting on his laurels in Washington, so save the tears," Mike quipped.

Kevin knew that arguing was fruitless, so he feigned compliance instead. "Alright, Mr. Mann, I'll see what I can do. Any other demands I can take care of?" he remarked, only half-joking.

"Nope! Just keep up the good work over there. Oh, by the way, we need that in two days, max. You can also tell Lincoln he won't need to dedicate any of his army to treaty enforcement. It'll be our pleasure to take care of that," Mike informed him in a matter-of-fact tone.

"Thanks for checking in and piling more on my plate," Kevin said.

"Roger that. Out, here," Mike transmitted.

Kevin and Joseph considered the request from Mike and Jon and knew in their hearts that it was the right course of action. Even so, they were concerned that with all the demands and requests thrust upon President Lincoln, this might overload his wagon.

"How about if we promise the US Government a share of the gold?" Joseph proposed.

"Kinda tricky to promise him gold if we're not even supposed to know there's gold there. And that might arouse his suspicion," Kevin replied. "We'll just have to appeal to his sense of humanity and strong-arm him if he doesn't see it our way," he concluded.

Joseph recommended that they try to meet with Lincoln right away; otherwise, they would have little hope of meeting Mike's two-day deadline.

"Hell, he's probably ready for some good news for a change, so we'll tell him we've settled the problem with the Sioux in the Dakota Territory. All he'll need to do is put pen to paper," Kevin reasoned.

With their course of action decided, the two set off for the president's office to request an audience.

President Lincoln was indeed glad to see the men and ushered them into his office on the spot. He spoke candidly, sharing his frustrations in dealing with the different delegations and their demands. Kevin pounced on the chance to inject his message about the Dakota Territory.

"If I may suggest, sir, how about you convene a joint session of Congress, the Senate, you, and your staff? I'll address them personally, eliminating any doubt as to the outcome if anyone should fail to get on board with your agenda."

Mr. Lincoln stroked his beard thoughtfully as he considered Kevin's proposal. "I am going to try persuasion a bit longer, although I am struggling with what I have to offer those states that are reluctant to remain in the Union," he submitted.

"Mr. President, you have the backing of a new army that has displayed an overwhelming fire superiority," Kevin pointed out. "You can lay out the pros and cons of choosing which side of that force they want to be on. I think they will be apt to listen to reason. In addition, my team is developing resources that will drastically alter the economic state of affairs for the entire country. In fact, that is one of the reasons we are here today. I have an urgent request from my team members that you immediately designate an exclusive area in the Black Hills of the Dakota Territory as a Sioux Nation reservation. The importance and urgency will soon become evident to you," Kevin intimated.

"In addition, my men will stay there and enforce the law with no need for US troops to be involved or stationed there, thus saving the government money." Kevin then launched into his appeal to Lincoln's human side before the president could respond. "Besides, the three of us know that along with the abolishment of slavery comes the obligation to treat the Native Americans with dignity and respect, to confer upon them the same rights as all other Americans. We owe them access to education and an active role in the future of this country. After all, how can we trumpet the freeing of slaves if we are simply going to shackle the Native Americans and swindle them out of their land and resources?" He met the president's gaze and held it firmly, clearly displaying the courage of his convictions.

President Lincoln mulled it over for several moments. He was not too proud to admit to himself that these men had valid points, although he could not discern how they had developed such a sophisticated worldview. What good would it do to free one subjugated people but continue the oppression of another? The Constitution did not support such hypocrisy. However, he knew all too well how much resistance they would meet. He was aware that neither lawmakers nor the public had any concern for Indian rights, particularly at such a turbulent time.

I suppose, he thought to himself, *that is the burden leadership must bear. We must demonstrate to the citizenry that we are willing to examine our own faults in reasoning and let those be a lesson unto them. For the moment anyone believes he has reached the pinnacle of understanding is the very moment he has proven otherwise.*

He turned to Kevin and promised to direct his staff to convene a meeting that would include the two men and outline the scope of their proposal. He vowed to sign it as soon as it crossed his desk. Kevin and Joseph thanked him, shook hands, and pledged their unflagging support to the cause. "I'll send a message to the appropriate authorities with my desire for urgency on this matter," Lincoln assured them.

Joseph nodded solemnly, adding, "Thank you, Mr. President, and God bless America."

Joseph and Kevin quietly made their exit and let out a celebratory "whoop!" once they were out of earshot of the most influential man in the nation.

Joseph grinned broadly and said, "Time to let Mike know that we are getting ready to serve up his tall order. You know he's champing at the bit to start cranking those mineshaft gears so he can issue us some more!"

Twenty-Nine

With the investigation concluded and the legal matters resolved, the *Sultana* pulled up the gangway and steamed back out into the swift Mississippi River channel. The journey to New Orleans had taken on a different mood since Vicksburg. Most of the passengers had begun to hold the two tall strangers in high regard, and other than an occasional show of thanks, they stayed clear and respected Jack and Dave's privacy.

That, however, did not apply to Elisha Root. He remained eager to see the handguns that Jack and Dave had used so deftly during the stickup. He was a constant presence whenever either of them was on deck, and he always joined them at the table during mealtimes. One day at breakfast, Dave asked, "Mr. Root, what are your travel plans from New Orleans to Texas?"

"I'm going to explore my options, but I hope to take a stagecoach to hasten my voyage," he replied.

"Good luck with that," Jack snorted. "With the marsh between New Orleans and Texas, that'd be tougher than stuffing a wet noodle up a wildcat's ass. I think you're in for another boat ride," he added.

Dave, slightly more patient than his companion, wanted to keep the door open to Mr. Root and the resources he might be able to extend them, whether now or at some point in the future.

"We're going to catch a boat from New Orleans to Beaumont if you're interested," he volunteered.

"What business have you in Beaumont?" Elisha inquired.

Jack, using the story that he and Dave had contrived, responded casually, "We're interested in buying land there to raise cattle."

"Is that so?" Elisha said, eyebrows slightly raised. "In that case, I just might be able to assist you. I have been doing quite a bit of business with Governor Murrah, so perhaps I can intercede to assist you gentlemen," he proffered.

"Very kind of you to offer," Jack answered right away, "and we may just take you up on that, but we're in a hurry to purchase the land and get started on behalf of our business partners."

He was wary of Mr. Root, just as he was wary of everyone out there who was upright. Eager to narrow the doorway that Dave had pushed open, he announced, "In the meantime, let's enjoy the trip to New Orleans and hope no more uninvited guests show up at the dock."

"Oh, I think your reputation precedes you, and I don't anticipate any more problems," Elisha commented.

No problems, Jack thought, *just a boatload more questions*.

The three chatted casually throughout the afternoon, and once dinner was over, they retired to their rooms. At daybreak the next morning, they chugged past several grand plantations situated along the river. Jack recalled seeing some of those beautiful houses before, at a time several sunrises and sunsets in the future. He was utterly amazed to see Oak Alley, a splendid plantation home on the west bank of the Mississippi, without the levee that existed when he had once toured the historic home. Jack had spent much of his life in Louisiana, and the familiar landscape made him feel nostalgic, if only for a few brief moments.

"We're just upriver from New Orleans," he declared, "so let's grab breakfast before we get there. If my geography is correct, we should arrive by midmorning."

"You know," Dave teased, "I can always check on the laptop."

Jack rolled his eyes in mock exasperation. "You know, Dave, some of us don't need maps or welcome signs to recognize home. We just pay attention to what's around us, Tennessee Titan."

As they ate breakfast on the starboard side of the boat, they watched the workers toiling in the fields of the nearby plantations.

"What do you think is going to happen to these plantations without the workers to care for the fields?" Dave mused.

"Not sure, but it will work itself out," Jack said offhand. Then he paused to consider the actual possibilities. "Maybe we propose to Kevin that some of the money generated from the oil discovery goes to purchasing the plantations. Then we can help establish cooperatives, allowing former slaves to eventually become owners of their own operations," Jack suggested.

"That's a great idea! Now let's just strike oil. Literally," Dave retorted.

"Working on it, bud," Jack quipped. "Seriously, though, Mike hired some stevedores off the docks in New Orleans to go to Deadwood with them and help with that project. Maybe we should do the same," he added. "They could learn the oil business from the ground floor and become self-sufficient and successful. How about we keep an eye out for candidates?"

It wasn't long after they finished eating breakfast that the porter came around announcing that the boat would dock in New Orleans in 15 minutes. Jack and Dave returned to their room to pack their gear, and when they brought it on deck, they were met by Elisha, who was flanked by his two employees.

Jack stepped up next to him. "Are you still interested in traveling together to Texas?"

Mr. Root replied, "I am indeed."

Jack suggested that the two set out to find a ship that would take them all to Beaumont. Mr. Root was agreeable and asked the others to keep an eye on the gear before hiring a buckboard to haul it to the dock once they found a suitable vessel for the trip.

In the meantime, Dave kept alert for a few hardworking men to hire. When he considered that the oil industry was in its infancy, he wasn't quite sure what he was looking for; as a result, he simply observed the stevedores as they labored. His gaze fell upon a group of six young men who appeared to be hard workers with good attitudes. Moreover, they seemed to work well with one another.

Dave moved closer to the group of workers and asked, "Are any of you interested in a job?"

"How much you pay, mister?" came the immediate response.

"More than you're making here, and we're offering a future as well," Dave countered.

"What'll we be doing?" one of them asked.

"You'll search for oil and then become involved in the business," Dave answered.

"We don't want to go on whaling boats," the spokesman said definitively.

"No, not that kind of oil. It comes from the ground," Dave explained, shaking his head. The men exchanged quizzical looks, but none of them spoke up. "Now, are you interested or not? My partner and I will be catching a boat to Texas soon, so if you're up for an adventure and an opportunity, we'll pay your way, as well as for any of your family who wants to go along. Just meet us at the boat before we leave," Dave instructed.

The six talked it over as they continued to unload 100-pound bags of coffee onto a wagon. They were cautiously curious about the tall stranger. They had heard rumors that the war was over, but none of them had ever been approached by a white man and spoken to directly, and in such a respectful manner. They could tell from his accent that he was from somewhere else, but they suspected that he was a Southerner.

After a brief discussion, they decided to throw in their lots with the polite gentleman. The leader of the group approached Dave to inform him that all six wanted to accept his offer to work. Then they all set off purposefully to collect their day's wages and gather their meager belongings and any family members who wanted to join them. A short while later, Jack and Elisha marched down the dock to where Dave and Elisha's assistants were waiting with the gear.

"We've secured passage on a steamer leaving in the morning for Beaumont," Elisha informed everyone.

"Great. We'll have a few others accompanying us," Dave responded.

"How many?" Jack asked.

"That's yet to be determined, but tentatively six, plus any family members that are coming with them. I told them we'd pay their way, too," explained Dave. "Mr. Root, I'm not sure how you feel about traveling with Black folks, but they're working with us now, so we're gonna consider them friends."

Elisha nodded his understanding. "I have no issue with that. In fact, I am considering hiring some folks myself as soon as Mr. Lincoln decides what he's going to do after the overwhelming defeat of the Union Army."

"He's going to unify the country," Jack stated, brimming with confidence. "Dave, why don't you wait here for them, and we'll go get rooms at that hotel three blocks down the dock. I'll book six extra rooms, and we'll be the first to integrate a hotel in New Orleans."

"Might get interesting," Dave bantered.

"Chances are," Jack laughed, "and if so, we'll just have a little fun."

The hotel clerk was slightly suspicious when Jack asked for eleven rooms for one night, especially since only two men stood before him. He set his reluctance aside when Jack produced a wad of bills to secure payment, and that settled that—for the time being, at least. Jack decided to let Dave handle the situation when he arrived with the rest of the men. He would just stand by to alert any curious onlookers that he was Dave's backup.

Fortunately, he didn't have to wait too long for the show. Dave led the group into the lobby, where Jack quickly handed him nine room keys and said with a grin, "Have fun."

The clerk rushed out from behind his desk, bypassing Dave altogether and making a beeline for the group of dockworkers. "You men know you're not allowed in here! Now get out or I'll call the sheriff," he threatened.

"I'm the new sheriff in town," Dave bellowed, "and these men work for me. They'll stay in the rooms my friend just purchased for them, and if you have a problem with that, I suggest you take it up with Mr. Root there. He'll give you an introduction to me and my friend."

The clerk looked hesitantly at the smartly dressed businessman, who set his jaw to suggest that the matter was settled. With that, Dave led the entourage upstairs, walked everyone to their rooms, and instructed them to bathe and be ready to go buy some new clothes in two hours.

Jack knew it would not be that easy, so he stayed in the lobby to watch and listen to the people beginning to gather there. When he spotted the sheriff at the entrance, he knew there would be trouble.

"Where are they?" the sheriff inquired in a gruff voice.

"They went to their rooms, but that man there is the one who paid for them," the manager said, pointing at Jack.

The sheriff turned toward Jack and took a few steps in his direction before he realized what he was up against. Jack had a look of cold determination on his face, but his unflinching glare was white hot. The sheriff hesitated and stammered, "I'm the sheriff here, and Negroes aren't allowed in this hotel. There's a rooming house down the street for colored folks. It's the law."

"Well, Sheriff, I'm Jack Morrison, and those men work for me and are staying in this hotel. I would venture to guess that you haven't gotten the word yet, so let me be the first to tell you *and* New Orleans that the war is over. That means slavery is over as well, and all men are to be treated as equals. How y'all regard those fellows doesn't say much for your definition of equal."

The sheriff stuttered while he considered his options. He glanced around and saw Dave, Elisha Root, and the two Colt assistants standing shoulder to shoulder, wearing looks of resolve on their faces and pistols on their hips. His sense of survival ultimately overruled his ego. He backed up and told the manager that he would look into the strangers' claims and get back to him, and then, he quickly departed. Jack gave Elisha and his men an appreciative nod before informing Dave that he would accompany them on the shopping expedition.

The men strode into a dry goods store that was normally off-limits to African Americans, and they became keenly aware of the judgmental looks being cast their way. Jack kept watch for any misguided troublemakers while Dave helped the men select some clothes to work in, as well as dress attire. It took a while to get everyone fitted, but the sense of pride in each man's face was well worth it to Jack and Dave. They returned to the hotel in their new outfits with bundles under their arms, only to encounter the disapproving eyes of the guests in the lobby.

"Never mind them. You'll be able to buy this hotel pretty soon," Dave declared loudly as they ascended the stairs to their rooms.

The next morning, they boarded the ship for the short trip to Beaumont. While on board, Jack and Dave decided to talk shop with Elisha for the purpose of arming their new team. They asked how many pistols he had in his possession and if any were available for purchase.

"We might as well teach them to shoot now before it's too late," Dave said, shrugging. It was a sizable risk to assume, but then again, so was the venture they had undertaken.

Elisha agreed to sell them six revolvers, but he had little ammunition to offer alongside the firearms. They would have to shoot sparingly if they wanted to keep any ammo on hand. Their challenge clearly laid out, Dave and Jack set about teaching their new employees the fundamentals of shooting. The men made swift progress, although they didn't have holsters to practice their draws.

"We'll have to get holsters when we get to Texas," Dave announced.

The novice marksmen were visibly excited, for they had never shot firearms before, much less had one to call their own. The crew that would land in Beaumont was sure to be a more confident bunch, bedecked in new clothing, peacemakers, and spirits. Jack and Dave were more buoyant, too, as they witnessed the power of tangible change, one small decision at a time.

Thirty

Tom kicked into high gear coordinating the plans for the medical facility while he developed new ones for the supporting industries necessary to sustain the operation. He knew that as the scope of the project increased, they would need further financial backing and some technical support to complete the job. He was not one to let the grass grow under his feet, so he convened a meeting to hammer it out with Frank and Jan.

The consensus was that Tom would travel to New York to seek out the additional resources he felt were required. What, specifically, he planned to do was anyone's guess. Jan and Frank knew that Tom was a master of improv, and he had a knack for reeling people in with his words and charisma. It was fruitless to argue with him once he had an idea in his head, but they also understood how this trait would benefit them all as the maestro's grand plans unfolded. Tom, for his part, relished the thought of going to the city, and he made arrangements to stop in Washington, DC, on the way. How could he pass up the opportunity to meet President Lincoln? The answer was he couldn't, so during their next radio communication, he informed Kevin of his plans.

Frank had readily agreed to relocate with Elisabeth to the plantation in Blackstone and supervise construction. That way, he could work simultaneously on building the medical facility and firing up his tobacco operation. However, Elisabeth insisted on staying at one of the other buildings on the property. "It wouldn't be proper for an unmarried woman, and a widow at that, to sleep in the same house as a gentleman."

Activity in Blackstone began buzzing as the train made daily stops to unload supplies and equipment. Frank soon recognized the need to purchase more land before the boom was in full swing. He took his idea to Mr. Winslow, pitching to him the benefits of acquiring more property.

"Why don't you come stay at the plantation with Elisabeth and me while we decide how much land to buy?" Frank suggested. Mr. Winslow was a shrewd man, and he was fully in the throes of a philanthropic transformation.

"That's a good idea," Robert conceded. "I can take the short train ride from there to Richmond to discuss it with William, my banker. I don't doubt that his bank would be happy to finance the property."

With Tom on his way to Washington and Frank relocating to Blackstone, Jan was the lone remaining team member at HQ. Jan, as always, was preoccupied with his medical practice and left the security and other responsibilities to Edwin and Silas. He trusted them supremely, and everything hummed along without any hiccups.

In recent days, Jan had started to embrace the idea of the new venture, and he was now impatient to move and embark on the journey before them. His head was full of ideas and visions of what he could accomplish, most notably, the tremendous strides that could be made in the realm of medicine as soon as they had the proper facilities.

During Frank's infrequent trips to HQ, Jan pestered him constantly. "When are you going to be ready for me to move?"

Frank did his best to exercise patience when the news was essentially the same as the last time they had talked. "I've got to complete the main building, and then it'll be ready for you. We can finish the other structures after you're already in place. You don't want to move before it's ready, do you?" Frank asked.

"Seeing as how I'm operating out of a barn, anything would be an improvement," Jan replied, oozing sarcasm.

"It won't take long," Frank reassured him. "Initially, it's gonna be a wooden structure. Just give me another week."

"When's Tom due back?" Jan quizzed, which was beginning to chafe his team member's nerves.

"Once he gets to New York, he may never come back," Frank said with a sigh. He decided to turn the tables on Jan and give him a taste of his own medicine. "And what about our two wayward crews roaming the Wild West? Heard from them?" Frank rattled off before Jan could fire any more queries at him.

"Not since Tom left. I don't monitor the radio like he did. I try to go to his office every evening, but I haven't caught their comms check yet. Last I heard from Tom, they were pretty close to their destinations," Jan reported.

"Well," Frank declared as he stood up and moved deliberately toward the door, "I'm gonna head back. Tell Tom I'm getting a wagon to come pick up a drum of gas and haul it to the plantation. We'll need it over there. And if you *do* talk to Jack and Dave, tell them to get off their asses and drill an oil well. Our supply's not gonna last forever."

"Will do," Jan agreed. "And I'll tell them to build a refinery while they're at it. Hey, by the way," he threw in, "when's the wedding?"

"Sometime in the future," Frank shot back, turning beet red as he made a hasty exit.

If Tom expected a lot of fanfare upon his arrival, he was sorely disappointed when the train pulled into the station in Washington, DC, and not a soul was there to meet him. With his expectation of the red-carpet treatment dashed, he hailed a buggy to take him to the White House. Arriving there, he spotted Kevin and Joseph seated in wooden chairs on the manicured lawn and expressed his displeasure at not being met at the train station.

"If this is all you two have to do, then we could use you back at HQ."

Kevin had a response at the ready: "Not likely. We're busy ruminating on the future of this great country, and as it turns out, that takes a lot of time and energy. Not to mention the hard work we put in lobbying and exerting our influence. I never knew that being a politician was this hard."

"I don't have time for the luxuries of political life," Tom snapped, "and I want to meet President Lincoln and be on my way to New York to get to the *real* work of this nation."

The three entered the White House, and Kevin headed straight for the president's office and knocked. The deep voice of Abraham Lincoln called out from within. "Enter."

Tom was, for once, speechless as Lincoln approached, and it was a sight to behold, the two towering figures standing 6'5" and 6'4", respectively.

President Lincoln shook Tom's hand heartily, stating, "A friend of Kevin and Joseph's is a friend of mine. What can I do for you, Tom?"

"It's an honor, Mr. President. It's not what you can do for me, but what we can do for you," Tom declared, hardly able to believe his eyes.

"If you can get these congressmen and senators to put their petty politics aside, I would appreciate that," Mr. Lincoln said chuckling.

"I'm sorry to say, but I think we're stuck with that until the end of time, Mr. President," Tom said reluctantly as he remembered his history. Then he continued, the tone of his voice instantly optimistic. "But what I can offer you is hope for the future. Our men are exploring options that will enable you to extend financial incentives to states and territories that cooperate with your agenda. It's too early for me to divulge those, but you designating the Dakota Territory as a reservation is much appreciated, and you will soon see the value in that. Meanwhile, I am en route to New York to secure financing for a new hospital in Virginia, and I would like to take this opportunity to nominate one of my teammates as the chief medical officer of the United States. He will serve you in good stead and will advance the medical knowledge of the entire world. It is our intent to develop this new facility into the world's most advanced medical complex, and it will surely attract doctors, scholars, students, and patients from around the world. I am proposing to name it the Lincoln Memorial Hospital in your honor, Mr. President."

Kevin and Joseph were taken aback by Tom's discourse. "Maybe we should let him stay here in Washington," Joseph whispered to Kevin.

"He's too valuable in his present job," Kevin whispered back. "Besides, if anyone can drum up money from investors, it's Tom."

Although Tom was enjoying his audience with Abraham Lincoln immensely, he was also keen to resume his trip to New York. He bade the president farewell and assured him that an invitation to the opening of the Lincoln Memorial Hospital would be delivered very soon.

As he made his exit, he said snidely over his shoulder to Kevin and Joseph, "Never mind the ride to the station, I'll catch a carriage."

"As you wish," was Joseph's derisive reply.

Tom boarded the train with a head full of confidence and settled in for the trip to New York, where he intended to make more acquaintances and strong impressions so he could grab the world by the tail.

Thirty-One

The trip westward up what would become known as the Cheyenne River was happily uneventful. The escort by the Sioux chief, whom Mike would later learn went by Red Cloud, ensured their safety, and they soon came to a fork in the Cheyenne and Belle Fourche rivers, as they were labeled on Mike's laptop.

"Keep west," Mike said confidently.

The boat departed the Cheyenne River and continued to the area where Whitewood Creek turned south. Through his map study, Mike was able to reasonably determine the location of the mouth of the creek, which put them approximately 20 miles north of their destination.

"This is the end of the line, guys!" Mike shouted.

Soon, the steamboat docked on a sandbar, and everyone leaped into action, unloading the animals and supplies.

Mike continued to motivate the crew. "Let's set up camp on the riverbank and figure out what we can pack in the morning for our trip to Deadwood."

Just then, Eagle Feather and Gray Wolf arrived at camp with the 10 other Native Americans who had escorted the steamship along the river. With a campfire blazing, they roasted the buffalo Gray Wolf had killed and cleaned. Jon broke out some beans and cornmeal to make bread, and they prepared a great feast. As they ate, Gray Wolf interpreted so Mike and Jon were able to convey to Red Cloud their intentions, including their offer to split the spoils 50/50 with the indigenous people for the right to mine the gold. In addition, Mike promised the chief that his people's rights would be protected.

"I guarantee that we will prevent any further land grabs by settlers. We will partner with you and preserve the streams and land. I know that you do not fully understand the benefits or consequences of this partnership right now, but you must trust me that it is in your best interest. President Lincoln has declared that this territory is yours, and we will act with you to defend it."

Red Cloud remained silent for most of the evening before he accepted Mike's offer. Neither man desired or felt the need to put anything in writing. This was a deal between men of honor. At this point, Red Cloud had no reason to expect otherwise, but internally, Mike reflected on just how far men of old had deviated from that commitment on the first go-round.

Mike pulled Jon aside. "Look, I know the time will come to formalize the agreement; nevertheless, for now, I think this is the best arrangement for everyone."

"I agree," Jon said. "It will put them in a good position once it's official."

Everyone slept soundly that night without worry or needing to post a guard.

Dawn broke along the river, illuminating the crude campsite as the men loaded up the mules for the trek up Whitewood Creek. The arduous journey took most of the day, and all the while, Otis kept a keen eye on the creek bed for gold flakes or specks. Any time he spotted a few, he began panning in a small number of select pools where the gold had settled. Some were successful and others were not, but he stayed true to his mission.

By the time the party arrived at Deadwood—an area that Jon remembered having visited in what seemed like another lifetime—the old prospector came to life.

"This is it! I knew it was around here somewhere. I could feel it in my bones!" Otis immediately waded out into the creek and started panning for gold like his life depended on it. Soon, he was whooping and hollering again.

"Boys, you were right! This place is the mother lode! There's gold everywhere! Beautiful, dazzling, amazing gold! Tomorrow, I'll determine where the veins are feeding the gold into the creek, and we'll start mining."

Red Cloud and his men were amused by Otis' antics. They had lived here for years and merely regarded the gold nuggets as ornamental pieces with no intrinsic value. He did, however, trust what Mike had told him: The settlers prized it immensely, and many more would come and try to take it once the word was out. He felt comforted that Mike's guarantee would hold fast, and that his people could continue their peaceful coexistence with these strangers who had come to collect the yellow stones.

To no one's surprise, Otis was up before sunrise full of pep and energy as he followed Whitewood Creek to determine where the veins of gold were hidden in the surrounding hills. His sharp eye and knowledge of how to spot the precious metal led him to a hill on the creek's west side.

"Looks like we found our spot!" he said gleefully. "First shaft ought to go right about here."

He feverishly gathered sticks of dynamite while Mike quickly unpacked the plastic explosives. Mindful of the ruckus they were about to create, Mike motioned to their Sioux companions to cover their ears.

"Fire in the hole, fellas!" he bellowed.

Soon, the earsplitting detonations rocked the earth, sending chunks of dirt and rock spiraling in every direction. They had exposed a huge gash in the hillside that gleamed with the freshly revealed gold-ladened vein.

Jon let out a "Hell yeah, brother!" as Mike beamed from ear to ear. Otis looked more excited than he had probably been in five decades...or ever.

The Sioux looked on in wonder, completely unaware of the gravity of this discovery. Yet, somehow, they knew in their bones that from now on, things would be different.

Mike could hardly wait to share the news, so he hustled the radio and antenna to the top of the ridge and set it up to report into HQ and give Kevin the update.

"You may inform the president that we now have a massive income stream that is partially at his disposal. I believe 'a shitload' is the technical term," he joked. "As per our agreement with the owners of the land, we are splitting the take 50/50, and I suggest 30% be dedicated to integrating and educating the neglected citizens of this country. Jon and I plan to remain here to protect the reservation and ensure the equitable distribution of assets that we promised." He paused briefly to let the news sink in.

"That's incredible," Kevin replied. "Keep us posted and let me know how we can help facilitate the development and transport of the gold. You know it's not going to be a piece of cake keeping it quiet while we try to get it out of there."

Mike answered pensively, "I'm aware of that. When we have enough to ship, I'll get you to telegraph St. Louis and we'll have the steamboat that brought us upriver meet us and return to St. Louis under guard. We'll stay in regular contact. Can you let everyone else know of our plan?"

"Will do," Kevin responded, "and keep your powder dry."

As the mining continued, the gold stacked up at a staggering pace. Before long, they had hundreds of pounds of it, which presented a problem for Mike. He was getting uncomfortable sleeping at night with that much treasure sitting unsecured. Although he trusted everyone in their party (with the exception of Otis), he still had lingering doubts, a holdover from his previous life.

Even in a simpler time with fewer resources at hand, people were still human, and a boatload of unguarded gold was enough to tempt even a righteous man. Mike would simply rely on the fact that Otis knew what would happen if he tried to abscond with any of the treasure. To avoid any confusion, he decided to make that point crystal clear.

"You're welcome to leave anytime you decide," he announced to the prospector, "and I'll make it well worth your time if you choose to do so." He trained his steely gaze on the old man and continued slowly. "But also, know this: If you leave and take any of the gold without my knowledge, I will hunt you down myself."

Otis was quick to assuage Mike's concerns, insisting that he was in this venture for the duration.

"Good choice," Mike said nodding. "In that case, you're the foreman. Let me know what supplies you need brought up from St. Louis, because I'm going to send for the steamboat soon."

During Mike's next contact with Kevin, he received an update on everyone else's progress. When Kevin brought up Jack and Dave's chance meeting with Elisha Root of Colt Manufacturing, it hit Mike like a ton of bricks.

"Can you arrange a shipment of rifles, pistols, and ammo on the supply boat from St. Louis? We're going to need a way to guard the shipment back down the river. We've got the bodies, but we'll need to have some more firepower."

"I'll take care of it," Kevin assured him.

Mike added hastily, "And perhaps you should arrange for the Army to meet the boat to take possession of the government's share. I want that liability off our hands ASAP."

"Copy that," Kevin transmitted. He was positively ecstatic, as he knew President Lincoln would also be. He could not wait to hand deliver such a momentous political victory. How could the president deny his value and advisement after such a triumph? Moreover, he was eager to finally set the wheels of justice and goodwill in motion and get this legislative show on the road.

Thirty-Two

The steamship docked at the wharf on the west side of Beaumont, a gritty town on the banks of the Neches River in southeast Texas. Although it didn't resemble the 21st-century bustling city on the interstate between Houston and Lafayette, Louisiana, that Jack had visited once upon a time, he was still confident that he could navigate them to the future site of history's first major oil well discovery.

The Lucas Gusher, as it was initially named, blew 100,000 barrels of oil for nine days before it was brought under control. That breakthrough ushered in the oil age in the United States in 1901. Jack intended to tweak history just a bit by "discovering it" 36 years sooner.

The odd group of men that disembarked from the boat puzzled onlookers, and not one of them could have imagined the turn the men's fortunes were about to take. They were a band of eleven, three white men in suits, six African Americans wearing their Sunday best, and two unusually tall figures who didn't quite look like anyone else.

Dave tracked down a wagon to transport their gear to a nearby hotel, where he rented rooms for the entire crew. No one dared step forward to challenge them for violating the hotel's segregation policy, and they were grateful for a smooth check-in, tinged only by the persistent stares that had grown routine by that point.

Dave immediately went up to the roof and set up the radio and antenna to call in a commo shot to alert everyone of their arrival. The only person he could reach was Kevin since Tom was still in New York. He informed Kevin that all was well and gave him a headcount of their group.

"Are you still in contact with Elisha Root?" Kevin wanted to know.

When Dave answered that they were, Kevin relayed the request for guns and ammo to be picked up in St. Louis and delivered the news of the gold strike.

"I'll talk to him as soon as we're done here. How many guns and how much ammo?" Dave asked.

"Five hundred pistols, 500 rifles, and 100,000 rounds of each caliber. You can tell him we have a guy in New York who can arrange the delivery to the US Army in St. Louis and the payment in gold wherever he chooses. Also, be sure he knows it's a rush order," Kevin instructed. "By the way," he added, "you might want to tack on some for your guys. I'll bet it's going to get ugly there, too. Have you gotten a progress report yet?"

Dave said, "Jack is out taking a tour south of town to locate the site from memory. Then we'll purchase as much of the surrounding land as we can. I'll handle the land deal while he locates the crew and equipment to drill the well. Both may take a few days, but I'll keep you posted. Meanwhile, send some gold this way, would you? Jack has plans to buy land farther north where another major oil strike occurred. His intention is to purchase as much as possible in any of the oil discovery areas that he knows about."

"Roger that," Kevin shot back.

Dave took down the antenna, turned off the radio, and went downstairs to talk to Elisha. He found Root and most of the others in the saloon on the first floor of the hotel.

After Dave recounted Kevin's message, Elisha said, "One problem. Colt does not make rifles. However, I have a friend named Oliver Winchester who is starting up a rifle company. If it would help, I can telegraph to see if he could fulfill the request. I can handle the ammunition for the pistols and ask Oliver to do the same for his rifles."

Jack, meanwhile, had located the well site quicker than he'd imagined. It was just south of town at a small mound that was impossible to mistake. The land was unremarkable, and he reasoned that they'd have no trouble buying a large tract that would encompass the entire field where many wells could soon be drilled.

He returned to the hotel to report his progress to Dave. They decided that the two of them would revisit the site the next morning so Dave could put eyes on it prior to facilitating the purchase.

"Then I'll locate a water well driller, and with some modifications, we can start the process," Jack said.

Elisha, for his part, had almost forgotten his reason for coming to Texas since the deal he had just made with Dave far surpassed that which he had hoped to make with the Texas Rangers. He knew, too, that he would have to gear up production to fill the order, but he assured Dave he would send as many pistols as he could right away. He then rationalized that there was no further point in remaining in Beaumont. He approached Dave and Jack with the news.

"I'm planning to return to Connecticut to get busy on the order," he said.

Dave nodded, "That makes sense. By the way, one of our men named Kevin McKenzie will be the point of contact in Washington."

The next morning, Jack and Dave split up to pursue their separate missions. They took three employees each to acquaint them with the business they were pioneering. Dave had no trouble locating the owner of the land, and he soon negotiated a fair deal. The men went to the land office to sign the deed for 5,000 acres at a price of $2 per acre. Jack found a water well guy who said his equipment was capable of drilling a well to approximately 200 feet. Jack remembered that the oil was over 1,000 feet below the surface, but he figured that with his knowledge of modern oil drilling techniques, they could improvise and reach that depth with this equipment. He also found some blacksmiths and a welder to build a crude device to prevent the oil from gushing out, along with some tanks to capture and store the oil for transport out of the nearby port.

Things are really coming together, he thought happily.

They spudded in the well a few days later, and Jack insisted that they rotate the crew in order to work 24 hours a day from then on. He and the water well driller took 12-hour shifts, assisted by three of Jack's employees. With slight modifications, they were able to pierce through the soft ground rather quickly. Jack even constructed a small on-site cabin to sleep in so that he was readily available for a consult with the water well driller if questions arose. There was no room for error, and he was hell-bent on a successful mission.

Jack's past study of drilling allowed the team to circumvent a host of problems that the original Lucas drillers had encountered. They were able to run casing to isolate zones, and the drilling progressed at an impressive pace. By monitoring the fluids that returned from the bottom of the well, Jack could ascertain what material they were drilling through. He also knew how to monitor the density of the fluid that was pumped through the drill pipe and then flowed up on the outside to offset the pressure at the bottom of the hole. In this manner, he would be able to keep the well from freely releasing the oil in the form of a gusher.

By day nine, they were nearly 1,200 feet down when Jack saw large amounts of oil in the returns from the bottom of the well. He knew right away that they had finally hit the large oil deposit below. He drilled down a few more feet and then waited for the crude to enter the well and make its way to the surface. It was not nearly as spectacular as the gusher that had erupted in 1901, but Jack planned it as a matter of course to be more economical and environmentally friendly than the original eruption.

The gravity of the discovery, and perhaps more crucially, the way in which they had precipitated it, did not escape Jack. This would pave the way for a vastly different oil drilling industry, as well as accelerate the machine age that loomed on the horizon. Dave, who was standing by that day, offered Jack a hearty "Congratulations!"

"Get on the horn and tell HQ to call me Jed Clampett because we've discovered black gold," Jack exclaimed triumphantly, "and ask 'em how they like their Texas tea!"

Never content to revel in the victories of the present, he then turned his eye to survey the vast land that unfurled in front of him and imagined the untold barrels of undiscovered oil coursing beneath the surface.

Thirty-Three

Kevin and Joseph were ecstatic with the news from Beaumont. The discovery of oil, in tandem with the Deadwood mine, which was producing hundreds of pounds of gold a week, gave them the financial clout they needed in Washington. Senators and congressmen who had been reluctant to agree to President Lincoln's terms of reconciliation would now face economic isolation in the capital. Projects aimed at training, education, health care, and infrastructure could now be used to persuade them to ratify his national reunification plan. Any state that still insisted upon secession would face the wrath of its citizens for forfeiting their seat at the table of prosperity. Kevin was excited to share the news with President Lincoln, so he and Joseph scheduled an appointment for later that day.

"Let's get our ducks in a row," Kevin suggested. "Joseph, would you reach out to the team and inform everyone of Jack and Dave's success? We need to get Tom thinking about how to properly organize and structure the oil company. We should also talk to Jack and Dave about how we're going to distribute the profits from that venture. It's going to take a lot of capital investment to bring this to fruition because Jack wants to start buying huge tracts of land where he knows oil is yet to be discovered. Move over, Rockefeller."

Joseph was able to get through to Tom and advise him of the situation. "Tom, I know you're hungry, so we're going to pile some more on your plate. Jack and Dave have struck oil, and it looks like that's going to be huge. Kevin wants you to start thinking about forming a corporation to handle that business. Jack intends to buy as much oil-producing land as we can and develop it at a rapid pace. The potential is mind-boggling. Although it will take a lot of capital, there should still be plenty left to funnel into projects geared toward bettering the lives of citizens who have been devastated by the war on both sides."

Tom feigned being overwhelmed by the new project when, in reality, he quite fancied the idea of becoming the most prominent businessman in the United States, perhaps even globally. He could see himself heading the largest oil company the world would ever know, while simultaneously controlling interests in the gold mining and medical industries. He had dollar signs in his eyes, and he decided that he didn't much mind living in the past, after all. Joseph got through to HQ a little later to let them know Tom would probably be delayed in New York to attend to the business ventures, although for how long was anyone's guess.

President Lincoln greeted Kevin and Joseph with his usual cordialness, and the two got right to the point. Kevin addressed him formally, but on the inside, he was practically giddy with excitement. "Mr. President, we are pleased to inform you that our colleagues have not only been mining gold in the Dakota Territory but have also discovered a huge deposit of oil in Texas. It is our intention to share the revenue from these two ventures with the US government in order to promote social programs that will reintegrate the nation's many disaffected citizens. We plan to fund education, health care, and infrastructure, which we encourage you to dangle in front of those legislators who are still straddling the fence of reunification. You may also stress that in choosing the path of independence, states will do so to their own detriment. They need to understand the growing influence and capability of the organization that is driving this train."

He paused, not wanting to appear too heavy-handed, but then he remembered the image of the big stick. He accepted that with great power also comes tremendous responsibility, and that was a fact that he did not—and would not—bemoan. "I will be glad to relay this message myself for emphasis if that is what you desire; otherwise, you are free to use the leverage as you see fit," he then added, putting the matter in the president's hands.

Abraham Lincoln, who typically refrained from displaying his emotions, was visibly pleased with the news. He thanked Kevin and Joseph for their support, pledging that he and the United States Army would do everything possible to support and assist their team. "With this knowledge and authority, I am confident that I can persuade everyone to be reasonable and ratify the reunification of our country," the president stated.

At that point Joseph spoke up, emphasizing their unflagging loyalty, "Mr. President, we are here to support you in any way possible. Please do not hesitate to ask. We are at your service."

Kevin and Joseph then triumphantly exited the president's office, high fiving each other as soon as the door shut behind them.

"I think we blew the doors off the problem," Joseph declared.

"True, but now the work of implementing these plans begins," Kevin cautioned. "Fortunately, they who have the guns, the money, and in our case, the scruples, shall prevail."

Thirty-Four

Frank, Elisabeth, and Robert Winslow were now settled at the new plantation house in Blackstone, and the temporary hospital building was nearly complete. The news that both teams had been successful in their search for gold and oil infused renewed energy into the project. The prospect of almost unlimited resources was surreal to Frank and Jan. In light of that, Frank stepped up construction of the stone building that would serve as the permanent hospital. He scoured the area for construction labor with the promise of on-the-job training and long-term jobs. He also started planning to build a school in the town and petitioned the mayor to expand hotel and restaurant facilities to temporarily accommodate the projected influx of people until more suitable housing could be completed.

In his next radio communication with Kevin, he asked, "Can you see if Tom can locate an architect in New York to design this campus?"

Kevin agreed and then added, "Tom is looking into office space in New York, and I don't think he'll be spending much time in Blackstone. He's keeping busy with all the corporate and legal business."

"I knew it was only a matter of time," Frank said with an exasperated sigh. "Next, he'll be building a skyscraper that he can name after himself." They both laughed, and behind the humor lay a mound of truth. "Meanwhile," Frank continued, "Jan and the rest of the crew should be relocating here this week. It'll be a logistical challenge, but the two of us will manage. How are things in our nation's capital, boss?"

"We're making progress," Kevin responded, "and all the states should be on board very soon. In the midst of his wining and dining financiers, Tom is setting up bank accounts that will allow you and Jan to access funds from the Bank in Richmond. I'll let you know as soon as that's complete. As for now, just keep on using Winslow's cash, and we'll arrange to reimburse him when the first shipment from Deadwood hits the bank in St. Louis. Joseph and I hope to take the train down as soon as we get things here running smoothly."

Frank was skeptical. "I suspect that, like Tom, you've found your home elsewhere and will only be here for a brief visit, but regardless, Elisabeth and I will keep a room for you to stay in."

"That's very generous of you, Frank," Kevin said, expressing sincere gratitude. Yet, not willing to let Frank off that easily, he threw in casually, "By the way, I've been meaning to ask you, when's the wedding?"

"Maybe in the future, my friend," Frank said slyly. "You never know."

"Well, get that tobacco growing, Holland, 'cause I'll be expecting a celebratory cigar from you soon," Kevin bantered.

"Roger that," Frank replied. "Now let me get back to work, and you and Joseph can return to shaking hands and kissing babies, or whatever it is y'all do all day."

Frank signed off, and he and Elisabeth rode the four-wheeler back to HQ to check on the status of things there. Jan met them at the porch with news.

"I'm happy to report that the remaining patients are ready to move as soon as Frank can arrange the wagon transport for all of them, plus the equipment and supplies, to Blackstone. He inspected the building earlier in the week and was satisfied that they could occupy it."

"I'll hire the wagons as soon as we get back," Frank assured Jan. "Expect the move in two to three days, max."

Jan knew that after all they'd been through, a couple of days was not much more to wait, but recently, each one seemed to drag on. "The patients are all stable enough to move, and Elisabeth, Mattie, and Annie are capable of caring for them while I go to New York to recruit doctors and staff," Jan declared.

"And establish an office there to run the operation from, I suppose," Frank remarked snidely. "Before you know it, I'll be the only one in

Blackstone. Speaking of, let me get back there so I can get some tobacco in the ground and start planning my own Big Apple excursion."

Thirty-Five

As the stockpile of gold continued to grow, Mike and Jon discussed the ever-increasing danger they faced in housing and guarding their treasure. They were confident in the Sioux's ability to protect the assets, but that was partly because almost no one outside of the immediate vicinity knew anything about the discovery. They understood that as soon as the steamship docked in St. Louis and sacks of gold were unloaded, word would spread like wildfire. That would open them up to the threat of criminals, prospectors, and settlers who would clamber to snatch up a piece of the pie.

Guarding the shipment on its journey downriver would require several men. After all, the cargo included a couple of hundred pounds of gold. They were hesitant to get the government involved, yet they were willing to consider Kevin's offer to request temporary army support until they were fully capable of providing their own security. Mike and Jon brainstormed at length because they wanted to be overprepared, rather than the alternative.

"What if we train some Native Americans to shoot guns using what we have available? Then you, Jacob, Stevenson, Samuel, and Emmanuel can accompany the shipment to St. Louis, and I'll stay back with Red Cloud, Eagle Feather, and Gray Wolf to supervise operations here," Mike suggested. "We can adjust our plan depending on whether Kevin manages to get any guns and ammo on the boat. I'd rather have plenty of firepower on board in case anything goes south. Better to have it and not need it, ya know?" Jon nodded in agreement.

"When we receive the munitions shipment, we'll get an armed force trained and equipped to secure the territory, as well as the mine and shipments," Mike continued. "In addition, I gave Kevin a list of the supplies we need, so I'll have you coordinate with the army commander in St. Louis on that. You can also have Kevin ask the president to send some of those troops on board if you think we need them," Mike concluded.

"Might not be a bad idea for the first shipment," Jon mused.

"This is going to become a busy place very soon, and it might be better to have the army aware of our location and familiar with us in the future," Mike pointed out, always thinking two steps ahead. "That would also leave more of us here to secure everything. Besides, some of that gold belongs to the government. Let's make them earn it. I'll get on the radio this evening and ask Kevin to see what he can do," Mike said reassuringly. "Meanwhile, I'll talk to Gray Wolf and see if we can come up with a training schedule for shooting instruction."

He had always hated staying still and was insistent upon making schedules for all tasks to be completed, regardless of how large or small.

"We have a fortune in gold sitting here and nothing to spend it on," Jon opined.

"We're rich in the natural beauty of this place, though," Mike reminded him, "but let's endeavor to protect both. There soon may come a time when both will be under siege."

The Native Americans took to the mining process quickly, and they showed proud ownership over the gift Mike and his crew had given them. As the gold deposit grew daily, Mike and Jon waited for word of the boat's arrival.

Red Cloud had charged a small band of Native Americans with watching the river from high upon a ridge, and they had instructions to notify him when they saw the vessel approaching. A few days after they had been sent to keep watch, one of them rode down to the mining camp with news that the boat was headed upriver, carrying several mounted soldiers. Red Cloud was angry and immediately confronted Mike about the unwanted soldiers' arrival.

"I will handle them," Mike assured the chief, "and I give you my word that they are only coming to transport the gold, not to stay."

The two had developed a strong sense of trust, and Red Cloud, although instinctively wary of trusting white men, accepted Mike's response. For his part, Mike assumed that the government was just being overly cautious so as not to take any chances with its portion of the gold.

"Oh, well, the cat's going to claw its way out of the bag soon any-way," he reasoned. Then he turned to Jon and said, "Let's get the gold down to the river to expedite the process. The sooner it's in the right hands, the better."

The next morning, the mule train carrying the gold to the river departed, and with the Native Americans keeping a close watch on the trail, the transport went off without a hitch. When the steamboat arrived the next day, it was quickly unloaded and replaced with new cargo, as well as Jon and his men. As Mike had promised Chief Red Cloud, all of the soldiers the boat had carried remained aboard. Jon and his men disembarked with roughly 200 pounds of gold in tow, and they departed just as swiftly as they had arrived. Jon assured Mike that everything would go smoothly, but in any case, he promised to send a telegraph from the army post in St. Louis when he arrived. The trip downriver with the current would go much faster, although it would still take a few days.

Mike and Red Cloud loaded the mules for the return trip to Dead-wood and made plans for another group to return for the remaining supplies.

"We might as well build a camp here to serve as a supply base since this is going to be a routine," Mike proposed to Gray Wolf for him to translate for Red Cloud. "We're going to need some help from the out-side," Mike said cautiously, looking at Red Cloud as he spoke, "but we'll leave it up to you who is allowed to get off the boat," he promised.

Eagle Feather volunteered to take charge of organizing the base camp operation since he was fluent in English and because the chief trusted him to screen the arriving passengers.

Things were looking up for Mike, and his confidence in the venture grew by the day. He felt that he could step back a bit since Red Cloud, Gray Wolf, and Eagle Feather seemed up to the task of running the day-to-day operations. He felt his only remaining obligation was to train the Native Americans to protect the mine and their land. He vowed to remain on-site until he was certain the situation was under control. He looked forward to spending his newfound free time hunting and fishing the abundant wildlife while pondering his next move.

The arrival of a large boat laden with gold set off a frenzy of activity in St. Louis as rumors about the discovery ignited and spread with wild abandon. Jon found the bank where Tom had made all of the arrangements in advance, and presently deposited all but the government's share of the gold. Then he tracked down the Army commander, to whom Mike had instructed him to hand over the government's take. After heaving a long sigh of relief, Jon went to a hotel and booked a room. He ascended the stairs to the roof, where he strung up the antenna and made a commo shot back to HQ and Kevin to report his success.

On the street below, townspeople flocked to the saloon, where they enticed the soldiers who had made the journey with drinks in an effort to uncover the secretive location of the gold strike that they had heard rumors about. Evidently, several of the soldiers ended up spilling the beans because soon there was frantic activity on the waterfront with people rushing to charter boats for an urgent trip up the Missouri River.

Jon had already spoken with the captain about their return expedition, and he was anxious to get underway. However, he still had to purchase the supplies and arrange for the guns and ammo to be delivered by the Army. Once he had done so, he asked the commander to authorize another escort for the return passage.

"I will only need them for this next trip. After that, my men will secure the shipment," he informed the commander.

Now that Jon had witnessed the first wave of hysteria throughout the city, he began thinking about alternate methods of transportation in the interest of volume and safety. He inquired at the rail station about the closest track to the Dakota Territory, and the yardmaster told him that Sidney, Nebraska, was the nearest stop. By using the map on his laptop, Jon reckoned that Sidney was almost 200 miles from the mine. He made a note to see if Tom could get a rail spur to Deadwood built in order to hasten and secure the shipments in transit. For now, he would have to endure the long boat ride back upriver. He patted his SIG instinctively and thought, *yes, sir, better to have it and not need it. And I really hope I don't need it.*

Thirty-Six

With the first well up and running and plans for subsequent ones to be drilled nearby, Jack and Dave discussed the next phase of their expansion. Jack knew that oil would soon be discovered in Corsicana, Texas, a small town about 60 miles south of Dallas. Its discovery in the late 1890s eventually ushered in the petroleum age in Texas, when oil companies began cropping up left and right, along with the state's first refinery. Jack remembered the story of how the town had initially hired a company to drill a well for water, but they hit oil instead, forever altering the landscape of the tiny, dusty town.

"Funny part is, they only paid them half of the agreed-upon price since they didn't hit water," he told Dave. "As I recall that land didn't have significant value until then. How about you coordinate with Tom to buy as much land as we can in the area and keep buying to the east as well? There's plenty of oil there. I'll stay here and keep things cranking while you head up to Corsicana and handle the business end of things."

"Sounds like a plan," Dave replied. "I can probably find a bank in Dallas to handle the purchase. I'll get on the horn to Tom and get him in gear."

"While you're at it," Jack added, "get him thinking about sending some ships down here to transport all the oil to the northeast. He might even want to consider getting some oil tankers built specifically for that purpose."

Dave departed the next morning on horseback for the long trip through east Texas to Corsicana. He would have to negotiate the rough dirt trail leading west to the area just north of what would become Houston before turning north for another 200 miles. The entire ride would be through sparsely settled country, where Dave knew to stay alert for bandits plying their trade along the route.

As his horse's hooves beat rhythmically on the path, Dave's thoughts kept drifting to Elisha Root's offer to work for Colt. Dave had a passion for guns, having grown up hunting with his dad and brother in the Tennessee wilderness. His interest had transformed into a real talent, and this led him to select weapons as his Special Forces Military Occupational Specialty (MOS), or career field. It dawned on him that he was now the most knowledgeable gunsmith in the entire world. He also had in his holster a gun that was decades ahead of its time. *Maybe when we get caught up here, I'll take him up on that offer,* he mused.

Jack, meanwhile, kept up the pace of drilling, and he was able to start the new well inside a week's time. For the next one, he calculated an even more condensed timeframe as the workers continued to hone their craft. He talked to Tom regularly for an update on when they could start shipping oil out of Beaumont because the storage tanks were already full.

"We're making as many as we can as fast as we can," he told Tom, who, in turn, said it was out of his hands.

"It's on them, Jack. I've already sold the oil, and the money is in the bank. From now on, we're charging them storage fees, so relax and keep up the good work. I'll transfer funds to a bank in Houston and start making plans to open our own branch in Beaumont. Rest assured that things are progressing smoothly, and that money is no issue. Do whatever you need to keep things moving down there. I've also been in touch with a bank in Dallas, and we can use them until we need to start our own in Corsicana if that's successful, too."

"You might as well start opening that bank because Corsicana's going to be bigger than this oil strike," Jack guaranteed. "We're going nationwide, and then maybe worldwide, so get ready. Send lawyers, guns, and money, partner, and step on it!"

Dave rode into Corsicana in the morning and went straight to the land office, claiming to inquire about buying acreage for his timber and cattle company. He was pleasantly surprised at the availability of huge tracts in and around town. Tom had arranged for the bank in Dallas to send a letter of credit to the local bank, guaranteeing unlimited funds with which to buy the land. Word soon spread that a tall stranger was in town and interested in buying up all the available property. It didn't take long for the people of the region to seek him out with offers to sell. In next to no time, he was flush with land deeds.

He then found a spot to set up the antenna to fill Tom in, and he monitored the radio for progress reports on everyone else. Having made quick work of his business in Corsicana, he decided to depart for Beaumont the following morning. On the way back, he scouted the Trinity River as a possible outlet to the Gulf of Mexico. His survey of the river, which ran just east of town, led him to believe that the shallow draft steamships that ran the river could be converted to tankers to haul the oil to the Gulf. He also kept his eyes and ears open for the outlaws that surely knew by now that he was a man of means traveling alone.

Dave's watchful eye served him well his second night on the trail. As he sat beside a small fire pondering a future with Colt Manufacturing, three shady figures crept out of the darkness with plans to ambush him. They were certain they had caught him unaware, and that he would be completely outgunned.

One of the renegades yelled, "Drop your gun and hand over those saddlebags!"

Dave drew his SIG before the robbers could even blink, and in three quick flashes, they all lay dead where they had stood. Dave mulled over his options of spending the night there or putting out the fire and moving on to avoid the coyotes that would soon converge on the large feast. He decided that lighting another fire was the best option. He saddled his horse and rode a couple of miles before dismounting, getting another fire going, and settling in for the night. The next morning, he mounted up and continued his journey south.

Jack had been busy training their employees to operate the drilling rig, and they were picking it up quickly. He was now comfortable letting them try their hands at running the project, which would be replicated from one site to the next. He paid them well, and he soon acquired a reputation as a fair and honest man. As people saw the successful Black men, they began to inquire in droves about working for Jack. In a further effort to provide the employees with ownership over the enterprise, Jack handed over control of the hiring to the de facto leader, whose name was Eli.

"We're going to need plenty of good men soon, Eli. Train them up, and I'll accept your recommendations about who we keep and how much we pay them," Jack announced. He went on, "I'm going to make you the foreman of operations in Beaumont. You'll stay here and run things while we head north in search of more oil."

The young man beamed with pride and thanked Jack for the chance to work harder and earn more. In short order, he and his five counterparts had gone from laboring on the docks in New Orleans to becoming financially independent pioneers in the oil industry.

Dave returned to a well-organized operation that required neither his nor Jack's daily involvement.

"Things are looking good," he told Jack, "and the oil's ripe for the drilling. We are now the owners of more than two million acres of east Texas land, and still more to come. As soon as we're satisfied that we have all we want—or should I say—can afford, we can move up the Trinity River and start drilling in Corsicana."

Thirty-Seven

Jan arrived in Washington, DC, by train in the early afternoon. He had radioed Kevin with his travel plans, and Joseph had arranged to take a carriage to pick him up at the train station. The old friends were glad to see one another, and in spite of the fact that none of the team members was the sentimental type, the men greeted each other with a big bear hug. Joseph helped Jan load his luggage in the carriage, and they set off for the White House.

"Just to let you know, Kevin has been lobbying President Lincoln to appoint you as the Surgeon General of the United States. Be prepared for that offer to come up when you meet him," Joseph told his friend.

"Thanks for the heads up because I need to figure out how to graciously decline," Jan thought aloud.

Joseph was slightly taken aback by Jan's response. "You don't want to become the top dog in US medicine? Think of all the influence you would have on the nation's future: policy you could change, diseases you could help cure..." His voice trailed off as he gazed at Jan, clearly perplexed.

Jan looked Joseph in the eye and said, "You know politics isn't my gig. Someone like Kevin or Tom is more cut out for spinning policy and addressing lawmakers. Besides, I would venture to say that even now, there are already enough politicians in the world. Since you've spent some time in DC, wouldn't you agree?"

Joseph paused to consider before responding. "You know, there's a lot of truth to that, Jan. It's taken so much time to make any meaningful progress, and that really only happened once we got the money from gold and oil in the mix. I think all the states are getting on board with the president's plan to move forward, but it all comes down to money and power. Seems like whoever has more of one will find a way to get the other," he said, a hint of resignation detectable in his voice. "Anyway," Joseph asked, eager to change the subject, "what about you? How are things your way?"

"The construction is going smoothly," Jan replied. "Frank is handling that, and the money has definitely sped up the progress. I'm headed to New York, and possibly Boston, to recruit staff and students for the hospital and research facilities. That's the best way to ensure that we make a lasting impact on the future of medicine," he said with conviction. "Look, Joseph, I think you're doing a hell of a job here, and you will be remembered throughout history for your influence," Jan articulated, "but at some point, we all have to decide what we want from the future and get busy heading there."

Joseph nodded slowly as he thought about how each of his team members *had* seemed to have carved out niches for themselves. "I don't think we'll be seeing much of the others from here on out," Jan continued. "Everyone else seems to have found his destiny in this age, and I can't find fault in that. But you, too, my friend, need to discover your own fulfillment."

The carriage dropped them off under the portico at the White House, and Kevin and Jan exchanged hearty greetings. As they crossed the threshold into the presidential residence, Kevin asked about Jan's expectations for the recruiting trip.

"I'm not sure how I'll be received, but I have to try. I can't pull this off by myself. Frank is handling all the construction and building admin, but I need medical staff. I'm also going to stop in and see Tom. I've got to drop off that spare laptop he requested. I guess he's got a lot of irons in the fire, as usual, and he wanted me to bring it up to him. Then, I'm going to make my rounds of the hospitals and universities in New York."

"Before you get too involved in headhunting," Kevin interjected, "I want you to know that there might be another opportunity for you."

He informed Jan that the president was expecting him, and the three of them proceeded to the Oval Office.

Jan was humbled to come face to face with Abraham Lincoln, a man he had always admired, and he shook the imposing leader's hand, managing to get out a shaky "It is my honor, Mr. President."

President Lincoln then addressed Jan directly. "Kevin has told me a lot about you, and I am duly impressed. Word of your medical exploits has filtered back to Washington, and you are held in high regard here. With that in mind, I would like to offer you the appointment to the post of Surgeon General of the United States."

Although Jan had prepared for this moment, he was still stunned by the reality of it. "Mr. President," Jan began with hesitation, "I am deeply honored, but I must respectfully decline this appointment. As you must know, I am establishing a medical center in Blackstone, Virginia, and that is, in fact, why I am here. I stopped on my way to New York and Boston to recruit staff for what will become the leading medical facility in the world. I have an obligation to fulfill there. I believe that my contribution to public health in the United States will be maximized in that role."

President Lincoln looked disappointed, but he hid his feelings rather quickly. "I understand," he responded regretfully, "but perhaps I can one day visit this new hospital and see the good work you are doing."

"Thank you, Mr. President," Jan stammered. "I would be honored to have you attend the opening ceremony of the Lincoln Memorial Hospital. I am certain that you will be pleased with the facilities and our mission."

The three of them dined that evening with the president, his wife, and a few members of Lincoln's staff. Jan was awestruck and considered this to be one of the highlights of his life. After the meal, Jan, Kevin, and Joseph talked well into the night, sipping ale and reflecting on the surprising direction their lives had taken. Finally, Jan stood up and said he had to get some sleep since he had a train to catch the next morning.

When the butler woke him early the following day, he quickly washed up and packed his things before boarding the carriage that took him to the train station. Once on the train, he immediately fell asleep until the porter woke him in his room to inform him that they had arrived in New York.

Tom had a carriage waiting at the station for Jan, and a driver holding a sign with his name on it. *That's Tom for you,* he smiled to himself. The driver promptly delivered him to a three-story brick building, where a doorman ushered him inside. The doorman led him down the hall to a large office, where Jan saw Tom seated behind a huge wooden desk. The doorman hesitated, but Jan barged right in, amidst the doorman's protestations. Jan had no intention of stopping and briskly took the few steps to the rear of the desk. The doorman immediately began spewing apologies.

"It's OK," Tom assured him, after which the doorman muttered something about "distasteful manners" and then made a hasty exit.

"Buddy, you might have them fooled, but you're not impressing me one bit," Jan teased.

After a few pleasantries, Tom asked about the laptop. Jan promptly pulled it from his bag and handed it over.

"And the solar charger, did you remember it?" Tom inquired.

"Of course," Jan replied. "What's the hurry?"

"I've got a million things up in the air, and I need this laptop to help bring some order to the myriad business ventures that keep getting heaped on my plate," Tom replied, a hint of impatience in his voice. "Now, remind me again what's on your agenda while you're here in New York," he said in a businesslike tone.

"How about we discuss everything over dinner? I want to get a hotel room, get cleaned up, and then have a good meal," Jan explained.

"OK, I'll have the doorman escort you to the Metropolitan Hotel just down the street. Register under my name, and it'll all be taken care of. I'll send a carriage for you at 6:00."

Jan dutifully did as he was instructed and thought, *Oh, Tom...he's in his heyday here, and we are* definitely *never gonna catch this guy in Blackstone again.*

Thirty-Eight

Construction of the medical campus was moving right along, thanks in large part to an abundance of labor from the area, as many of the men were eager to resume work after the long war. Frank strived to hire veterans and former slaves, and he insisted that the men work together amicably and respectfully. In addition, he provided meals prepared by the local women, and they, too, were a multiracial group. As part of his daily routine, Frank made a point to circulate among the crews, address everyone by name, and demonstrate a top-down standard of equality. His leadership cultivated a sense of acceptance on the farm, and before long, he observed the same behavior in his workers. Word of mouth lauding the fair treatment, great pay, and good working conditions soon encouraged workers from afar to come and join Blackstone Enterprises.

Frank constantly juggled the building of new structures for the hospital and the tobacco plantation. The town itself had become a hive of activity, with workers and their families arriving daily to take part in various aspects of the fledgling commercial scene. Housing soon added to the construction activity, and Frank kept the railroad active hauling supplies for the booming town. The temporary hospital was complete, and the permanent stone building was well underway. Hotels, stores, and restaurants were stood up as quickly as the materials arrived.

Frank scarcely had a free moment to contact Kevin or any of his other teammates, and the time flew by. He, Elisabeth, and Robert Winslow shared their evening meals at the plantation with two former slaves, whom Frank had hired as permanent workers to tend the tobacco crop. They all felt a deep sense of satisfaction knowing that Blackstone would serve as a model for the rest of the country in repairing the rift that had divided the United States for the past five years.

In a further effort to spur economic recovery, Frank promoted foremen and administrative staff to handle the ordering and unloading of the massive amounts of supplies that arrived daily. Many of the workers and townspeople, seeing the increased demand for services, soon became their own bosses by opening small businesses to fill the growing needs of the ever-expanding township.

Joe and Mattie had become well-respected members of the emerging community, and they built a beautiful brick house on the edge of town, where they settled in with Silas and Annie. Silas eagerly awaited Jan's return so that he could resume his medical training. A growing queue of people wishing to be admitted was also keen for Jan to get back. As for the few patients that remained under treatment, the majority no longer required extensive care, mainly just the changing of bandages and monitoring of wounds.

The tobacco plantation was also becoming a tourist destination. People flocked to the farm and watched in amazement as the four-wheelers pulled their plows along, effortlessly tilling the fields. The two newly freed young men sat up straight and waved good-naturedly, swelling with pride as they passed the assembled crowds observing them from the edge of the fields.

Frank relished the peace and serenity he had created in Blackstone, as well as the sense of accomplishment he derived from building something from nothing. These were things he had never experienced in his previous life. Moreover, he was grateful for having met someone he truly loved in the midst of such tumult. As much as he may have had to give up, he had no regrets about the hand that fate had dealt him.

"I wouldn't change a thing," he promised Elisabeth.

However, he had a lingering desire that he was unable to quell. *I do wish I could share my story with you,* he longed to tell her, *but I know you wouldn't—you couldn't—understand.*

Thirty-Nine

The Native Americans who had scouted the river from atop a large hill sent a messenger down to the resupply camp as soon as they spotted the approaching steamboat. Gray Wolf was stationed at the camp, Red Cloud at the mine, both awaiting news of the ship's arrival. The men at the camp unloaded the equipment and supplies straightaway before turning over the next shipment of gold to the soldiers on board. After much deliberation, Mike resolved to let the soldiers escort the gold without Jon or any of the tribe members accompanying them.

"The soldiers would be bat-shit crazy to try embezzling on their first load," he had reasoned to Jon. "If they do, their first trip will be their last."

As such, he decided not to expend the manpower just to keep the soldiers company on the long trip.

The wagons transported the load of supplies and equipment to the mine site, where the Sioux would learn to crank up the mining machinery to crush the ore and extract the gold. This process would be far more efficient than using the crude tools they had purchased with Otis. Modernizing their equipment would serve the dual purpose of ratcheting up the mine's output while reducing the need for manual labor. The workers stood in awe of the mechanical improvements taking place, but none was more pleased than the chief himself. In fact, Mike asked Otis if there were any other operational improvements that could be made.

"Well, now," Otis said, scratching his head, "if you and that magic map can just keep telling me where to go next, I think we'll be in business."

Red Cloud may have lacked a formal education, but he was a wise man with a genuine desire to take care of his people. He recognized right away that the labor-intensive work of mining could be carried out much more efficiently by the machines Mike had shipped in. In light of Red Cloud's open arms to the concept of technology, Jon decided to float his idea about the railroad spur by the small assembly of decision-makers.

"Red Cloud," he asked directly. "would you allow the railroad to build tracks from Sidney, Nebraska, to Deadwood?"

Red Cloud agreed to let the trains pass through their territory, but he made it clear to Mike that he would like the tribe to own and operate that section of track. Mike felt confident that he could facilitate the chief's request, and he volunteered to talk to Tom and Kevin about beginning initial discussions with the railroad.

Mike and Jon's next task was to inspect the shipment of guns that were delivered courtesy of the US Army. Mike was impressed that all of the rifles and pistols were new, packed carefully in wooden crates to protect them from the elements. The ammunition, too, was sealed, and all requested units were accounted for.

"Damn, Jon, the postal service could learn a lot from these guys," he said only half-joking.

Mike was itching to get the men trained on how to use them. Not only was he looking forward to organizing a training regimen, but he also knew that they would need to be ready for action when the next steamboat docked.

He approached Red Cloud, requesting twenty men for the first weapons training class. It would be a weeklong course, which he would repeat until he and Jon had issued all 80 weapons.

Just four weeks to go, then I'm due for a long vacation, Mike told himself as he drew up a curriculum for the tribesmen. *Jackson Hole sure sounds nice right about now.*

Although Mike was happily looking down the road at his next mile marker—in typical Mike fashion—he remained focused on training the men to properly handle the weapons and become expert marksmen. This was, in fact, what he enjoyed most about his military role. As the team sergeant, he was responsible for a great deal of planning and training. After the day's work was done and the sun had set, he and Jon used their evenings around the fire to discuss the future and reflect on the past.

One night Mike told Jon, "This has been great, but I, for one, could use a break from all these civic duties and the industrial renaissance. I'm thinking about taking my money and buying a spread near Jackson Hole. I'd build a cabin where I can hunt, fish, shoot shit...you know, just take it easy for a bit."

Jon, for his part, said he hadn't decided on his next move. "Getting to rewrite one of my favorite stories from history has been incredible for me. When I brought up the idea of a Deadwood expedition, I only halfway believed it could actually come to fruition. Think about it: We singlehandedly prevented the massacre at Wounded Knee with what we've done here. As for now, I plan to stay here and see this thing through. Once the railroad is completed, though, I may travel some. Who knows?" he said with a shrug, yet clearly content with his current lot.

The mine continued producing gold at an astounding rate, and the money accumulated in the bank just as quickly. In an effort to set his people up for their own long-term success, Red Cloud asked Jon to advise him on projects that would help them maintain and protect their sovereignty, while simultaneously allowing them to step confidently into the future. Jon had an abundance of ideas, and he quite liked being the tribal counselor.

Meanwhile, the money continued to flow to Washington, guaranteeing the Sioux influence and protection from the government. The mutually beneficial arrangement between the parties illustrated what Mike and Jon had hoped to accomplish when they set out for Deadwood: to usher in an age in which *all* Americans could coexist and have the opportunity to prosper.

Forty

Jack and Dave arrived in Corsicana by steamboat, by way of the Trinity River, hauling two drilling rigs and crews to run them. They left Eli in charge in Beaumont to continue drilling in that field. By now, they had a business model in place, with Jack selecting two sites for the first two wells to be drilled and Dave buying more land. Then, they set up a homegrown office to train people from the community to run the drilling operation. Once Dave had acquired as much land as the two of them desired, they decided that Dave would set his sights on Oklahoma and obtain as much land as he could in that region. Jack knew that the area around Tulsa had turned Oklahoma into one of the leading producers of oil in the early 1900s. Jack's guidance was to focus first on the towns of Sapulpa and Glenpool, and then concentrate on Muscogee and the land north of Tulsa, which would later become Bartlesville.

"That's all Native American territory, and you'll need to sign a contract with the respective tribes for a revenue sharing agreement," Jack explained. "We can use Mike and Jon's deal as the model. We'll make them the same offer to train and employ their people, and we'll prepare them to defend their land, both with weapons and in the halls of Washington, DC."

Dave set off for the Oklahoma Territory with the intention of seeking out Quanah, the fierce leader of a band of Comanches who had gained a reputation as the most feared tribe in the Texas-Oklahoma frontier. He had elected to confront the issue head-on and try to convince Quanah that he wished to be an ally. *If I'm lucky (and still alive), he'll trust me, and hopefully help me gain an in with the Creek and Cherokee tribes*, he reasoned. Having a feared and respected chief on his side would undoubtedly win him trust in the tribal communities. He stopped in Dallas to consult with some of the buffalo hunters who were known to have had run-ins with Quanah and his men. He wanted their advice as to where and how he should seek out the legendary chief.

"If you're that determined to die, I'll lead you to a place near Wichita Falls, and he'll find you. For a price, of course," one old hunter told Dave.

They agreed on an amount and soon headed northwest on the trail to Wichita Falls. When they arrived, the old man instructed Dave to set up camp on the banks of the Red River, where Quanah would make quick work of rooting him out.

"Maybe, *just* maybe, you'll have a chance to speak to Quanah before they scalp your ass," he warned Dave. Then he took his payment and bade Dave goodbye and good luck.

The hunter knew what he was talking about because Dave awoke the next morning with the distinct feeling that he was being watched. He sat up, fully alert and listening intently, and he soon detected the presence of humans around him. He remained calm but vigilant, and in a matter of minutes, he saw a man on horseback approaching with several others close behind. Dave waved his hand to show that he was not reaching for his gun as the man rode closer. He then stood up slowly, and the rider dismounted his horse.

He was a lean figure with sharp gray eyes, taller and lighter-skinned than the others who gathered behind him. When he spoke, his English was good, and Dave introduced himself.

The man said, "My name is Quanah, and if you come in peace and leave without claiming any land, I will allow you to leave."

Jack had told Dave the story of how Quanah's mother was abducted as a child by Comanches during a raid and later married the tribal chief. Quanah had become a fierce fighter and a revered leader at a young age.

Dave began his pitch slowly, keeping his voice even. "I come in peace to ask for your help." The chief had dealt with white men before, and he knew what offering his "help" might cost him. He remained silent and stone-faced as Dave continued. "I want to invite you and other tribal leaders in the region to sign an agreement to cooperate in drilling for oil on tribal land. This will help to bring prosperity and security to all of the tribes of Oklahoma. We have done the same for the Sioux in the Dakota Territory, and I give you my word that we will back you both here in Oklahoma and in Washington, DC. My men and I pledge to do everything in our power to help you and your people."

Quanah sensed Dave's sincerity and admired his bravery for choosing to come meet him alone. He agreed to accompany him farther north into the territory and seek out the leaders of the other Indian territories. The Comanches were known for riding great distances on horseback, and Dave was grateful for the partnership, but quickly developed a sore keister after covering so much ground in only two days.

They met first with the Creek leaders and then were escorted into the Cherokee Nation, where all the tribal council members sat and listened to Dave's presentation. As Dave had predicted, Quanah's presence conveyed a great deal of trust and credence to his words. The leaders conferred with each other at length, weighing the pros and cons of entering into an agreement with the strange white man. Ultimately, they decided that his proposition was the most likely path to independence and prosperity that they had been offered thus far, and they agreed to the same terms as the Sioux. With a handshake, they all sealed the deal, and Dave promised to put in writing the terms that were acceptable to everyone.

Dave used the rest of his time to scout the Arkansas River to assess its viability for transporting oil. The river was certainly suitable, and he made notes to take with him to Corsicana. The ride back was uneventful, with Quanah's presence offering an added layer of protection from external threats. They covered the section that Quanah rode with him in record time, his backside feeling the effects once again.

Dave made a pit stop in Dallas to inform the Commander of the US Army Cavalry there that he had met and forged an agreement with Quanah. He said that Quanah had agreed to cooperate with him, and as a result, he felt the Comanche raids would soon cease. He also shared Quanah's commitment to abide by the treaty that established the Oklahoma Territories if the army would fulfill its role of preventing any further encroachment by settlers. As an added measure, Dave conveyed his intent to relay this message to Washington.

Jack was excited to hear of Dave's victories and urged him to get on the radio right away to tell Kevin and Joseph. "Let's notify Tom, too, so he can start making arrangements for shipments out of there," Jack threw in. "While you were gone, we completed the first two wells here in town, and they're already producing. Tom struck a deal to sell all of it, and we hope to start shipping some out next week," he informed Dave.

"Wow, you've been burning the midnight oil, I see," Dave commented.

"Yep. And furthermore," Jack continued, "there are hundreds, maybe thousands more to drill. The town is growing by the day." Dave was pleased with the progress report, but his face betrayed a hint of exhaustion. Jack kept going in spite of this, as he was on a roll, his consummate energy on full display. "Dave, how would you feel about going to California and buying land for the next strike?"

"Only if I get to keep the frequent traveler miles, and only after my butt heals," Dave replied halfheartedly. "After that, I'm thinking about taking Elisha Root up on that offer to go work for Colt."

Jack nodded his understanding. "Once we get the oil fields into production in Oklahoma and California, I'm thinking about taking a break, too. The money's rolling in faster than Tom can count it, and I figure you and I are wealthy men by now."

Dave managed a slight smile.

"Keep your chin up, Dave," Jack said in an encouraging tone. "We'll get there soon, brother. In the meantime, just imagine how many lives you've changed and how many guns you'll be able to buy."

"Guess my sore ass is a small price to pay," Dave laughed.

Forty-One

Jan made the rounds of the New York hospitals and then traveled to Boston to do the same before visiting Harvard Medical School. There, he met with the faculty to interview prospects for his staff. Then, he invited all the doctors that he felt were a good fit to visit the facility in Blackstone. Many were intrigued and accepted the invitation with promises to make the trip down soon. Satisfied that he had a promising start, Jan returned to New York. That night at dinner, he shared his story with Tom.

"I think we have a solid candidate pool to build from. Several other physicians I talked to are planning to come see the hospital, and I asked them to recruit nurses to come along. I plan to make them offers they can't refuse."

"That's great," Tom said. "When do you expect to be up and running?"

"At the rate they were going when I left, the building should be complete by the time I get back. Then it's just a matter of furnishing it, so, I'd say a month at the most," Jan estimated.

"Wow, that soon?" Tom remarked.

"I think so. We'll have to plan an opening and invite President Lincoln and anyone else we think might want to attend. Maybe some of the European ambassadors to stir up interest in the international community," Jan proposed.

"Sounds like a good way to gain exposure," was Tom's off-handed response. Suddenly, Tom changed the subject in abrupt fashion. "I think I'm going to go back with you," he declared. Jan raised his eyebrows in disbelief. "Do you remember the laptop you brought me?" Tom asked.

Jan nodded. "It came with the XLIMTR. I managed to hack into it, and I found something very interesting. You may also remember that the tech rep who showed us the XLIMTR said not to use the laptop for anything else." Jan's attention was now fully engaged. "It looks like Kevin took it with him while he was doing his master's thesis on the Civil War. And here's the strange part: He uploaded the coordinates for the Battle of Sayler's Creek to it, along with the manifest for the equipment that we infilled with in Afghanistan. That's got to be the origin of our voyage through time. I mean, it can't be a coincidence that we ended up at Sayler's Creek."

When Tom concluded, the men simply stared at one another, unsure of the implications of Tom's words. Finally, Jan managed to stutter, "I-I-I don't know what to say. I don't know...what we should do."

Tom, of course, had been sitting with the information for a time, so he had already begun wrapping his brain around it. "I'm going back with you to investigate, but for now, let's just keep it between us," he told Jan.

"Deal," Jan mumbled as he started to lose himself in his thoughts. They spent most of the train ride in silence as both pondered the possible repercussions of the startling discovery.

The train pulled into Blackstone that evening, and dozens of passengers got off with Tom and Jan. Both of them were stunned by the progress that had occurred in such a short time. Blackstone was now a flourishing community, and the construction was expanding in every direction. They could barely recognize the town and had to ask for directions to Frank's house.

They flagged down a carriage to take them there and soon arrived at the newly renovated plantation home. No one was there, so they let themselves in and waited. Tom, impatient to investigate the XLIMTR, decided to look around for where it might be stored. Frank had meticulously stowed the team's unused equipment in large, unoccupied bedrooms throughout the house. Tom came across the XLIMTR in one of the rooms, along with some of their weapons and surveillance equipment. He shuffled things around to get to the almost-forgotten apparatus. He racked his brain for the instructions, and finally, he remembered how to power it up and do a functions check. As he fiddled with some of the controls, the XLIMTR suddenly activated, whirring and flashing to life.

After a while, Frank and Elisabeth returned home and were surprised to find Jan waiting for them.

"Why didn't you let me know you were coming?" Frank wanted to know. "I would've arranged to meet you at the station, and we could've had dinner at one of the new cafes in town."

"After I finished my recruiting trip, Tom and I decided to head down on short notice," Jan explained.

"Tom's here, too?" Frank said excitedly. "Never thought I'd see the day! Where's he at?"

"He's in the other room looking for some equipment," Jan responded.

"Tom!" Frank yelled, making his way down the hall to the closest bedroom used for storage. With no sign of him, Frank continued through the house, peering into doorways and shouting Tom's name. Jan and Elisabeth helped Frank search the house's interior and, unable to locate him, they decided that he must have made a run to the outhouse. They shrugged it off and sat down to catch up on the progress of the hospital and the town.

"Looks great, Frank. I'm impressed with the development," Jan complimented his buddy. "You ought to run for mayor next. You'd have an excellent platform, that's for sure."

As they continued their discussion, Jan felt a nagging sense of uneasiness creep into his mind. "Frank, let's go check the room again for Tom," he said, concern detectable in his tone. Jan asked Frank where he had stored the XLIMTR, and Frank led them to the room where Tom had found the device situated among some of the other equipment.

"In here with the other stuff," Frank muttered as they combed the room to no avail. He looked around in confusion, certain of where he had stored it. "It was right here," he insisted, "but looks like it's gone now."

The color started to drain from Jan's face. "And so is Tom," he pronounced, his voice catching in his throat. "Frank, I have something to tell you," Jan said as he took a deep breath. "Tom told me that when Kevin used the laptop that we were issued with the XLIMTR, he somehow loaded the coordinates for Sayler's Creek on it, along with the list of equipment that we deployed to Afghanistan with." Frank's apprehension mounted as he stared blankly at his teammate. Jan went on, "Tom was sure that was how we ended up here in the first place. He said he was just going to find it when we came back. I had no idea he was going to experiment with it."

The two of them sat speechless for several minutes until finally, Frank asked the question burning in both of their minds: "What in the hell do we do now?"

Forty-Two

Tom woke from a fog, not sure what had happened or where he was. As he shook the cobwebs from his head, he looked around and gradually realized that the scenery had changed to something eerily familiar. Clearly, he was no longer in the 1800s, but where was he? Tom scanned the landscape and quickly recognized where he and the XLIMTR had transported. Somehow, he just knew that he was back "home." As he conducted an investigation of the perimeter, he discovered that he was on the grounds of a large complex of some kind. He walked toward a huge, ornate stone building that seemed to be the center of activity.

Just then, two men walked by, and he stopped to ask the name of the building.

"Why, it's the Winslow Memorial Cancer Center," came the reply.

"Are you looking for someone?" the other man asked.

"Can you tell me the date and the name of this town?" Tom replied.

"It's June 7, 2018, and you're in Blackstone, Virginia," one of the strangers replied as they continued on, whispering between themselves.

Tom quickly made his way back to the XLIMTR and pondered his fate. He remembered experimenting with the XLIMTR and guessed that he had activated it again and somehow transported himself forward in time. Now that he had identified the mysterious power of the XLIMTR, he was faced with an excruciating decision. Should he immediately activate the XLIMTR again and try to go back in time to notify the team of his discovery, or should he stay put and continue to gather data?

As he considered his options, he realized that he had no money or transportation. Looking around at the immaculate grounds of the cancer center, he shuddered at the thought of leaving the XLIMTR unattended. If something were to happen to it, his decision would be made for him. There would be no more travel, and he'd probably never see his buddies again. He grappled with the decision, but his sense of duty to his teammates ultimately won out. He knew that he had to go back and inform them of his discovery. Tom figured out that Captain McKenzie had unwittingly entered the coordinates for Sayler's Creek into the XLMTR while doing his Civil War research, triggering the system to transport them far from their intended landing spot in Afghanistan, year 2018.

As he closely examined the XLIMTR, Tom also realized that the scanning setting could be used to determine the size of the area, which could then be included in the transportation through time. Tom adjusted the setting to include only himself and the XLIMTR. It was now a matter of reprogramming the machine to its previous setting. Now that Tom felt confident that he had figured out how to control the XLIMTR, he leaped into action and soon found himself again hurling through time and space.

He wasn't sure how much time had passed, but Tom emerged from the bedroom and ran into a stunned Frank with Elizabeth not far behind.

"Where the hell have you been?" slid out of Frank's slack jaw.

"Believe it or not, I just took a quick trip to 2018, *Quantum Leap* style!" Tom said slyly. "I'll tell you more about it later, but first we need to get on the horn and tell everyone the news! We can get home!" Tom blurted out as he shook Frank by the shoulders emphatically.

Frank slowly backed away. "That's amazing, buddy. Would you go tell Jan? I need to talk to Elisabeth," he said softly.

Tom was a bit puzzled. "Sure, and I'll get on the radio and let everyone know as well. I'm sure they'll want to get back here as soon as possible so we can get moving."

"No need for that; everyone's already on their way. We put out a call as soon we noticed you missing. We were planning a team meeting to discuss the situation," Frank explained.

Tom nodded and quickly found Jan not too far away. The teammates greeted each other with a bear hug and Tom excitedly told Jan about figuring out the XLIMTR and how they could now return to their original lives. He encountered the same reaction. Jan was pensive, and Tom was at a loss for the lack of excitement from yet another teammate.

"Hey, buddy, did you hear me? We're going home!" he shouted.

"I know," Jan replied. "It's just that there's lots of unfinished business here."

"Don't tell me you want to stay," Tom said in disbelief. He'd never even considered such a scenario.

"It's just so sudden," Jan answered, a hint of disappointment in his voice.

"It's what we've been talking about from day one of this madness!" Tom cried incredulously. "What about everyone else? What do you think they'll have to say?"

"Well, everyone is on their way back due to your disappearance, so you can ask them yourself," Jan retorted.

"It shouldn't take that long, thanks to the new railroads into Texas. Jack and Dave should be here in two or three days, and Mike and Jon are taking the express route from Deadwood to St. Louis. There, they will board a steamboat to cross the river, and then it's a two-day train ride. Kevin and Joseph are due in tomorrow," Jan explained. "I need to make rounds and check on the progress of everything. Let's discuss it further over dinner."

Tom was confused, and he wondered if everyone else would regard the news with as much uncertainty as Jan and Frank had. He hadn't been around to see how close Frank and Elisabeth had grown, nor how entrenched Jan had become in the community as a result of the hospital's preeminence. Would the others be as engrossed in their endeavors as Jan and Frank? Would everyone want to stay here instead of returning to their 21st-century lives?

To be honest, Tom relished the newfound fame and fortune he had created in his brief time here. He could certainly understand their trepidation in returning to a time and place where they felt more like a spoke in a wheel, a little fish in a big pond. Each man, regardless of his personal life, had been a soldier in the US Army Special Forces, and with all due respect, had been merely a pawn for the politicians to deploy around the world at their discretion.

In the 1800s, each was an important person with the ability to shape the world and its future, to have a real and tangible impact that was simply impossible in the present day. It suddenly dawned on Tom that it would be a daunting decision each man would have to make for himself. The trouble was, if the decision wasn't unanimous—if not everyone wanted to return—what would that mean for the team and its bond? Would this be the end?

Later that evening, Frank approached Tom and Jan to ask that they avoid discussing the situation in front of Elisabeth. "Can we just talk about where we're at now, and the progress of things?"

"Sure," Jan offered while patting his buddy on the back. "We understand it's a sensitive subject for her...and you," he added with a small smile.

Alone with his thoughts that night, Tom reflected on what he would be leaving behind and what unknowns he would return to. He also knew that Jan, Frank, and the rest of his teammates would soon face the same dilemma.

"Time will tell," he said aloud before dozing off, heavy under the weight of his quandary.

The next morning, Kevin and Joseph arrived and somberly walked into the HQ. They were awestruck upon seeing Tom sitting there in a chair like he didn't have a care in the world. Greetings had to wait until Kevin and Joseph cleared their heads and were able to speak.

"What happened?" Kevin asked incredulously. "Where have you been, man? Don't tell us that you..." His voice trailed off.

"Yeah, I briefly went back to 2018, and now I'm here again. I figured out how to do it, and it's a repeatable process. We can all return to our lives! Can you believe it?" Tom exclaimed. "DoorDash and Hulu, here we come!"

Kevin and Joseph were taken aback at the thought of leaving so suddenly.

"When?" was the only word Kevin could muster.

"Jan said everyone is on their way here, and we'll have to talk about it," Tom replied. "Frank has asked that no one discuss it in front of Elisabeth, so we're trying to let everyone do their own reflecting, and then have a team meeting in the next day or two."

Kevin and Joseph took time to observe the construction and all the progress that was made in their absence. They marveled at the completed structures and the others under construction. Jan toured them around, proudly explaining in detail all of the projects that he and Frank had launched, as well as the training programs they had instituted.

"Very impressive," Kevin said, glancing around in awe.

"I'd like to see Frank's operation," Joseph said.

Jan nodded. "If you can catch Frank alone, I'm sure he'd love to show it to you. He's very proud of it, as he should be."

"But that may be hard for him to do. He's wrestling with some big decisions, like everyone else, because he and Elisabeth are clearly in love. That's something that none of the rest of us is dealing with," Jan added. "It adds an extra wrinkle to the equation."

Jan paused briefly before continuing. "Jack and Dave radioed on the train ride, and they should be here tonight. Mike and Jon are about to board the train in east St. Louis, and that's scheduled to arrive tomorrow night."

Now Kevin and Joseph reflected on their situations and considered what they wanted to do with the rest of their lives. Unlike Jan and Frank, neither of them had built anything or achieved success in the traditional sense of the word, even though they had made a huge impact on the proceedings in Washington, DC. Joseph was touched by the progress that was made for African Americans in such a short time, and he regretted leaving before more was accomplished.

Kevin, meanwhile, basked in the bit of influence and position he had managed to create in Washington, an achievement he could only dream of in the 21st century.

Jack and Dave arrived at the new train station in Blackstone and caught a carriage for the trip to HQ. They, too, were amazed at the progress that was made in their absence, and they were quick to congratulate Jan and Frank on the fruits of their labor.

They were informed of Tom's return when they made their radio call, so they'd had plenty of time to think about what came next. Nevertheless, they were excited to see him and hear the details of his discovery. Tom was thrilled to have a couple of teammates who were visibly excited about the possibility of returning to their previous lives. He had started to feel sort of alone and feared that he might be the only one willing to leave the past behind.

"Let's see how Mike and Jon feel," Jack mused. "You never quite know how money and power will change a person."

Once the final two arrived, everyone was ready to sit down as a team and finally sort out their individual and collective emotions. More importantly, each man had a decision to make. Who would stay, and who would go? It was time to decide.

For their part, Mike and Jon were fascinated by all of the developments that took place while they had been out west. After the vastness of Deadwood, they felt like they were back in civilization.

Tom wanted everyone to see all the changes that had taken place, but they just didn't have time. They had important things to discuss. He proposed that after dinner, they retire to the porch and have a team meeting. They agreed to keep the conversation casual until then, so dinner was filled with tales from around the country as each man shared highlights of his trip.

It was refreshing for the guys to relax and shoot the shit. They were proud of each other's accomplishments and the undeniable mark they had made on the past. But they all knew that the time was rapidly approaching when they would each have to make a critical decision. This meeting would most likely be the last time they sat down as a group and shared the camaraderie they had established in what felt like another lifetime. The moment was bittersweet.

As they enjoyed the last few minutes around the table, Mike motioned for the team to follow him out to the porch, and then called the meeting to order.

Kevin was the first to speak. "To steal a line from Patrick Henry, I know not what course others may take but as for me, I choose to stay here and continue to try and influence the shaping of our great country." The guys glanced at each other as the weight of the statement hit them with full force.

Frank, relieved to hear that he was not alone in his decision, chimed in next. "I, too, am staying. I've found not only the love of my life but also my calling here on earth. My only regret is that I won't be able to stay in touch with those of you who choose to leave. It's been a pleasure and an honor to serve with and know all of you, but here is where I belong."

Jan was next to speak. "I also have an obligation to stay here and finish my work. I share the honor of serving with everyone, and if any of you ever make it back here by any means, you've got friends and hospitality forever in your grasp, not to mention a medical community ahead of its time."

Tom waited to let those announcements sink in and then asked tentatively, "Anyone else choosing to stay?" No one broke the somber silence.

Joseph and Jon found their eyes watering as they contemplated leaving behind the people they had come to know and trust with their lives. Hugs, handshakes, goodbyes, and even a few tears flowed as they huddled up to share one last moment of fellowship.

Then Mike spoke. "I'd like for those of us who are leaving to have a word together."

After Jan, Kevin, and Frank had left, Mike addressed the remaining team members.

"Men, we don't know what awaits us upon our arrival back to the future, but I suggest we make a pact not to discuss any of this with anyone. Let's agree to find a place to lock the XLIMTR away and forget about it. Is everyone on board?"

With no objections, they returned to the room where the XLIMTR was stored, and Tom made a few quick adjustments to the dials as the others watched in amazement. They all inhaled and braced themselves as the device sprang to life, preparing to take them to a time and place that perhaps they only thought they knew. The walls shook, the air turned icy, and darkness enveloped them, immediately shuttering all thoughts. It was over in a flash.

When the earth below their feet was solid once more, the men glanced around at each other and let out a collective sigh. The A-Team had completed their unthinkable mission, and they are forever blessed with the wisdom of hindsight.

I would like to thank my agent Diane Nine at NineSpeakers.com and Mike Acheson for his support and help moving this forward. And thanks to Dave Smitherman for all the great help. Also David Hill, Carl and Patty Saucier and Greg Mulligan.

A special thanks to my daughter Melissa and most importantly to my wife and soulmate for all of her help, understanding and encouragement throughout this endeavor.

Printed in the USA
CPSIA information can be obtained
at www.ICGtesting.com
LVHW020059120923
756292LV00032B/257